SO-ASI-221

A BLACK HAT AND A PAIR OF GUNS

The outlaw working this side of the aisle had gotten a little behind his companion, and that might prove to be a problem. It would just have to be dealt with, though. The bandit on the other side reached the young man, and he growled, "Shuck that gun and toss it here, too." The young man hesitated. Staring down the barrel of the bandit's gun, he had no choice but to do as he was told.

That made the situation even worse, since the man in the black hat had been counting on the youngster for a little help. But not impossible. Just . . . trickier.

The other outlaw paused beside the man. "Come on, old-timer," the outlaw said impatiently. "Let's have the loot."

"Sure," the man said mildly. "Here you go."

With a movement so smooth and deceptive that it didn't seem to happen, each of the man's hands slid underneath his coat and then came out as he uncrossed his arms. There was an ivory-handled Colt gripped in each fist, and his thumbs eased back the hammers as the barrels tipped up. The bandit barely had time to widen his eyes in surprise before flame and smoke belched from the barrels of both revolvers.

Books by James Reasoner

Wind River
Thunder Wagon
Wolf Shadow
Medicine Creek
Dark Trail

Available from HarperPaperbacks

ATTENTION: ORGANIZATIONS AND CORPORATIONS

Most HarperPaperbacks are available at special quantity discounts for bulk purchases for sales promotions, premiums, or fund-raising. For information, please call or write:
Special Markets Department, HarperCollins*Publishers*,
10 East 53rd Street, New York, N.Y. 10022.
Telephone: (212) 207-7528. Fax: (212) 207-7222.

DARK TRAIL

JAMES REASONER

HarperPaperbacks
A Division of HarperCollins*Publishers*

If you purchased this book without a cover, you should be aware that this book is stolen property. It was reported as "unsold and destroyed" to the publisher and neither the author nor the publisher has received any payment for this "stripped book."

This is a work of fiction. The characters, incidents, and dialogues are products of the author's imagination and are not to be construed as real. Any resemblance to actual events or persons, living or dead, is entirely coincidental.

HarperPaperbacks   *A Division of* HarperCollins*Publishers*
10 East 53rd Street, New York, N.Y. 10022

Copyright © 1995 by James M. Reasoner and L.J. Washburn
All rights reserved. No part of this book may be used or reproduced in any manner whatsoever without written permission of the publisher, except in the case of brief quotations embodied in critical articles and reviews. For information address HarperCollins*Publishers,*
10 East 53rd Street, New York, N.Y. 10022.

Cover illustration by Rick McCollum

First printing: August 1995

Printed in the United States of America

HarperPaperbacks and colophon are trademarks of HarperCollins*Publishers*

❖ 10 9 8 7 6 5 4 3 2 1

For Michael and Kelly Davis

There was one thing to be said about being the deputy marshal of Wind River, Wyoming Territory, mused Billy Casebolt: you never knew what in blazes was going to happen next.

With that thought, he threw himself forward and grabbed for the old Griswald & Gunnison revolver holstered on his hip.

He landed hard and painfully on the platform of the Union Pacific depot as a bullet thudded into the wall above his head. He was getting too damned old for fandangos like this, he told himself. But when you were packing a badge and a corpse-and-cartridge session broke out right in front of you, there wasn't any way to avoid taking a hand. Over the roar of gunplay, he shouted, "Hold on there, you two! Drop them guns!"

The two miners ignored him. Dressed in rough work clothes, they stood about twenty feet apart on the platform and continued to blaze away at one another. So far, neither man seemed to have been hit. That wasn't too surprising. At any distance over ten feet, the old cap-and-ball pistols they carried were notoriously inaccurate. The two gunmen were probably in less danger than the other folks on the platform, who were all scurrying for cover. No one wanted to get hit by a stray bullet, which were flying around the platform plenty right now.

Casebolt's lean, grizzled features twisted into a grimace. He didn't want to shoot either one of those fellas, but he might have to if they didn't run out of ammunition pretty soon. He winced as another shot slammed into the wall a couple of feet above his head. Luckily, the depot was built solidly of stone blocks and timber beams, and the walls were thick enough to stop just about anything short of a cannonball.

"Damn it, I'm warnin' you!" Casebolt called again. "Drop them shootin' irons!"

The miners still paid no attention to him. One of them stopped firing—but only because his gun was empty. He stood there with the weapon extended, pulling the trigger and cursing as the hammer clicked repeatedly on empty cylinders.

The other man stopped shooting, too, but only long enough to let out a chuckle as a savage grin wreathed his bearded face. "Looks like you're plumb out of luck, Harry," he said. "You're sure as hell out o' bullets. But I got at least one left, and I been savin' it for you."

He aimed carefully and drew back the hammer. The other man stared at the muzzle of the gun—which had to look as big around as a rain barrel right about now—and licked lips that had gone dry.

"So long, you son of a bitch," said the man who still had bullets in his gun.

He had gloated too long. Billy Casebolt scrambled to his feet, lunged across the platform, and lashed out with the revolver in his hand. The man saw him coming and tried to twist around to meet this new threat, but Casebolt was surprisingly fast and spry for a man of his age who appeared to be made out of sticks and twine. The barrel of the old Confederate revolver thudded against the man's skull and sent him stumbling toward the edge of the platform. Casebolt struck down with the gun then, cracking it across the man's wrist. With a howl of pain, the man let go of his pistol. It fell to the platform and discharged with a loud bang, making Casebolt jump even though the ball whined off harmlessly.

Casebolt glanced around at the other man and saw that he was frantically trying to reload. The deputy brought up his gun and eared back the hammer. "Put it down, mister!" he warned. "I ain't in no mood to fool around with you boys. I'll shoot you if I have to, sure as hell."

The man must have believed him, because he gulped and bent over to place the revolver on the platform. Then he stepped back and lifted his hands. "Take it easy, Deputy," he said nervously. "It's all over."

"It ain't over until I *say* it's over!" snapped Casebolt. His heart was pounding in his thin chest, and he was still angry. He had been on intimate terms with danger for many years, but it still made him mad when he nearly got shot over something stupid.

And there wasn't anything much more stupid than a couple of men arguing over a whore.

"You ladies can come on out now," he called to a couple of women who were crouched behind a stack of baggage.

They emerged somewhat hesitantly, and Casebolt

couldn't blame them for that, considering how much lead had been whistling through the air around here only moments earlier. They straightened their fancy silk dresses and brushed themselves off, and the tall, willowy brunette said, "Thank you, sir. I can't imagine what got into those two men."

Casebolt could. To men who had been up in the mountains lucklessly searching for gold and silver for months on end, the sight of a pair of women like these two was enough to make them downright crazy.

The brunette was wearing a red dress with a matching hat, and despite her slender figure, she had plenty of curves to show off in the outfit. The blonde with her was a couple of inches shorter but probably twenty pounds heavier—although you didn't discuss such things with ladies, not even *nymphs du prairie* like these two. That made the blonde even more lushly proportioned than her companion, and the light blue traveling gown she wore displayed that lushness just fine. There was a smile on her round, pretty face as she came up to Casebolt and said, "Oh, thank you, sir! You saved our lives."

Casebolt grunted. "Not hardly. I just waited until one of those ol' boys ran out of powder and shot."

"What are you going to do with them?" the brunette asked.

"Take 'em down to the jail, I reckon. They was disturbin' the peace real good. That'll earn 'em a few days behind bars to simmer down."

"You mean you're going to lock them up?" the brunette asked. She sounded surprised.

"That's generally what we do around here with folks who go to shootin' off guns for no good reason," Casebolt replied grimly.

Both women looked disappointed. The blonde said, "We were hoping that once the gentlemen had calmed down, we might, ah, enjoy their company."

Casebolt tried not to roll his eyes. It wasn't bad enough that the two soiled doves had ignited a shoot-out with their mere presence. Now they were trying to drum up some business from the very gents who had been trying to kill each other a few minutes ago.

The morning hadn't started out badly. It was a crisp, late summer day here on the high plains of Wyoming Territory, and since there was a westbound train due to come in at ten o'clock, Casebolt had ambled down here to the station to see who got off. That was part of the routine he and Marshal Cole Tyler had established. One of the lawmen tried to be on hand at the depot every time a train came in, just to make sure no troublemakers disembarked. More than one desperado on the dodge from the law had been caught by an alert star packer keeping an eye on the train and stagecoach stations across the West.

There weren't any stage lines serving Wind River yet, but there was the Union Pacific, which in fact was the settlement's reason for existing. Wind River had served as the railhead for a time the year before, until the construction of the UP moved on west. Earlier this year, the final link between the Union Pacific and the Central Pacific had been completed, with the so-called Golden Spike being driven at a place in Utah called Promontory Point. Casebolt had read all about it in the *Wind River Sentinel*.

With the transcontinental railroad completed, the rail traffic through Wind River was heavier than ever. Westbounds came through four times a week, eastbounds twice. It had gotten to where it was impossible for Cole

Tyler and Billy Casebolt to be on hand for the arrival of every train.

But Casebolt was glad he had been here this morning. Otherwise somebody would have likely been hurt, maybe even killed.

He had been leaning against the wall of the station, enjoying the shade cast by the roof over the platform, when the big Baldwin locomotive pulled in with the squeal of brakes and the hiss of steam. The train stopped so that the passenger cars were next to the platform, and after the conductor and a couple of porters placed portable steps at the rear of each car, travelers had begun to flow out onto the platform. Some of them were leaving the train here, while others were just stretching their legs before their journey continued on to Rock Springs, Reno, or beyond. Some folks might be going all the way to San Francisco, Casebolt had thought, and in a way he envied them. At his age, he was glad to have settled down in a growing community like Wind River, but he remembered some wild times on the Barbary Coast when he was younger . . .

Then the two women had gotten off the train. And all hell broke loose.

Like a lot of people in small towns across the frontier, the two miners had evidently come down to the depot just to pass the time of day and indulge their curiosity. The arrival of a train was still an event in a place like Wind River. Casebolt had seen the two burly men around the town's saloons the past few days and knew from talking to some of the bartenders that they had been up in Montana Territory for the past eight months doing some prospecting. Judging by the threadbare condition of their clothes, they hadn't struck it rich—but then neither did most of the men who sought their fortunes that way.

Both men had looked rather bored until the blonde and the brunette got off the train, and then they had perked right up. In fact, they had leaped forward with offers to carry the ladies' bags, and it hadn't taken but a minute for them to start squabbling over who was going to escort which of the women. The argument had been sheer contrariness, Casebolt knew, because he had heard the men swap positions several times as their voices got louder and angrier. Both of them wanted the blonde, then both decided to switch to the brunette, and they didn't have a chance to work it out before their tempers got the better of them and they reached for the pistols stuck behind their belts. A second later, the platform was echoing with the sound of gunshots and the acrid stink of powder smoke filled the air.

Now, Casebolt was the only one still holding a gun, and he motioned with it to the two miners. "You fellers get movin'," he ordered. To the women, he said, "Sorry, ladies. I don't reckon you'll have any trouble findin' some other 'gentlemen' around here to keep you company, though."

"I'm certain we won't, Deputy," the brunette said coolly. "By the way, my name is Lucy."

"And I'm Irene," the blonde added.

Casebolt reached up with his free hand and tugged on the brim of the battered hat that sat on his thinning gray hair. "Pleased to meet you, ladies . . . I reckon. I'm Billy Casebolt."

The brunette called Lucy smiled. "Just what is it you 'reckon', Deputy Casebolt? That you're pleased to meet us—or that we're ladies?"

Casebolt took a deep breath and said, "No, ma'am, you ain't gettin' me into this conversation. I got me some prisoners to tend to." He gestured again with the revolver and said to the miners, "Thought I told you two boys to get movin'."

Grudgingly, the men marched through the lobby of the station with Casebolt following behind them, gun in hand. They had just reached the porch on the front of the building when a well-dressed, very attractive woman with dark hair came up to the little group. She asked, "What's going on here, Billy?"

Casebolt tugged at his hatbrim again. "Howdy, Miz Simone. Just arrestin' these fellers for disturbin' the peace. Figured the marshal'd want us to extend the hospitality of that spankin' new jail of ours to 'em for a day or so."

"Just what were they disturbing the peace over?" Simone McKay asked.

Casebolt hesitated, then jerked a thumb over his shoulder toward Lucy and Irene, who had corralled a porter into bringing their bags into the station for them. Simone looked at them, and Casebolt saw her mouth tighten.

"I see," said the widow of one of the town's founders. Simone was also one of the richest women in the territory, thanks to the deaths of her late husband and his partner. She owned several businesses, including the hotel, the general store, and the newspaper, as well as about half of the real estate in the rest of the settlement. Over the past year and a half, she had settled comfortably into her role as the matriarch of Wind River, despite her relative youth. She looked back at Casebolt, gave him a little smile, and continued, "Well, carry on with your duties, Deputy, by all means."

"Yes, ma'am," Casebolt said. "Move along, boys."

As they headed west along Grenville Avenue, Wind River's main street, toward the squat stone building that had been only recently constructed, Casebolt thought about the encounter with Simone McKay. Simone was a lovely woman, the sort who looked as if she ought to wear lace and sit in a fancy parlor all day, but she had steel in her. Casebolt knew that.

And he had seen the way she looked at those two soiled doves. Simone hadn't been happy to see them. Which meant that *somebody* was in for some trouble.

Not for the first time, Casebolt was glad that he was just the deputy around here.

Before he came to Wind River and accepted the marshal's job—pinning on a law badge for the first time in his eventful life—Cole Tyler never would have believed that he could actually like a jail.

But by God he liked this one, he thought as he leaned back in the chair behind his desk. This was *his* jail.

Well, actually it belonged to the town, since the citizens of Wind River had paid for constructing the building. Until recently, the marshal's office had been located in the front room of the Wind River Land Development Company, and whenever he and Billy Casebolt had needed to lock somebody up, they'd been forced to use a smokehouse or the storage room of some business, any place that had a sturdy door and a lock.

Now he had an actual office, with his desk and chair moved over from the room in the land development company, along with the old sofa, plus a new filing cabinet and a gun rack on the wall. A black, cast-iron stove sat in one corner, and there were several extra chairs in the room as well. In the wall behind the desk were two doors; one led to a back room with a cot and a rear exit, while the other opened into a cell block containing four cells, two on each side of a short hallway. The bars of the cells had been freighted in on the UP, like some of the other furnishings, and they were supposed to be escape-proof. The small window in each cell was also heavily barred. Jesse James himself couldn't break out of this jail, Cole thought proudly—not that Jesse was likely to be up in these parts any time soon. He and his brother Frank were busy robbing banks down in Missouri, Arkansas, and Kentucky.

At the moment, nobody was locked up in the cells except the two men Billy Casebolt had brought in a little earlier for shooting up the platform down at the Union Pacific depot. Cole had agreed that the men needed some time behind bars to cool off. One of them complained that Casebolt had broken his wrist by whacking it with a gun barrel, and Cole had promised to have Dr. Judson Kent come by and take a look at it later. He wasn't in any hurry to do so, however.

In fact, Cole thought, as he propped his booted feet on the desk and leaned back in the chair, he was going to sit right here and contemplate matters for a while longer before he did anything.

He was a muscular, medium-sized man with sandy brown, square-cut hair that fell nearly to his shoulders. His features were permanently tanned by years of exposure to the sun and wind, and his gray-green eyes were alert and intelligent. He wore a buckskin shirt over denim pants that were tucked into high-topped boots. The gunbelt that was usually strapped around his waist was hung on a peg on the wall behind the desk, the Colt conversion revolver resting snugly in its holster. A Winchester '66 model, like the revolver a .44, was propped in the rifle rack next to a Sharps Big Fifty. The only weapon Cole was carrying at the moment was a heavy-bladed Green River knife sheathed on his left hip. He looked every inch the seasoned frontiersman that he was—even though he was a little sleepy.

That lassitude vanished abruptly as the front door of the office opened and Simone McKay came in.

Cole sat up hurriedly, his feet and the front legs of his chair thumping to the floor about the same time. He stood and put a smile on his face as he said, "Hello, Simone." Some people might have smiled anyway when confronted with the person who was, in effect, their boss, but in Cole's case the expression was genuine. He had grown quite fond of Simone over the months that he had known her. He would never forget that she was the one who convinced him to take the marshal's job after her husband was murdered.

"Hello, Cole," she said, returning the smile. He thought she looked very attractive in a pale gray skirt and jacket over a white shirt with ruffles at the throat.

"What can I do for you?" he asked, feeling a little tongue-tied. Simone had that effect on him sometimes.

She came into the office and closed the door behind her. "Deputy Casebolt brought some prisoners in a little while ago," she began.

Cole nodded. "That's right. A couple of miners who caused some sort of ruckus down at the train station. We've got 'em locked up back there. After a couple of days behind bars they'll likely think twice before causing any more trouble around here."

"I'm sure they will . . . but do you know what they were fighting over? Or perhaps I should say *who* they were fighting over."

Cole frowned and felt a touch of embarrassment. "Well, the way Billy explained it to me, there were a couple of, ah, young ladies involved . . . "

"Prostitutes, you mean," Simone said matter-of-factly.

"That's right," Cole said. He supposed if she wanted to be blunt, so could he.

"I asked around at the station, and I found out those women came in on the westbound today. Do you know just how many of those so-called soiled doves are already in Wind River, Cole?"

He had no choice but to shake his head and shrug, wondering what she was getting at. He said, "I wouldn't have any idea."

"Nor do I. But I can tell you this," declared Simone, "there are dozens of them. Perhaps even scores."

"Well, now, I'm not so sure about that," Cole said dubiously. "A couple of dozen, maybe—"

"It doesn't matter," Simone said sharply. "However many there are . . . there are *too* many."

Suddenly, Cole knew where she was headed with this discussion. An unhappy expression passed across his face as he said, "Simone, you're not about to ask me to run all those girls out of town, are you?"

"It's not just the prostitutes. There are all sorts of undesirable elements coming into Wind River these days. You know as well as I do that the town is full of gamblers and gunmen and . . . and painted women."

Cole wasn't sure what to say. Simone obviously wasn't in the mood to hear that the settlement had been that way right from the start. In fact, it was more peaceful now than it had ever been. When the railhead had first arrived, bringing with it the hell on wheels that followed right along the path of the Union Pacific, things had been a lot worse. Cole knew that for a fact because he had been in Wind River then, had worn a badge and dealt on a daily basis with the chaos that arose from the proliferation of saloons and gambling dens and bordellos, most of them housed in big canvas tents that were eventually taken down when the railhead was transferred to Rock Springs. Sure, there were still a lot of saloons in Wind River, and it was a rare week when somebody didn't get shot or robbed—or both—but that was a far cry from the flood of violence and greed and lust that had swept over the town in its early days. Cole thought he and Casebolt had done a pretty good job of bringing law and order to Wind River.

On the other hand, Simone's current concern was perhaps a testimonial to that very fact. Early on, most of the citizens had been more concerned with mere survival. Now that things had settled down a little, folks could start to worry about actually civilizing the place.

"I understand how you feel," Cole told Simone, "but Wind River's not just here for the folks who live in town. You've got your railroad men passing through, and all the cowhands from the ranches around here, and even a few prospectors drifting down from Montana Territory, like those two locked up back in the cells right now. When they come into town, they all want to have fun."

"Fun," Simone repeated with a touch of contempt. "You mean getting drunk and carousing and gambling."

"Well, they do seem to enjoy it," Cole said mildly, "at least until they wake up hung over and broke. And despite that they still come back the next time they've got two coins to rub together. That may not be the way it is back east, but it's the way of the world out here on the frontier."

Simone sighed. "I suppose you're right."

"And there aren't any laws against drinking and gambling. If I was to try to shut down the saloons, I'd have Hank Parker and his kind in here yelling like a buffalo was standing on their feet. As long as folks are a little discreet about their activities—including those two women who came in on the train today—there's not much I can do about them. Of course, if anybody breaks the law . . . "

"Of course," Simone said, a touch of angry sarcasm in her tone, despite the fact that she was agreeing with him. "All right, Cole, I see your point." She turned toward the door, then looked back at him. "But there *will* come a day when Wind River will no longer tolerate such behavior. And I intend to be here when that day comes."

"Me, too, Simone," said Cole. "Me, too."

But as she went out and he sat down behind the desk again, his good mood gone, Cole had to think about what he had just said.

Would the day really come when a man couldn't buy a drink or sit in on a friendly game of poker or even pay for the companionship of a pretty lady if he wanted to?

If that day ever came . . . it might just be the day that Cole Tyler finally took off that lawman's badge and rode on.

Lon Rogers whistled a tune to himself as he strode along the boardwalk connecting several of the businesses on the south side of Grenville Avenue. The young cowboy was in such a good mood he felt like breaking out into song, but he knew that if he did, folks would look at him funny. He settled for giving a big grin and a cheerful "Howdy" to everybody he passed.

Lon was slicked up good today, being as it was a special occasion and all. He had washed his pants and shined up his boots and put on his best shirt, the one his mama down in Texas had decorated with some fancy stitching. He had even brushed off all the dust from the hat that was pushed back on his curly brown hair.

"Whooo—eee, boy!" one of the hands in the Diamond S bunkhouse had called to him as he was leaving earlier. "You goin' courtin' . . . or did you get yourself all purtied up for us?"

That gibe had brought hooting laughter from the

other punchers scattered around the big room, but Lon had shot back, "You boys wouldn't know pretty if it came up and gored you like a wild-eyed longhorn!"

"That's the way you look right about now, Lon—plumb wild-eyed with love!"

He had given up and got out while the getting was good, saddling up one of the horses from the remuda and riding into Wind River as the sun slid toward the mountains on the horizon. He wouldn't be the only one of Kermit Sawyer's cowboys who came into town tonight, he knew, but he was getting a head start on the others. He wasn't going to gamble and drink and get into fights, though.

He was going to have him some supper at the Wind River Café.

In fact, there was the place now, the yellow glow from the lamps already shining warmly through the big, cheerfully curtained windows in the gathering twilight.

Lon hesitated, torn between his desire to go into the café and see the proprietor, Rose Foster, again, and a sudden nervousness that went through him. He had hinted pretty strongly to Rose on a number of occasions how he really felt about her, but although she had always seemed friendly to him, she had never taken advantage of the opportunities to let him know that she returned his affection.

Which likely meant she didn't feel the same way about him at all, Lon thought glumly.

But, as he took a deep breath, he told himself that his mama hadn't raised him to be a quitter. Nor had his boss, Kermit Sawyer—the man who had been like a second father to him—instilled in him anything less than sheer determination to get what he wanted out of life. Sawyer hadn't particularly wanted him to make the trip up here to Wyoming Territory from the ranch on the Colorado River down in Texas, but Lon had been determined then, and he had gotten what he wanted. Over the long months that had passed since Sawyer had established the Diamond S up here with those longhorns from Texas, Lon had grown in the eyes of the middle-aged cattleman. Sawyer respected him now; Lon was sure of it.

If a stubborn man like Kermit Sawyer could change his mind, so could a woman like Rose Foster. Lon squared his shoulders, put a smile on his face, and pushed open the door leading into the café.

Rose was tired, a bone-deep weariness that came from being on her feet nearly all day every day. Running a busy café wasn't easy, especially when the only full-time workers were herself and old Monty Riordan, the cook she had hired away from the Union Pacific. The growing business had prompted her to hire a couple of part-time waitresses recently, but most of the time it was just her and Monty, going from can to can't.

And now as she stood behind the counter and glanced up, she saw just about the last person she wanted to see at the end of a long day.

Lon Rogers was coming into the café, dressed up in his best clothes and wearing a big silly grin on his face.

Rose suppressed the sigh of irritation that began to well from inside her. Lon was a sweet boy, he really was, but she had neither the time nor the inclination to deal with his courting tonight. Every seat at the counter was full and most of the tables were occupied, too. The cowboys and farmers who patronized the café didn't have much money most of the time, but they had hefty appetites. When they could afford to buy a meal, they wanted all the trimmings with it. Rose had been hopping all evening, waiting on tables and ducking into the kitchen whenever she had a chance to lend Monty a hand. Now, when she was taking advantage of the first opportunity in a while to pause and catch her breath, Lon had to wander in so that he could make calf eyes at her and drop hints about wooing her.

If he knew the truth about her, she suddenly thought, he wouldn't have been so quick to fall for her.

She looked down as the thought made a bitter grimace pull briefly at her mouth. Then she raised her head, ran her fingers through her thick, strawberry-blond hair, and managed to smile a little. One of the men at the counter had finished his meal and got up to leave, and Lon slid smoothly onto the stool he vacated.

"Hello, Rose," Lon said as he grinned at her. "Mighty pretty evening tonight . . . almost as pretty as you."

"Thank you, Lon," she said. "What can I do for you?"

"I'll have the usual. Fry me a steak with all the fixin's."

"Sure." Rose turned her head to call through the little window into the kitchen, "Another one, Monty."

She waited until the elderly cook nodded and made a gesture of acknowledgment, then turned back to Lon.

"And a cup of coffee," he said before she could ask.

She got a cup from a shelf behind the counter, picked up the blue tin coffeepot from the stove with a thick leather potholder, and poured the strong black brew for him. The men here in Wyoming Territory liked their coffee sturdy enough to get up and walk off with the cup if they didn't keep an eye on it.

Rose suddenly remembered *café au lait* in delicate china cups with beautiful designs filigreed on them, sipped in elegant dining rooms in the best homes in the city . . .

She put that thought out of her mind with a tiny shake of her head. That had been a thousand years ago, in a place a million miles away.

Turning her attention back to Lon, she kept the smile on her face as he said, "You know, Rose, I've been thinking—"

"That's good, Lon," she cut in before he had a chance to go on. "A man needs to think. But right now you've got to excuse me. I've got customers who need tending to."

"Oh." He made a visible effort not to appear too crestfallen. "Sure, Rose. You go right ahead and do what you need to do."

She hated to cut him off that way; she knew she had hurt his feelings a little. But he would get over it, and at any rate, she had known what he was about to say. He had been planning to say something about the two of them getting together sometime. She had recognized the look in his eye of a man who had finally worked up the courage to do something that scared him half to death.

For the next few minutes Rose moved among the tables, making sure no one needed anything else. She carried several coffee cups behind the counter, refilled them, and returned them to the customers. She went into the kitchen to dish up bowls of apple cobbler for some of the men. As she worked, she could feel Lon's eyes on her, following her around the room, watching her as she went about her tasks. There had been a time when she had reveled in such rapt male attention.

No longer, though. Now she just wanted to do her work and be left alone.

By the time Monty slid the plate containing Lon's steak, potatoes, beans, and cornbread through the opening from the kitchen, Rose's weariness had deepened to a steady ache across her shoulders and the back of her neck. This time she didn't return Lon's smile as she put the plate in front of him and said, "There you go."

"Thank you, Rose. It all looks mighty good. And so do—"

The door opened, and the jingling of the bell that hung over it cut into what Lon had been about to say. He looked irritated. Rose checked to see who was coming in and saw a tall, heavily muscled man with massive arms and shoulders. His face was round and a little flushed, and he had thin, pale hair. He wore work clothes and shoes rather than boots, but he had taken off the leather apron he usually sported while he was working in the blacksmith shop he owned. Jeremiah Newton was Wind River's only blacksmith, in addition to being the settlement's only preacher, although he had never been ordained in any organized church. His sermons were of the hellfire-and-brimstone variety, as hot and sulfurous as the flames in his shop's furnace. When he wasn't spreading the Gospel, however, his voice and demeanor were gentle and mild.

"Good evening, Sister Rose," Jeremiah said as he came up to the counter. "I was wondering if I might get something to eat?"

Rose glanced around the room. "We're full up right now, Jeremiah," she said apologetically. "Maybe in a little while . . . "

"I don't mind waiting," he said.

The man sitting to Lon's left wiped up the last bit of

gravy from his plate with a piece of cornbread and popped it into his mouth. As he chewed, he said, "Here y'go, Jeremiah. You can have my place. I'm finished."

"Why, thank you kindly, brother," Jeremiah said. He thumped a ham-like hand on the man's shoulder in gratitude, staggering the gent a little as he stood up.

Lon looked less than happy about having the massive blacksmith sit beside him, but he didn't say anything.

"Well, Jeremiah, what can I get you?" asked Rose.

Jeremiah grinned. "A freshly baked loaf of Brother Riordan's bread, perhaps, and a side of beef? It's been a long, busy day at the shop."

"You settle for fried steak and all the trimmings?"

Jeremiah held up two long, thick, blunt fingers. "Two steaks."

"You've got 'em." Rose turned and called to Monty Riordan, "Two for Brother Jeremiah!"

"Praise the Lord," grunted Monty sarcastically, and Rose cast a glance over her shoulder at the counter. Jeremiah didn't appear to have heard, and she was thankful for that. The big blacksmith might not have taken the comment too well.

Jeremiah had turned to Lon Rogers, and he said, "Hello, Brother Lon. Haven't seen you at services lately."

"We've been pretty busy on the ranch," Lon answered, sounding a little defensive. "Cows don't know the Sabbath from any other day."

"I suppose not. Maybe what I ought to do is start riding around to the ranches in the area one Sunday a month and hold services right out there on the range."

"Well, that's an idea," Lon said noncommittally. Clearly, he was a little uncomfortable with the conversation.

Rose felt sorry enough for him to come to his rescue

by asking Jeremiah, "How are the plans coming along for the new church?"

"Just fine, Sister Rose. There's almost enough money in the bank now to start construction, and I've got my eye on a piece of land that'll do just fine."

For more than a year, Jeremiah had been taking up collections at the weekly services he held underneath a big tree on the western edge of town when the weather was nice. During the winter, the services had been moved inside to a vacant store. Jeremiah made no secret of the fact that he wanted to build an actual church, however, and the money taken up at the services had been saved for that purpose, along with all the profits from his blacksmith shop that weren't necessary to pay for his simple living expenses. He probably hadn't eaten at the café more than half a dozen times in the past year, Rose recalled.

Recently, a bank had opened in Wind River, the first such financial institution in the settlement. Simone McKay was backing it, and an experienced banking official from the East had been brought in to run it. The bank and the new jail were signs that progress was really taking hold in the town, and there was even talk of building a school. A church would be just what Wind River needed to make it complete, Rose thought now as she listened to Jeremiah talk about his plans. He had deposited all the funds he had collected in the bank, and as soon as he decided where the church should be located, he could buy the land and get started on the construction. Wind River was getting more civilized all the time, Rose mused.

Of course, it was still a far cry from a place like New Orleans . . .

That thought took Rose back again in time, and she was deep in reverie when she became aware that Monty was talking to her and both Lon and Jeremiah were frowning at her.

Lon pointed at the window to the kitchen. "Jeremiah's food's ready," he said.

"Oh. Oh! I'm sorry, Jeremiah," Rose said quickly as she turned around to gather up the plates full of steak and potatoes. "I'm afraid I was woolgathering."

"That's all right, sister," the big man assured her. "Sometimes I find myself doing the same thing. I promise you, it's better to do it behind the counter of a café than while you're standing behind a horse that doesn't particularly like being shod."

Rose smiled. "There you go." She placed the food in front of Jeremiah, then glanced at Lon. He had almost finished his supper, and he looked like he was girding himself up again for something.

It came as no surprise to her when he asked a moment later, "Rose . . . I was wondering if I could walk you home after you close up for the night?"

"Well, that may be a while, Lon." She gestured around at the busy room. "You can see for yourself, it doesn't look like the place will be clearing out any time soon."

"I can wait—or I can come back. Whatever you want."

Rose hesitated. On more than one occasion, he had walked her back to the boardinghouse where she rented a room, and she didn't really mind his company as long as he didn't try to get too serious. Despite the tiredness she felt, she couldn't find it in herself to refuse his offer tonight.

"Sure, Lon," she told him with a smile. "That would be fine."

His face lit up like the sun rising in the morning.

Rose hoped she hadn't made a mistake.

Lon didn't wait in the café, preferring to come back later when the place wasn't so busy. That was all right with Rose, because it not only gave her an empty stool at the counter which could be filled by another paying customer, but it saved her from having to work all evening under the watchful, love-struck eyes of the young cowboy.

With any luck, walking her home was all that Lon had in mind tonight. But one of these times, he was going to try to kiss her. Rose was sure of that. She wasn't certain, though, how she would handle the problem when it came up.

Lon was back a little before ten o'clock. The evening's rush was finally over. There were only a few customers left, and they were finishing up their meals. Rose had already propped the *Closed* sign in the window, but that didn't stop Lon, of course.

"You about ready to go?" he asked as he came up to the counter and smiled at her.

"Well, I've still got a few customers . . . " Rose began.

From behind her, Monty Riordan said, "Aw, go on, Rose. I can handle things here and close up for you." Then he chuckled.

Rose cast a glance over her shoulder at the old man and saw the big grin on his face. Monty was pretty sharp; he knew how she regarded Lon as a good-hearted nuisance. She frowned at him so that Lon couldn't see the expression, then sighed and turned back to the young Diamond S puncher.

"All right," she said. "I guess we can go."

She had a shawl hanging behind the counter. She draped it around her shoulders and let Lon take her arm as he escorted her to the door. It was still summer, but on these high plains, the nights could get chilly. Rose was grateful for the shawl as she stepped out onto the boardwalk.

For the most part, Wind River was quiet at this hour. The saloons on the east end of town were doing a brisk business and light and noise spilled through their batwinged entrances, but most of the other buildings in the settlement were dark. Rose saw a lamp burning through the window of the *Wind River Sentinel* and knew that editor Michael Hatfield was probably in there working on the next issue of the newspaper. Likewise, there was a lighted lantern hanging from the awning over the porch of the new jail and marshal's office. Rose spotted a figure moving along the boardwalk on the other side of Grenville Avenue, pausing to make sure all doors were locked, and she recognized the man as Marshal Cole Tyler. Her eyes flickered back to Cole as she and Lon passed on the other side of the street, going in the opposite direction.

Cole Tyler was a handsome man in a rough way, and although there had been some friction between him and Rose from time to time, she found herself admiring him. It wouldn't ever go beyond that, though, she knew, because Cole only had eyes for Simone McKay. A woman could tell those things.

And besides, he was a lawman, and she could never afford to let a lawman get too friendly with her. She couldn't take that chance . . .

Lon was talking to her, his words fast and nervous,

and Rose realized she had better start paying attention to what he was saying when she heard, " . . . be your beau, Miss Rose."

She gave a little shake of her head. "What? What did you say, Lon?"

"I said I'd sure be proud and honored if you'd allow me to be your beau, Miss Rose. I . . . I reckon you know how I feel about you by now, what with all the courting I've been doing."

She stopped, knowing that she couldn't put this off any longer. Here on this darkened boardwalk, with no one else around, might be the best place for it, too.

"Lon," she said quietly, "I know you've been trying to court me, but honestly, I'm just not looking for a beau right now."

"You're not?" He sounded amazed.

"No. I'm sorry, but I just think of you as a friend."

"A friend," he repeated slowly. "Well, if you just give me a chance, maybe I'll grow on—"

"No, Lon." Rose's voice was firm now. "You can't be my beau, and if you think you're courting me by walking me home like this, well, we'll just have to stop that."

There was enough moonlight for her to see how stricken his face was, and for a second she felt a surge of guilt. He was really a decent young man, and she hoped she hadn't hurt him too much. She said, "I'm sorry if you think I've led you on . . . "

"No, ma'am, Miss Rose," he said quickly. "If anybody's to blame here, it's me. But you know how it is. I'm just a thick-headed ol' cowboy. I get these foolish notions in my brain, and before you know it, I'm spouting off things that I shouldn't ever say. I'm purely sorry, Miss Rose, I really am."

"You're not offended?"

"No, ma'am. And I'll be glad to walk you home any-time, as your friend. Shoot, I may be around even more now that we've got things straightened out between us."

Damn! That wasn't what she wanted at all. She had thought that by telling Lon he couldn't court her any-more, he would be around less, not more. Rose took a deep breath and said, "I don't think that would be a good idea."

"Why not?" Lon asked stubbornly.

She was going to have to hurt his feelings after all, Rose realized. She said, "Because I don't want you to. I . . . I want you to quit bothering me so much."

"Bothering you?" His voice was brittle with surprise and pain.

"That's right. My God, Lon, I thought you would have figured it out by now."

He let go of her arm and stepped away from her. "Like I said, I'm just a dumb cowboy. But I reckon you've made it clear. I won't bother you anymore, Miss Rose. Now, if you don't mind, I'll take you on to your board-inghouse so I can get started back to the ranch."

"I can get home all right by myself, thanks."

"No, ma'am. I'll escort you."

He was just being chivalrous, though. Rose could tell that much from his voice. She had finally gotten through to him, but only by being brutally honest with him.

And not completely honest at that, she thought as she took his arm again and they walked on down the street in strained silence. Under other circumstances, she might not have minded a little innocent flirtation with Lon Rogers, even though he was too young—and, to be truthful, too innocent—for her.

But not now. Not yet. Despite the quiet, peaceful existence she had led for over a year, the past could still catch up to her. The secrets were still lurking back there behind her.

And secrets, as she knew all too well, could be deadly. Not just for her, but for anyone unlucky enough to be close to her . . .

A couple of days later, another train was rolling west toward Wind River from Rawlins with a good head of steam built up as it traveled across the Wyoming plains. From a high ridge to the south of the tracks, the train was plainly visible to the man who sat there on horseback. The man pulled a piece of a broken mirror from his saddlebag and angled it so that the reflected sunlight flashed toward another ridge almost a mile to the west.

Another man stood on the second ridge waiting for the signal. When he saw the brilliant shard of light reflected from the other man's mirror, he grinned broadly and took off his hat. He waved the hat back and forth over his head.

At the base of the ridge, where the tracks of the Union Pacific ran, a third man saw the signal, smiled, and called to his companions, "Fire it up, boys."

"You bet, Lew," one of the other men responded eagerly. Several of them held torches made of pitch-soaked rags wrapped around tree branches. One of the men scratched a lucifer into life and held the flame to his torch. After a moment, the rags caught fire, giving off a black, oily smoke. The other men lit their torches from this one.

Then they plunged the flaming brands into the pile of brush that was heaped on the tracks.

Lew Stanton threw back his head and laughed as the dry brush caught fire and blazed up brightly. The fire was just to get the attention of the approaching train's engineer, and all those flames and smoke ought to do the job nicely. It was the massive pile of boulders and broken cross-ties stacked in front of the fiery brush that would force the train to come to a halt or risk derailment.

Once the train was stopped, Stanton and his men could really go to work.

The leader of the outlaw gang was a tall, broad-shouldered man with curly brown hair and a wide mouth that could quirk into a charming grin whenever he wanted it to. That charm never quite reached the flat, dead gray eyes, however. Stanton peered down the tracks to the east. The twin lines of the rails curved around the shoulder of a hill about a quarter of a mile away, and Stanton knew the locomotive ought to be coming into view at any moment. He couldn't hear the humming of the rails because of the crackling and popping from the blazing pile of brush, but when he put his booted foot on the steel, he could feel the faint shudder that heralded the approach of the train. He waved an arm at his men and called, "Let's go, let's go! Everybody in your positions!"

At times like this, Stanton almost fancied himself a military man once more. This was like being at war again, like the days when he had captained a troop of cavalry and fought the Rebs. He could still smell the smoke and the blood. At times he even seemed to hear the crash of cannon, the crackle of small arms fire, the screams of dying men and horses.

How could a man go back to an Iowa farm and be happy after that? Lew Stanton couldn't, and he had known it as soon as the war was over. That was why he had headed west, seeking something to replace the thrill of battle.

Robbing trains and banks wasn't as good . . . but it would do until something better came along.

The outlaws scattered, spreading out along both sides of the railroad tracks, using clumps of brush and the little gullies that crisscrossed this part of the country to conceal themselves. Stanton dropped behind a small mound of rocks and drew his gun. He pushed his flat-crowned black hat off his head so that it hung on his back from its chin strap, then lifted his head a little to watch and wait. A moment later the locomotive came into view, rounding the curve in the tracks, smoke and steam puffing from its diamond-shaped stack.

A wide grin spread across Lew Stanton's face as he heard the sudden squeal of steel against steel. The engineer had spotted the fire and the barricade and hit the brakes, throwing the drivers into reverse. The train shuddered and bucked as it skidded toward the deadly pile of rocks and cross-ties.

The sudden lurch threw passengers forward in their seats, made women scream, prompted curses and shouted questions from the men.

One man, who had been dozing in his seat with his

head leaned forward and his broad-brimmed, high-crowned black hat tipped over his eyes, had to lift his hands quickly and catch himself against the back of the seat in front of him. He lifted his head, revealing weathered, mild-looking features and piercing blue eyes that narrowed in speculation. Such a sudden stop could mean only one thing, he knew.

Trouble.

He started to get up as the train jolted to a halt, but then the conductor came running through the car, yelling for everybody to stay calm and not to panic. The man in the black hat thought the conductor could have used some of that advice himself.

Then, from the corner of his eye, he spotted motion through the window next to his seat and peered out to see men leaping up from their hiding places and running toward the stopped train, guns drawn and ready to savagely cut down anyone who opposed them. A glance across the aisle and out the window on the other side of the train showed the same thing. There had to be at least twenty men storming the train, maybe more.

So it was a hold-up, the man in the black hat told himself. Several of the bandits would leap into the cab of the locomotive first thing, taking the engineer and fireman captive. Another group of outlaws would concentrate on the express car, while the rest of the gang would spread through the train, taking over each of the cars and looting everything of value from the passengers.

Typical. The man in the black hat had seen it all before. He leaned back in his seat and tipped his hat down again, then crossed his arms over his chest. Might as well take it easy until the desperadoes got around to him, he thought.

All the yelling and uproar going on around the man didn't appear to bother him. He might have been dozing, for all the concern he showed. But as a wild-eyed young passenger brandishing a gun started past him toward the front of the car, the older man's arm suddenly shot out. With surprising strength, he grabbed the gun-toter's coat and shoved him into the vacant seat opposite.

"Sit down and put that gun away, you damned fool!"

The sharp tone of command made the young man gape. "What—"

"Save it until it can do some good," said the man in the black hat. "You go running out there now, they'll just gun you down and you'll have died for nothing. Now put it away!"

The young man swallowed, looking confused, but then he did as he was told and slipped the pistol back into its holster. The older man crossed his arms again and resumed his waiting.

It didn't take long. Three men clattered up the steps at the front of the car and leveled guns at the frightened passengers. All of them wore long dusters and had bandannas tied across the lower halves of their faces. The tallest of the three called out, "Just stay in your seats and stay quiet, folks, and nobody'll get hurt! I reckon you've already figured out this is a robbery!"

An uneasy silence fell over the car. The man in the black hat sent a warning glance at the younger man across the aisle. Now wasn't the time to try anything.

"All right," the tallest outlaw said in satisfaction. "Looks like you're all going to be smart and behave yourselves. Now in just a minute, my pards are going to be coming down the aisle with some sacks. All valuables go in the sacks, understand? Wallets, purses, watches, jewelry . . .

anything you got that's worth anything, in it goes. We find anybody who tries to hold out, they die. It's that simple." To his two companions, he added in a quieter voice, "Get started, boys."

That one had to be the boss, mused the man in the black hat. Despite the roughness of his tone, there was something in his voice . . . an intelligence that not every outlaw possessed. Maybe not educated or cultured, but more than a simple killer or thief. A former military man, perhaps. That was a pretty good guess, the man in the black hat decided.

The two outlaws carrying burlap bags were making their way down the aisle, holding the bags while the passengers deposited their valuables. Each of the men used only one hand to hold the bag, while the other hand still gripped a gun butt. They weren't watching the passengers that closely, however. The man in the black hat saw their eyes following the money clips, the wallets, the jewelry into the burlap bags. Greed had replaced alertness.

Stupid. Damned stupid.

The outlaw working this side of the aisle had gotten a little behind his companion, and that might prove to be a problem. It would just have to be dealt with, though. The bandit on the other side reached the young man, and he growled, "Shuck that gun and toss it in here, too." The young man hesitated, then, staring down the barrel of the bandit's gun, had no choice but to do as he was told.

That made the situation even worse, since the man in the black hat had been counting on the youngster for a little help. But not impossible. Just . . . trickier.

The other outlaw paused beside the man. "Come on, old-timer," the outlaw said impatiently. "Let's have the loot."

"Sure," the man said mildly. "Here you go."

With a movement so smooth and deceptive that it didn't seem to happen, each of the man's hands slid underneath his coat and then came out as he uncrossed his arms. There was an ivory-handled Colt gripped in each fist, and his thumbs eared back the hammers as the barrels tipped up. The bandit barely had time to widen his eyes in surprise before flame and smoke blasted from the barrels of both revolvers.

The bullets slammed into the belly of the outlaw, doubling him over from their impact. Before he had a chance to fall, however, the man in the black hat came up out of his seat, moving so fast it was difficult for the eye to follow him. His right arm, still holding one of the pistols, went under the left arm of the outlaw and caught him, holding him up as a makeshift shield. The tall boss outlaw at the end of the car cursed and fired, but the bullet thudded harmlessly into the back of his already-dead partner. The man in the black hat snapped a shot at the boss outlaw with his right-hand gun.

At the same time he twisted and brought the other pistol in line with the outlaw who had moved on down the aisle. That man was spinning toward him, startled, and trying to bring his own gun to bear. There wasn't time, because the ivory-handled Colt boomed again and the slug lanced into the outlaw's chest. The man was thrown backward to land in the lap of a shrieking woman.

The man in the black hat fired again at the outlaw chief and was rewarded by the sight of the tall man staggering back a step. The outlaw cursed again and sent one more futile shot screaming down the car, over the heads of the passengers who were all trying to crawl under the seats. Then he plunged out of the car's vestibule, leaping down the steps to the ground outside.

Shoving the corpse of the first outlaw away from him, the man in the black hat whirled and ran toward the other end of the car. Racing after the boss outlaw would just get him shot if he emerged from the car unwarily. He heard footsteps behind him and glanced back. The young passenger had reclaimed his gun from the outlaw's bag and obviously wanted in on this fight.

The two of them reached the platform at the rear end of the car, and the older man motioned for his companion to stop. The express car was farther back, and sure enough, some of the outlaws were already there. The man in the black hat ventured a glance toward the front of the train and was rewarded with a bullet that chewed splinters from the wooden trim at the corner of the car, about a foot from his head. He ducked back and grimaced.

A second later he heard the voice of the boss outlaw, bellowing, "Get up here, now!"

The bandit was calling to the other members of his gang, and the man in the black hat knew that pretty soon he and his companion were going to be caught in a crossfire. He said, "I don't know about you, son, but I think I'm going where it'll be a little harder for those outlaws to shoot me."

"Where?" the young man asked frantically.

Using the barrel of one of the ivory-handled Colts, the man in the black hat pointed up.

Rage filled Lew Stanton. One old man who looked about as dangerous as a plate of mush was going to ruin everything! Who would have thought that he'd have a couple of guns hidden under his coat—or that he would be able to use them so well? Stanton wasn't going to be happy until he had put a bullet in that bastard's face.

Two of his men were dead already, and Stanton himself had been clipped by a bullet on the top of his left shoulder. His left arm hung numb and useless at his side, and the crease itself hurt like hell. Blood stained the shoulder and sleeve of the duster.

After snapping a shot at the man in the black hat, Stanton looked down the train and saw several of his own men come boiling out of the express car. He counted them quickly, saw there were four of them, and let out another curse.

The damned fools hadn't left anybody behind to watch the guard, and there hadn't been any shots from down there so Stanton knew the man was still alive. Maybe the men had at least had the sense to clout him over the head with a gun barrel—

The next second, a man in a vest and string tie leaned out of the door of the express car, a rifle in his hands. He threw the rifle to his shoulder and pressed the trigger, and the bullet took one of the running outlaws in the back, pitching him lifelessly forward onto his face.

The idiots! Stanton fumed. Not only had they left the express messenger behind them, they hadn't even made sure there wasn't a gun in the car! It served them right that the Winchester was barking, cutting them down from behind. Another lesson of war, thought Stanton.

It was amazing how quickly even a well-organized plan could go to hell when a wild card popped up.

The man in the black hat ran to the other side of the platform, jammed both guns back in the holsters underneath his coat, and leaned out to grasp the ladder that ran to the top of the car. A quick glance as he swung onto the ladder told him that none of the outlaws who had been on this side of the train were in sight now. "Come on!" he called to the young man as he climbed.

Moving with a spryness that belied the weathered features and the thick white hair underneath the black hat, the man scrambled up the ladder and pulled himself onto the top of the car. His boots slipped a little on the curved surface, but he was able to fling himself forward and land on the six-foot-wide strip of flat roof that ran down the center of the car. He came up in a crouch and drew one of his guns as the young man followed him to the top of the car.

"Now what?" the young man gasped from hands and knees.

"Now we look for some more of those owlhoots to shoot," the man in the black hat replied. "By the way, my name's Dan Boyd."

"I'm Riley . . . Riley Colbert."

Dan Boyd grinned. "Glad to meet you, Riley. Can you use that hogleg?"

"Yeah. Pretty good, I guess."

"Come on, then."

Boyd started along the car, bending low so he wouldn't be spotted as easily from down below. He heard gunfire break out from further back along the train and knew that someone else was fighting back against the outlaws. Boyd was more concerned about what was happening at the front of the train, though, and that wasn't far away. He had been riding in the first passenger car, and there was nothing between it and the engine except the coal tender.

Suddenly a gun cracked in the cab of the locomotive,

and Boyd saw some frantic motion up there. The engineer and the fireman must have launched an attack of their own when their captors were distracted by the unexpected outbreak of gunfire along the train. Boyd wanted to get up there and help them, but Riley Colbert suddenly yelled, "They're behind us!"

Boyd turned around quickly but carefully, not wanting to lose his balance and fall off the train. He saw that several of the outlaws were in the process of scrambling up onto the car. "Get down!" he barked at Riley.

The young man threw himself flat. He stuck his pistol out in front of him and started firing as fast as he could, spraying bullets toward the outlaws. Boyd took his time, aiming and firing deliberately as Riley's bullets kept the outlaws occupied even if they didn't hit anything. Three times the ivory-handled Colt cracked, and each time one of the bandits went spinning off the top of the car.

The rest of them would think twice about trying to come up that ladder, Boyd knew.

He turned back toward the engine, wondering where that boss outlaw had gone. No more shots had come from up there, so Boyd said to Riley, "Stay here and keep your eyes open."

Then he holstered his gun and got a little bit of a running start before he leaped across the gap between the passenger car and the coal tender.

It was an easier jump than it might look, since the level of the coal was lower than the roof of the passenger car. Boyd caught himself as he landed on the stuff and began to clamber over it toward the engine. The coal immediately turned his hands black as he scrambled to keep his balance, but the stains didn't show much on his dark clothing.

When he slid down from the tender and landed in the

cab of the engine, going to one knee as he did so, he saw the fireman standing over one of the outlaws, shovel raised to strike again if he needed to. From the misshapen look of the outlaw's skull, that wasn't going to be necessary. Startled, the fireman turned toward Boyd and raised the shovel higher.

"Hold it!" Boyd snapped. "I'm not one of those desperadoes. I'm a U.S. marshal."

The fireman didn't lower the shovel immediately, not convinced that Boyd was telling the truth. But then the engineer, who was leaning against the side of the cab and clutching a bullet-shattered shoulder, said through teeth clenched against the pain, "I know this fella, Farley. He's tellin' the truth!"

Boyd came to his feet and went hurriedly to the engineer. "Was there just one of them?"

"The others jumped down and ran back to join the rest of 'em when the shootin' started," the fireman supplied. "That's when I grabbed my shovel and bounced it off this bastard's head. He managed to plug Hobbs there before he fell down, though."

"I'll be all right, Marshal," grated the engineer. "Just do something about them outlaws!"

"I have been," Boyd said. "And I'm about to do something else."

His coal-grimed hands went to the controls of the engine as his eyes flicked over the dials of the gauges. There was still plenty of steam up. He grabbed a lever and shoved it over, throwing the train into reverse. With a heavy jolt, it lurched into motion.

"Get down!" Boyd snapped at the crewmen as he drew one of his guns. "We'll be backing right past some of those owlhoots!"

Sure enough, a second later he caught a glimpse of men wearing dusters and firing at the engine as it passed. Bullets spanged harmlessly off the steel walls of the cab. He saw the tall man who had led the gang and threw a shot at him, but Boyd couldn't tell if the bullet found its target or not. Several of the outlaws were sprawled alongside the tracks, though, never to move again.

"Damn!" Boyd suddenly exclaimed as the train began to pick up speed. "I forgot about that boy Riley!"

Motioning to the fireman to take over the controls, Boyd turned and climbed the iron rungs leading to the top of the coal tender. When he reached the mound of coal, he was able to peer over it and see the young man's head at the front of the first passenger car. Evidently when the train had started moving, Riley had spread-eagled himself in the center of the roof and was hanging on for dear life.

Cupping his hands to his mouth, Boyd shouted, "Stay put, Riley! We'll be stopping in a minute!"

He turned and slid back down the coal to the cab. The train was rocking along at a good clip as it took the curve it had come around earlier. The outlaws who had been left behind were well out of range now. Boyd figured they must have had their horses hidden somewhere nearby, but it would take some time to fetch them. Meanwhile, he didn't know if any of the robbers were still on board the train. It was quite possible, he thought. He let the train roll another half mile or so, then said to the fireman, "Throw on the brakes."

The man did so, sending the train shuddering and squealing to a halt again. Boyd leaped down from the cab and ran along the train, both of the ivory-handled Colts in his hands now. The coal dust on his hands would soil those pistol grips, but they could be cleaned.

The conductor emerged from one of the passenger cars and ran toward Boyd, also holding a gun. He waved the weapon and asked, "Are there any more of them on board?"

"You tell me," Boyd snapped. "Nobody's taken a shot at me since we stopped."

The guard from the express car joined them, still carrying his rifle, and the three men began to go through the train, car by car. Quickly, it became apparent that except for dead men, none of the outlaws were left.

"We were damned lucky," the guard said. "Think they'll hit us again?"

"We killed nearly half of them, I reckon," said Boyd as he watched Riley Colbert climb down from the first car and go back inside, shaken but unhurt. "If they've got any sense, they've already taken off for the tall and uncut."

And that leader had sense, Boyd thought. The man wouldn't try to take over the train again with little more than half of his original force, not when there were well-armed men aboard and he had lost the element of surprise.

"Who started the shooting?" the conductor asked angrily. "I told everybody to stay calm."

"I did," Boyd replied. "And I *was* calm. If I hadn't been, I'd've wound up dead instead of those gents in the dusters."

"Who are you, mister?" asked the guard.

"Dan Boyd. Deputy U.S. marshal working out of the Omaha office right now." He turned to the conductor. "You can pull the train forward again and get some volunteers to start clearing that mess off the tracks. Your engineer's got a bullet in his shoulder and will need some tending to, but the fireman looked like he could handle the controls all right. We'll find somebody else to shovel for him."

"Hell, you just take right over, don't you, Marshal?" the conductor said, his voice full of resentment.

"I'm trying to wrap up a case I've been working on for a long time," Boyd told him, making an effort to hold on to his patience with the conductor. "I need to get where I'm going as soon as possible."

"Where's that?" asked the express guard.

"A town on down the line," Dan Boyd said. "A place called Wind River. And I sure hope the woman I'm looking for is still there . . ."

Rose Foster picked up a bolt of fabric with a bright, blue and white pattern printed on it. She was studying the material when a voice said behind her, "That's pretty, but I don't think it really suits you, dear."

Rose turned quickly, habits that she had thought were forgotten springing to the fore again. Those instincts had alarm bells clamoring in her mind.

Instead of the threat she had feared she would see, however, there were merely two young women, a blonde and a brunette, standing there, also looking through the bolts of material scattered over a large table in the Wind River General Store.

"I didn't mean to frighten you," the brunette said with a friendly smile. "I just don't think that fabric would make a very pretty dress."

Rose realized she was holding the bolt of cloth in front of her, almost like a shield. She turned and placed it on the table, then managed to smile back at the woman.

"That's all right. Sometimes I start thinking about things and I don't realize what's going on around me until somebody speaks to me. I was considering making some new curtains for my business."

"What business would that be?" asked the blonde.

"The Wind River Café," Rose said. "It's a couple of blocks down Grenville Avenue."

The brunette nodded. "Oh, yes, I've seen it. We'll have to stop there and eat sometime. You *own* the place, you said?"

"That's right."

"How remarkable. It's not often you find a woman owning any sort of business."

"Well," Rose said, thinking about Simone McKay, "it's not that uncommon in Wind River."

"We're working girls, too," the blonde said.

Rose wasn't sure how to respond to that. She had pegged them as soiled doves right away, and it didn't take a genius to figure that out. Their tight, low-cut, flashy gowns and the fancy feathered hats were evidence enough, even without the heavy makeup each of them sported. Rose didn't have anything against such women; unlike some of the citizens, she supposed that what they did even served some sort of purpose. But she didn't number any women like that among her immediate circle of acquaintances, either.

The brunette held out a gloved hand. "My name is Lucy," she said.

"And I'm Irene," added the blonde.

Trying not to appear too hesitant, Rose took Lucy's hand. "Rose Foster," she introduced herself. "I'm glad to meet you."

Before she even had time to think about whether that

statement was true or not, Harvey Raymond came bustling up, a tall, thin figure in his white apron. The manager of the emporium ignored Lucy and Irene, appearing not to even see them, as he said to Rose, "Good afternoon, Miss Foster. What can I do for you?"

"I haven't quite made up my mind, Mr. Raymond. Why don't you help these ladies instead while I look around?"

Rose wasn't sure where those words had come from, either, but she found herself enjoying the look of surprise and consternation that came into Raymond's eyes. The man sighed, then turned to Lucy and Irene and asked sharply, "What do you want?"

Surely they noticed his tone, but neither Lucy nor Irene showed any sign of being offended. Lucy asked, "Do you have any ladies' . . . unmentionables?"

"We go through so many, you know," Irene added sweetly.

Rose had to bite her lip to keep from laughing as a deep red flush began creeping over Harvey Raymond's features. He swallowed a couple of times, then said, "Ah . . . ah, right over there . . . on that counter."

"Thank you," Lucy said, then she and Irene sauntered toward the counter that the manager had indicated with a slightly trembling finger.

Raymond turned back to Rose, pulled a handkerchief from the pocket of his apron, and mopped his face. "The nerve of . . . of women like that," he hissed, keeping his voice low but not so low that Lucy and Irene couldn't still hear him. "I'm sorry if they were bothering you, Miss Foster. I don't know what their kind is doing in here."

"No one was bothering me," Rose said tightly, feeling a surge of unexpected anger.

Harvey Raymond leaned closer to her and lowered his

voice a little more, though it still wasn't a whisper. "I happen to know that they tried to check into the Territorial House. But Mrs. McKay sent them packing quickly enough, you can count on that! Women like them belong down at the other end of town, and they know it."

Rose took a deep breath. "I said no one was bothering me, Mr. Raymond, but that isn't strictly true."

The store manager raised his eyebrows and looked alarmed.

"*You're* bothering me," Rose went on quickly. "I'd appreciate it if you'd . . . if you'd go sell some licorice or something!"

She was surprised at herself, and she felt a twinge of guilt as she saw the shock and hurt appear on Raymond's face. She had always gotten along well with the man. She felt sorry for him, too, because he had lost his wife the year before when she died giving birth to a stillborn child, leaving Raymond alone. Rose understood, as well, that he worked for Simone McKay, who owned the emporium, and his employer naturally set the tone for Raymond's own reactions.

But still, she couldn't bring herself to agree with, or like, the way he had treated Lucy and Irene, and she felt a flash of satisfaction when, after standing there open-mouthed for several seconds, Raymond finally managed to say, "Well, I never! Pardon me for annoying you, Miss Foster!" He went to the other side of the store, his footsteps landing heavily on the plank floor.

Lucy drifted back over toward Rose and smiled. "You didn't have to do that," she said quietly. "We're used to the way most people treat us."

"That doesn't mean it's right," Rose said.

Lucy just shrugged eloquently, communicating without

words the undeniable knowledge that in the world she and Irene inhabited, right and wrong didn't matter that much. All that was important was what *was*.

"I want the two of you to come down to my café sometime," Rose went on. "Any time you want. Your first dinner there will be on me. Sort of a welcome to Wind River, you might say."

"That's awfully nice of you," Irene said. "We'll take you up on it, won't we, Lucy?"

"Of course we will," murmured Lucy. The two young women started to turn toward the door, but Lucy paused and looked back over her shoulder. "For what it's worth," she added, "I think that blue and white fabric would make nice curtains. There was a time when I made curtains myself."

For an instant, Rose thought she saw a flicker of something in Lucy's brown eyes. Regret, perhaps, sadness at a reminder of better days. But then it was gone and the cool facade was firmly back in place.

They went out, and Rose called through the open door after them, "Goodbye, ladies." Her emphasis on the last word was directed more toward Harvey Raymond, who was still sulking on the other side of the room. Rose ignored him and went back to the table full of fabric. Raymond would get over his resentment quickly enough once she was actually ready to buy something. The sight of a purse or a wallet being opened always made him perk up.

Outside, Lucy and Irene walked along the raised porch of the general store until they reached the steps to the boardwalk and the other stores along Grenville Avenue. When they were well out of earshot of the emporium, Irene asked quietly, "Well, what do you think?"

"It's her," Lucy said. "Oh, yes, it's her, all right."

"Then we'd better get down to the railroad station and send a wire," Irene said, excitement creeping into her voice. "He's going to want to know right away."

"He certainly is," agreed Irene. She paused and looked back at the general store, and once again an unreadable expression passed across her lovely features for an instant.

Then, her jaw tightening slightly, she walked across the street and turned east toward the railroad station, where the local Western Union office was located. Irene walked along beside her, hurrying a little to keep up.

Despite what they had said, Rose didn't really expect Lucy and Irene to take her up on her invitation. But a couple of days after meeting them in the emporium, the two women did indeed show up at the café, although they came in the middle of the afternoon when the place wasn't busy. Rose suspected they had chosen that time so as not to embarrass her, knowing that there wouldn't be very many customers on hand to see her being friendly with women of such dubious virtue.

As a matter of fact, there weren't *any* customers in the café when Lucy and Irene came in, and Rose wondered if they had been keeping an eye on the place, waiting for just such an opportunity.

"Hello, ladies," Rose greeted them as they came in and took seats at one of the tables. "It's good to see you again."

"It's good to see you, too, Rose," Lucy said, "and thank you for inviting us."

"What would you like? Today's menu is written there on the chalkboard, and remember, it's on the house."

"That's not necessary," murmured Lucy.

"No, I insist. What'll it be?"

Both women ordered chicken and dumplings, and Rose called Monty Riordan out of the kitchen to introduce him. "These are my friends Lucy and Irene," she said. "I want you to make sure those are the best chicken and dumplings you've ever dished up."

"Since when is any o' my cookin' not the best you ever ate?" Monty demanded testily. He turned to Lucy and Irene and gave them a big grin. "Howdy, ladies. We'll do you up proud. You got my word on that."

"I'm sure the food will be excellent, Mr. Riordan," Irene said.

"Call me Monty. You pretty ladies just sit right there, and I'll get them dumplin's." He hustled back to the kitchen, obviously not bothered at all by the fact that Lucy and Irene were prostitutes. After years of cooking for the Union Pacific in every hell-on-wheels railhead town along the line, there wasn't much that bothered Monty Riordan anymore.

"I'll get you some coffee," Rose offered, and when she brought it back, Lucy gestured toward one of the empty chairs at the table.

"Why don't you join us?" she asked.

Rose hesitated, then nodded. "Sure, why not? Let me get a cup for myself."

For the next hour, Rose had a fine time. She found herself forgetting about the profession that Lucy and Irene practiced. She simply enjoyed talking to them, and the café rang several times with the sound of their laughter. It was good to visit with someone who knew about the world beyond Wind River, someone who wasn't a farmer or a ranch hand or a freighter or a railroad worker. Lucy was obviously intelligent, and Irene was undeniably pleasant. Some people might look down on her for enjoying their company, Rose thought fleetingly, might regard her as no better than them for associating with such women. But she didn't care.

For one of the few times since coming to Wind River, Rose found herself relaxing.

Not to the point that she let herself answer some of the casual questions Lucy and Irene asked her, however. When Lucy wanted to know where she was from, Rose smiled and said, "Oh, I've moved around a great deal. But Wind River is home to me now. It's a fine place to live." Likewise, she was noncommittal when Irene asked her if she had ever done anything other than run a café. Old habits were hard to break, and the need for secrecy was ingrained in Rose by now.

During the conversation, Monty Riordan brought the bowls of chicken and dumplings from the kitchen and placed them on the table with a flourish. Lucy and Irene displayed hearty appetites as they dug in, and Monty grinned broadly at the compliments they paid him on his cooking. Rose sat, sipped her coffee, and smiled.

After the meal, Lucy said, "We may have to go back to the general store someday. Can we get you to go with us so you can say 'boo' to that storekeeper again?"

Rose laughed. "I'd be glad to. Any time you ladies want to go shopping, feel free to come by here first. I'd love to go with you."

"We'll remember that," Irene said. "Not everybody makes us feel as welcome as you do, Rose. You know, we couldn't even get a room in that fancy hotel, even though we could pay for it. We've been staying at Schirmer's Inn."

Rose knew the place, a one-story clapboard establishment run by a beefy, surly German. There were worse places to stay, she supposed, but it was hardly the same as having a room at the Territorial House.

Feeling the need to defend her adopted home, Rose said, "I guess people around here have decided that it's time for Wind River to be more . . . well, progressive."

"In other words, they don't need any more whores," Lucy said.

Rose frowned, hoping this enjoyable afternoon wouldn't wind up leaving all of them with a bitter taste in their mouths. "I can't blame you for resenting the way you've been treated," she said. "You just have to remember that not everybody around here feels the same way about *anything*. There are all sorts of folks in Wind River."

"We met a man named Parker yesterday," Irene said. "He seemed quite taken with us. He even said we could work in his saloon if we wanted to."

"Hank Parker?" asked Rose, her frown deepening.

"Why, yes, I believe that was his name," Lucy said. "Why? Do you know him, Rose?"

"Not well, but I know him. He's something of a troublemaker."

Irene shrugged. "He seemed nice enough to me."

"I wouldn't presume to tell you what to do, of course. But I'd be careful around Parker, if I was you."

Lucy smiled faintly and said, "We're always careful."

They finished their coffee and got up to leave, and as they did so, Lucy started to open her purse. Rose laid a hand on Lucy's fingers to stop her. "I said this was on the house, and I meant it," she said, her voice friendly but firm.

"All right," Lucy said. "Thank you, Rose. I'm sure we'll be seeing a lot more of each other."

"That's right," Irene added. "It's mighty nice to know another woman who's just a friend."

"Come back any time," Rose said as she showed them out. She gave them a friendly wave as they started down the boardwalk.

Then, feeling the touch of eyes watching her, she looked across the street and saw Simone McKay regarding her rather intently. Simone nodded but didn't smile, then moved on.

What in the world was *that* about? Rose wondered . . . then decided that maybe she didn't want to know.

"You wouldn't believe what I just saw," Simone said to Cole Tyler a few minutes later.

Cole was leaning against one of the poles that supported the awning over the boardwalk in front of the Wind River Land Development Company. Simone had come up to him a moment earlier, a frown on her lovely face.

"Around here it could be almost anything short of an elephant stampeding down the street," Cole said with a chuckle. "And I wouldn't completely rule that out."

"This is serious, Cole," Simone snapped, and he immediately regretted his attempt to lighten her mood. She obviously wasn't having any of it.

"Some sort of trouble?" he asked as he straightened.

"I'd say so. Do you remember those two women who came in on the train earlier this week?"

"The ones those miners were fighting over?" Cole had turned the two men loose a couple of days earlier. They had been embarrassed over their fracas on the depot platform and had headed north again almost immediately to do some more prospecting, vowing that they would never again allow a couple of calico cats to provoke them to gunplay. Cole hadn't believed that for a second, but as long as they didn't shoot each other in Wind River, it was none of his business.

"Those are exactly the ones I mean," Simone was saying. "I just saw them again."

"They've been around town," Cole said with a shrug. "I've seen 'em several times, and they've always been behaving themselves. What were they doing now?"

"They just came out of Rose Foster's café."

Cole almost asked what was wrong with that, but he held his tongue, sensing that Simone wouldn't take kindly to that reaction. Instead, he merely said, "And?"

"And Rose was being very friendly with them. Too friendly, if you ask me."

"Folks've got a right to choose their friends," Cole pointed out.

"Yes, but Rose isn't a . . . a harlot! She shouldn't be associating with them, not unless she wants people to start thinking that she has the same dubious moral character as those women."

Cole stiffened as he tried to control a sudden surge of anger. "I don't believe anybody's going to think such a thing about Rose Foster," he said tightly. "She's been a fine, upstanding woman ever since she came to Wind River."

"Yes, but what about *before* she came to Wind River? What do we really know about her, Cole?"

"I reckon we know all we need to. You're from back east, Simone, so you may not understand how things are out here on the frontier. Folks are judged by who they are and what they do *right now*, not by what might've happened in the past."

"Are you lecturing me, Marshal Tyler?" Simone asked coldly. "If you are, I ought to remind you that I've been in Wind River longer than you have. I only want what's best for this town, and I know that sometimes . . . sometimes secrets can be dangerous. Sometimes the past *can't* be ignored."

Cole didn't like being talked to that way, but he forced down any angry reply he might have made. And Simone had a point, he grudgingly admitted to himself. She had as much at stake in Wind River as anybody else, and more than most. Certainly more than a fiddlefooted drifter like himself who'd had to be coerced into pinning on the marshal's badge in the first place.

He said, "Well, you may be right. But I can't believe we've got anything to worry about where Rose Foster is concerned. A lady like her may have some secrets, all right, but nothing that's going to threaten the town."

Simone sighed. "I suppose you're right, Cole. I *know* you're right. I'm just upset to see so many people around who lower the standards of the community."

"Like those two ladies you saw with Rose?"

"I'd hardly call them ladies," Simone said.

"Well, whatever. I can't run 'em out of town, just like I can't make any of the other women like them leave, and I can't close down the Pronghorn or any of the other saloons. There's no law against any of it, Simone."

"You're right, Marshal. But perhaps we need to do something about that. Good afternoon."

With that, Simone went into the land development company, leaving Cole staring after her.

What in blazes had she meant by that comment?

Cole rubbed a thumb along his jaw. The more he thought about it, the less sure he was that he really wanted to know.

5

Michael Hatfield stood next to his wife Delia, his son Lincoln cradled in his arms. The boy was almost a year old now, and he was a good-sized lad for his age. Michael's arms were getting tired from holding him. He didn't dare put Lincoln down, however. The youngster would scuttle away immediately. Lincoln was possessed of the same insatiable curiosity that had proven to be a such burden at times in his father and his older sister Gretchen. It was a family failing of sorts, Michael thought.

Delia held tightly to Gretchen's hand to keep the little girl from wandering off. Gretchen was four now, and more than once her impetuous nature had led to trouble.

They were a good-looking group in their Sunday best: Michael a handsome, sandy-haired man in his mid-twenties; Delia a lovely redhead a couple of years younger; Gretchen, a lively, attractive child whose blond hair was slowly turning darker; and Lincoln, who already had a full head of black hair inherited from his maternal grandfather. Delia wore a bottle-green dress; Michael was in a suit and tie, with a stiff collar that was slowly wilting in the midday heat. Even under the shade of the big tree's spreading branches, it was quite warm today. Michael hoped that Jeremiah Newton would be finished preaching soon. It was too hot to expect people to stand through a lengthy sermon, Michael thought.

Jeremiah didn't seem to be bothered by the heat. Rivulets of sweat bathed his face and dripped from his chin as he stood on a stump, waved his thick black Bible in the air, and exhorted the congregation to godliness. The Bible was the massive type that was usually found sitting on a table in someone's parlor, but in Jeremiah's huge fist it didn't look so large.

Michael's mind was wandering, as it often did during these weekly services. He found himself glancing around at the other members of the gathering. He saw his employer, Simone McKay, and Dr. Judson Kent, the tall, bearded, distinguished physician who had come from England to practice in Wind River. Harvey Raymond was there, tugging at his collar to give himself some more room for his prominent Adam's apple, and Mr. Bradley, who ran the Union Pacific depot. Many of the other merchants from Wind River were there as well; no matter what their beliefs, it was good business to attend these makeshift church services, and they knew it.

Rose Foster was there, too, Michael noted with interest. He had been hearing some stories about Rose . . .

Nobody could dispute that the café owner had become friendly with a pair of prostitutes. Rose had been seen with the women more than once. What was in debate was the reason for it. Michael had heard people say that it was because Rose had known them before coming to Wind River. Most folks left unspoken the implication that

Rose herself had been a soiled dove, and that was how she came to know the two women called Lucy and Irene. Some weren't even that discreet and came right out and said that Rose Foster must have been a whore, too. Such talk didn't sit well with Michael. He liked Rose.

But he had to admit, if only to himself, that he didn't know a thing about her life before she had come to this growing settlement in Wyoming Territory . . .

He supposed everyone had things about themselves that they would prefer no one knew. That was certainly true in his case. There had been a time not long past when he had almost made a terrible mistake that would have hurt his family very much. Ever since then, Michael had been doing his best to lead an upright life.

Even if that meant standing here in the heat, holding a squirming infant and listening to Jeremiah Newton bellow scripture.

Finally, though, Jeremiah was finished, and a basket was passed to take up the collection. Michael shifted Lincoln to his left arm and used his right hand to grasp Gretchen's pudgy fingers. Delia opened her bag and took out a silver dollar that she dropped into the basket when it went by. There were quite a few coins in the basket, along with some greenbacks. Michael had heard that Jeremiah's building fund for the new church had grown to a sizable amount.

When the collection was complete and the basket had been placed on the ground next to the stump on which Jeremiah stood, the big blacksmith bowed his head and launched into a lengthy benediction, but that was finally finished, too, and the service was over at last. Michael sighed gratefully.

Simone McKay came up as he and Delia were turning

to leave with the children. With a friendly smile, she said, "Good morning, Michael. Hello, Delia. You look lovely today."

Delia had hold of Gretchen's hand again. With her other hand, she pushed back some of the thick red hair that framed her fair-skinned features. "Thank you, Mrs. McKay," she said politely. "So do you."

Michael knew that his wife wasn't overly fond of Simone, although Delia did admire the way the older woman had handled things after the deaths of her husband, Andrew McKay, and William Durand, the two men who had founded Wind River. For one thing, Delia didn't particularly like living on the frontier, and it was the newspaper now owned by Simone that kept Michael here. But being the practical sort that she was, Delia was always unfailingly polite when Simone was around.

Judson Kent sauntered up to join them. He tipped his bowler hat to Delia and then ruffled Lincoln's hair. In a hearty voice, he asked, "And how is the Hatfield clan on this beautiful day?"

"We're all fine," Michael said. "It's a little warm for my taste, though." He was hoping this conversation wouldn't be a long one. He wanted to get his collar and tie off.

"Compared to the cold and the damp where I come from, this weather is splendid," said the doctor. He drew in a deep breath.

"It was quite a good sermon this morning, don't you think?" commented Simone.

"Oh, excellent," Delia said quickly. "I always find Brother Newton's messages to be so uplifting."

"Indeed. I especially liked the part about how doing the Lord's work leads inevitably to progress and civilization. I think that's so true, don't you?"

"Absolutely," Michael said, although he didn't really remember that part of the sermon. Jeremiah must have touched on it while he was thinking about other things.

"I hear that Jeremiah is going to start building his church soon," Simone went on. "It's about time. And it's time we started thinking about a school, too. It's true that there aren't a great many children of school age in Wind River yet, and Abigail Paine has been doing a good job of teaching some of them in her home, but think how much better it would be if we had an actual school here in the settlement. That would be one more step toward becoming an actual city."

"No one can argue with you, my dear," Kent said. "You always make too much sense."

"It's time for Wind River to put its rough and rowdy past behind it," Simone went on. "This is a modern era—why, both sides of the continent are connected by rail now!—and Wind River should be part of it."

Despite his discomfort, Michael found himself interested in what Simone was saying. The things she was talking about—a church, a school, more progress coming to Wind River—those were things that meant stories for the newspaper, and Michael's instincts were those of a newspaperman.

"Those are good ideas," he heard himself saying. "I ought to put something in the paper about them."

"Oh, don't start editorializing on my account," Simone said quickly. "I've always told you that you have a free hand in the running of the *Sentinel*, Michael, and I meant it."

"A newspaper has a responsibility to the community," Michael said. "It ought to be in the forefront of any efforts to improve things."

"Well, of course. But you do what you think best."

He nodded, and he was frowning slightly in thought as Simone and Dr. Kent said their farewells and moved on, arm in arm.

"Michael," Delia said to him under her breath, "you've got that look in your eyes again."

With a little shake of his head to clear his mind, Michael said, "Nothing to worry about, sweetheart. I was just thinking."

"That's what I mean," Delia said ominously.

Michael wasn't quite sure how to take that, but the last thing he wanted to do was start an argument, so he smiled and said, "Let's go on home, shall we?"

The things Simone had said stuck in Michael's mind, however, and after Sunday dinner, while Delia was cleaning up, Lincoln was taking a nap, and Gretchen was outside playing, Michael went into the living room of their neat little house and sat down at a desk he sometimes used when he was working at home. He took paper and a pencil from the desk drawer and stared at the blank white sheet for a long moment before he started to write.

Our community is at a turning point, he wrote. *Will Wind River continue to be the rough and ready frontier hamlet it has been since its inception, or will it take the required steps to become a vital, growing, progressive city?*

Michael stopped and looked at the words he had written, and a smile began to appear on his face.

The Sentinel firmly believes that Wind River should— nay, must—take those steps.

The next edition of the paper would be published in three days. This editorial, once he'd finished with it, would go in a box on the front page, he decided, so that no one could miss it.

Wind River was going to enter that modern era Simone had talked about, Michael thought, even if the town had to be dragged kicking and screaming into it. A fiery editorial was just the thing that was needed to get things off to a good start.

And he was just the fiery editorialist to provide it.

Michael Hatfield wasn't the only one who was busy on what was a lazy Sunday afternoon for many of the people in Wind River. Jeremiah Newton hauled back on the reins of the two mules pulling his old wagon and brought the vehicle to a halt on top of a wooded knoll about a quarter of a mile southwest of the settlement. The wagon's springs creaked under Jeremiah's weight as the big blacksmith climbed down. He put his hands on his hips, looked around, and was pleased with what he saw.

The view from here was a sweeping one, despite the fact that the knoll itself wasn't particularly high. All of Wind River was visible in the distance, with the rails of the Union Pacific running almost due west from the town. To the east and southeast were plains, to the north was the rich rangeland where several huge ranches had been established. Even farther north were the snow-capped mountains of the Wind River range, which had given the town its name. The terrain to the west and southwest, while not as rugged as those mountains, was still less hospitable than it might have been, but even that part of the country possessed a certain majesty, a stark beauty that was ample proof the hand of God had moved on this land. Jeremiah knew beyond a shadow of a doubt that this community was where he was meant to be.

And he knew that this knoll, this piece of land with its

spectacular view, was where God meant for His church to be built.

It was the perfect spot. As he looked around, Jeremiah could see it in his mind, as clearly as if the building already stood there. Some of the trees would be cleared away, leaving a large open space, but enough of them would remain to provide shade. The church itself would be made of thick, whitewashed planks that gleamed with the light of the Lord in the sunshine. Stained glass windows, such as the ones that graced the giant, stately houses of worship back east? Perhaps someday, Jeremiah told himself. For now he would be content with plain glass, brought all the way from Omaha or St. Louis on the train. And a bell tower capped by a steeple, of course. A church had to have a bell, so that on the Sabbath the sound of its sonorous tolling could call the faithful to worship.

Inside, the sanctuary would be plain and simple, as befitted a place that was more concerned with the things of Heaven rather than those of Earth. Two rows of pews with an aisle between them, with a podium and pulpit at the head of the aisle and perhaps a large wooden cross on the wall behind the podium. Jeremiah paced off the dimensions, located the approximate spot where the pulpit would be, and turned to face the congregation that would also be there, their faces lifted, ready to receive the message he would bring to them. Ready to receive the Lord's blessings . . .

Jeremiah was so lost in his dream that he didn't even notice the presence of a snake slithering into paradise.

Not until a rough voice said from behind him, "Hey! What the hell are you doing up here, Newton?"

Jeremiah started and swung around, rage welling up inside him that someone could profane what was going to be a holy place like that. A good Christian was supposed to be slow to anger, though, so he took a deep breath and folded his brawny arms across his chest as he watched the man who had spoken climb down somewhat awkwardly from the back of a big, mouse-colored horse.

The man was a little awkward in dismounting because he had only one arm. The empty left sleeve of his coat was pinned up out of the way. He wore a flashy suit and a silk tie with a diamond stickpin, and a derby hat was on his bald head. He had a long, fat cigar clamped between his teeth. The muscles of the newcomer's arms and shoulders stretched the fabric of the suit, because he was just about as big and powerfully built as Jeremiah himself. He took the cigar out of his mouth and said, "I asked you a question, Newton."

"And I could ask you the same one, Brother Parker," replied Jeremiah, still keeping a tight rein on his temper.

Hank Parker leaned over and spat on the ground, then put the cigar back in his mouth and said around it, "I've told you before, preacher, I ain't your brother. Not unless your daddy got around a lot more than I suspect he did." Parker chuckled.

Jeremiah's jaw tightened, but he didn't lose control. He couldn't expect anything from Hank Parker except crudeness and belligerence. Parker didn't get along very well with anyone and hadn't since he had come to Wind River on the first train to arrive, bringing with him the huge tent and the barrels of whiskey of his portable saloon, which traveled from railhead to railhead with the rest of the hell-on-wheels contingent. Parker had evidently liked what he saw in Wind River, however, because he decided to stay. He bought a piece of land from the development company and erected a large, two-story building which was now the Pronghorn Saloon, Wind River's largest—and most troublesome. Parker was a thorn in the side of Marshal Cole Tyler, a fact that Jeremiah knew well since he had served from time to time as an unofficial deputy for Cole.

Perhaps Parker had his good side; he had ridden with several posses and was brave under fire, a fierce fighter who didn't shrink from long odds. From what Jeremiah had heard, Parker had served with distinction during the Late Unpleasantness, losing his left arm to Confederate fire during that long, awful, bloody day at Shiloh. But anything too honorable about the man was kept concealed most of the time, Jeremiah reflected now. Parker didn't just hide his light under a bushel; a rain barrel was more like it.

"I got a right to ask questions," Parker went on as he strolled toward Jeremiah. "A man rides out to take a look at his own land and finds some yahoo wandering around on it, he's got a right to be curious."

Jeremiah felt something colder than a Wyoming winter touch his spine. "Your land?" he said slowly.

Parker shrugged broad shoulders. "It's going to be, soon as I buy it."

Relief flooded through Jeremiah. He met Parker's slightly hostile stare squarely and said, "Then this land doesn't belong to you."

Parker took the cigar out of his mouth again. "Not yet, but I've got my eye on it," he snapped. "That's enough. Everybody else better just steer clear."

Jeremiah glanced around the knoll, unsure of just how much he ought to tell the saloonkeeper about his plans. Duplicity didn't come easily to Jeremiah, and it wasn't simply a matter of obeying the Lord's command-ment not to lie. Pulling the wool over somebody's eyes just wasn't part of his nature. So instead of lying, he merely said truthfully, "I like to come up here and look around. It's a beautiful spot."

"Yeah. I guess," Parker said in a tone that indicated he had never really noticed. He seemed to relax a little.

"What about you, Brother—I mean, Mr. Parker? What's your interest in this land?"

"Well . . . " Parker hesitated, then went on, "I look at it more as an investment."

"An investment?" Jeremiah repeated.

"That's right." If any man could seem to strut standing still, it was Hank Parker. He hooked his thumb in his vest as he continued, "I've been buying a little land around here. You know, a piece of property here, a piece there. There ain't no reason Simone McKay ought to rake in all the profits around here."

"I see," said Jeremiah, nodding.

And he did, at that. Hank Parker was an ambitious man. Owning a large, thriving saloon would make him well-to-do; there was no doubt about that, given the thirsts of all the cowboys and farmers and railroad work-ers in the area.

But if he could establish a land development company that was as successful as Simone McKay's . . . that would make him rich—pure, rolling-in-it rich.

Trying not to show the flood of emotions gripping him—anger, doubt, even a little fear—Jeremiah gestured at the knoll and asked, "What would you do with land like this?"

"Well, you see that slope over there?" Parker was warming to his subject. He pointed a blunt finger at the long, gentle, grassy slope that ran down to the plains from the east side of the knoll.

Jeremiah had envisioned that slope as the perfect place for the cemetery that would inevitably accompany the church, replacing the little burial ground on the east side of town. "I see it," he said quietly.

"I was thinking maybe some stockyards. The way the ranches are building up around here, it won't be long until Sawyer and the others are shipping a lot of beef back east. This place is close enough to town to make it handy for holding pens, but far enough away that the stink won't bother folks too much." A gleam of anticipation came into Parker's eyes. "Hell, if somebody could figure out how to keep those railroad cars cold enough, we could build our own slaughterhouse right here. No sense in shipping those cows all the way to Omaha or Chicago to butcher 'em when we could kill 'em just as well here. That'd save on the weight. And if there was a rendering plant to take care of the hooves and horns and hides, too . . . "

Parker's voice trailed away, and he sighed.

A huge shudder went through Jeremiah, shaking him so much that even Parker noticed. "Hey, what's wrong with you?" the saloonkeeper asked.

Jeremiah couldn't answer that Parker's gruesome vision had repulsed him to the core of his being. Instead, he said, "Maybe a touch of the summer grippe."

"Well, stay away from me. I don't need it."

"Don't worry, Mr. Parker. I'll be leaving now." Jeremiah started toward his wagon.

"Hey, preacher. You can still come up here for a while," Parker called after him, sounding magnanimous now. "Until I get those stockyards built, anyway."

Jeremiah didn't look back as he climbed into his wagon, took up the reins, and got the mules moving. He had to do something about this, had to stop Hank Parker from ruining what the Lord had led him to do. Jeremiah thought he knew where to start.

He had to talk to Simone McKay—and soon.

6

Cole Tyler and Billy Casebolt strolled down Grenville Avenue toward the Union Pacific station. It was Monday morning, and Cole felt pretty good about the weekend just past. There hadn't been any shootings, and only one knifing. And that fella was going to live, according to Dr. Kent. Not bad at all for a weekend in Wind River, Cole reflected.

"When's that westbound due?" he asked idly.

Casebolt pulled a fat turnip watch out of his pocket and flipped open its lid. "'Bout ten minutes from now," he said. "Want me to see who gets off?"

"We both will," Cole decided. "Things seem to be pretty peaceful around here this morning."

He knew as soon as the words were out of his mouth that he shouldn't have said them. He was tempting Fate.

And Fate responded with a yell and a couple of gunshots that shattered the morning air.

"What the hell!" Casebolt exclaimed.

Cole broke into a run as the gun roared again. The shots were coming from somewhere on the east side of town, past the depot. Cole hurried in that direction, with Casebolt doing his best to keep up. Both lawmen had drawn their guns without thinking.

It came as no surprise to Cole when a woman burst out through the batwinged doors of the Pronghorn and shrieked, "He's going to kill us all!" Hank Parker's saloon had always had more than its share of trouble, even when it was just a big canvas tent with planks laid across whiskey barrels to serve as a bar. Now that the place was permanent and supposedly more respectable, it had settled down a little—but not much.

"You reckon it's Parker?" Casebolt panted as he ran alongside Cole. The woman who just emerged from the saloon dashed on across the street, still screaming.

"Don't know," Cole replied. It could be that Parker had finally snapped and gone mad. Cole had known the man for quite a while, had seen other examples of Parker's violent rages. But somehow he doubted that the saloon-keeper would shoot up his own place.

More shots boomed inside the saloon. Folks had cleared both sides of the street within a block of the Pronghorn, not wanting to take the chance of getting hit by a stray slug. Cole vaulted onto the boardwalk in front of the saloon, then flattened back against the wall, his revolver gripped tightly in his hand. He began to edge toward the entrance. Casebolt followed suit.

Suddenly a man slapped the batwings aside and lunged out of the saloon. As he did, a gun barked behind him and splinters flew as a bullet punched through one of the batwings. It caught the man high on the right shoulder and spun him around. He yelled loudly as he clutched his shoulder, lost his balance, and fell to the boardwalk. But he had the presence of mind to roll quickly to the side, out of the direct line of fire through the doorway. That action brought him close to Cole and Casebolt.

Cole dropped to one knee beside the man, recognizing him as one of the gamblers who frequented the Pronghorn. His name was Ahern, Cole recalled.

"Take it easy, Ahern," Cole said quietly to the wounded man. He put his free hand on Ahern's uninjured shoulder. "I reckon you'll be all right. That slug just clipped you."

"Hurts like hell," Ahern said through gritted teeth.

"I imagine it does. What's going on in there? Who's doing that shooting?"

"Some drifter," Ahern grated. "He's been . . . playing cards and drinking . . . all night. Finally lost . . . one too many pots . . . I reckon. Said Brownie was . . . cheating. Bastard pulled a gun . . . shot Brownie . . . started blasting all over the room."

Cole grimaced. It was an all too familiar story. Some liquored-up hardcase had decided that his own failings at poker had to be due to the dealer slipping one off the bottom of the deck or from a hideout rig up a sleeve, and the reaction was a common one. Too many drifters had all their brains in their gunhand.

"Anybody else hurt in there?" Cole asked tightly.

Ahern managed to shake his head. "Just Brownie. Everybody else . . . hunted cover. I tried to . . . make a run for it. You saw what happened."

Another shot crashed inside, and glass shattered.

"Sounds like that feller's shootin' up the place for the fun of it now," said Casebolt as he leaned over Cole's shoulder. "What're we goin' to do, Marshal?"

"Stop him somehow," Cole said. "Give Ahern a hand and get him back farther away from the door."

While Casebolt was doing that, Cole straightened and stood with his back against the wall once more, next to the saloon entrance. He remembered the gambler called Brownie: a quiet, mild-looking man with the long, supple fingers of a professional card-player. Brownie had probably possessed the skill to cheat if he wanted to, but Cole had never heard any complaints about him. As far as he knew, Brownie had been a straight dealer.

He never should have congratulated himself on how peaceful things were, Cole thought with a trace of bitterness. This incident was a painful reminder of the savageness and brutality that lurked just under the surface of the town, of how quickly things could fall apart.

The badge pinned to his buckskin shirt meant it was his job to put them back together.

He took a deep breath and yelled, "Hey! Hold on in there!"

A moment of silence, then a man shouted, "Who's out there, damn it?"

"I'm Marshal Cole Tyler. There's been enough shooting, mister. Why don't you just put down your gun and come on out? Nobody's going to hurt you."

"Damn right nobody's goin' to hurt me! I'll shoot the first son of a bitch who pokes his head in here! And I ain't comin' out!"

Cole heard a noise beside him and looked over to see that Casebolt had rejoined him. The deputy had half-dragged, half-carried Ahern to the corner of the building, where several townsmen had ventured out to lend a hand as well. They were taking the wounded gambler down the street toward Dr. Judson Kent's office.

With that worry taken care of, Cole turned his attention back to the gunman holed up inside the Pronghorn.

"Listen, mister, unless you come out peacefully, you won't come out of there alive. I can promise you that."

"Go to hell! You think I don't know what'll happen if I give up? That tinhorn's friends'll string me up for gunnin' him! If I got to die, I want to take some more o' you bastards with me!"

Cole's mouth tightened. The gunman had a point. There wouldn't be any lynchings—Cole wasn't about to allow that in Wind River—but it was true the killer would be held for trial until the circuit judge came through and then no doubt hanged once he was found guilty. Cole had to admit, too, that going out fighting was a more appealing prospect than kicking your life away at the end of a rope. The gunman didn't have a damned thing to lose.

Leaning over to Casebolt, Cole said, "Go around to the back, Billy. I'll take the front. We'll go in at the same time. He can't drop both of us."

"Doggone it, Marshal, that feller's goin' to be watchin' the front door, and you know it!" Casebolt objected. "You'll be takin' a hell of a chance."

Cole shrugged and gave a half-smile. "It goes with the badge, I reckon," he said.

Casebolt frowned and was obviously getting ready to argue some more, but suddenly a woman's scream ripped out from inside the saloon. Both lawmen stiffened in alarm, and the thing they feared was confirmed a second later when the gunman called, "Hey, Marshal! A new hand's been dealt! Got me a pretty little gal here, and she's goin' to die if you don't let me walk out of here and ride away!"

Cole bit back a curse. Now that the gunman had a hostage, it changed everything. Probably one of the women who worked in the Pronghorn had been crouched behind an overturned table, hoping the drifter wouldn't notice her, but that hope had proven futile.

"Forget what I told you about going around back," Cole told Casebolt quietly. "I want you to stay out here. I'm going inside."

"Shoot, Marshal, you can't do that!"

"I've got to know what the situation is in there before I can figure out what to do about it," said Cole. He slipped his pistol back into its holster and turned his head toward the doorway. "Listen in there!" he called. "I'm coming in to talk to you, mister."

"Damn it, you stay away from that door! I'm warnin' you, Marshal—"

"My hands will be empty," Cole cut in. "There's no need for more shooting."

Then, before the gunman could protest again, Cole took a deep breath, turned, and stepped into the entrance of the saloon. His hands were held about shoulder-high, the empty palms turned toward where he thought the gunman would be. Cole pushed through the batwings, squinting his eyes as they adjusted to the relative dimness inside the building.

It took only a moment for him to scan the room and get the situation clear in his mind. The gunman was to his right, backed up toward the bar that ran down that side of the room. He had one of Parker's percentage girls held in front of him just as Cole expected. The drifter's arm was looped tightly around the young woman's neck. Her eyes were wide with fear, and her mouth was moving even though no sound came from her lips. One of the big mirrors behind the bar was broken, shattered by one of the man's bullets. Enough of the glass still remained to give a fractured, distorted view of what was going on in the room.

Several men had turned over tables and were hiding behind them on the far side of the room. Others peeked over the railing of the balcony that overlooked the room. No doubt some of the men were armed, but they couldn't risk a shot at the murderous drifter as long as he had that woman pressed so tightly against him. Anyway, most of them would figure that this was the marshal's job, not theirs, Cole knew.

Sprawled motionless on the floor near the gunman was the body of the gambler called Brownie. He was lying on his back, his arms outflung, a look of surprise and horror etched permanently on his face. He was wearing a shirt, vest, and tie, but no coat. The white shirt was stained darkly with blood.

There was no sign of Hank Parker. Cole wondered if he was hiding behind the bar.

The gunman had a long-barreled Remington pressed to the side of the young woman's neck. As Cole entered the room, the man jerked the barrel away from his hostage and leveled it at Cole instead. "Stop!" he shouted. "I told you not to come in here!"

"Just wanted to see if maybe we can work this out," Cole said, trying to keep his voice calm. The black hole of that gun barrel staring at him made his nerves twitch. He forced his feet to work and moved a couple of steps into the room.

"Nothin' to work out," the gunman said. "I'm leavin', and if anybody bothers me I'll blow this whore's head off. And I'll kill you, too, lawman."

"Killing a bunch more folks won't do you any good," Cole told him. The drifter wore ragged trail clothes and had a shock of greasy blond hair. He looked like hundreds of no-account saddlebums Cole had seen over the years . . . but that didn't make him any less dangerous.

"That tinhorn shouldn't have cheated me! This is all his fault!"

"Well, you've settled your score with him. Why make things any worse?"

The gunman gave an ugly grin and moved his gun back to the woman's neck. "They ain't goin' to get worse. They're goin' to get better. My horse is tied up outside, and I'm goin' to get on him and ride out of this damned town. Ain't nobody goin' to stop me, either."

"That's where you're wrong, friend," Cole told him. "Somebody will stop you. If not me, then my deputy. And if not him, then somebody else. We've got law and order here in Wind River."

"Law and order, hell!" the drifter shot back. "The only law that means anything comes out the barrel of a gun! Now get out of my way!"

At that moment, with the gunman's attention focused completely on Cole and the doorway behind the marshal, there was movement on the other side of the bar. From the corner of his eye, Cole saw a bald head come into view. Hank Parker was rising slowly and silently from concealment.

And the saloonkeeper was gripping a shotgun with the barrels cut down so that it could be handled more easily by a man with only one arm.

Cole tried to keep his eyes from giving away what he saw. At such close range, a blast from that sawed-off greener would just about take the gunman's head off. The only trouble was, it would probably kill the woman, too. Parker might not care about that, though. He might decide the risk was worth it if he could keep the gunman from doing any more damage in the saloon. Cole knew that busted mirror had cost Parker a pretty penny.

He wasn't sure what to do, how to warn Parker not to shoot. Then an even more astonishing thing happened.

Somebody whistling a merry little tune slapped the batwings aside and strode jauntily into the saloon, nearly running into Cole's back. The gunman flinched, and Cole took an involuntary step to the side.

"What the hell!" the gunman shrieked. He didn't pull the trigger, however.

Cole stared at the newcomer, who looked equally startled. The man was middle-aged, dressed in a dark suit with thick white hair under the black hat he wore. The hat's high crown was creased in a Montana pinch. He looked around the room with keen blue eyes and said heartily, "Say, I seem to have walked into something here."

Cole just had time to wonder how the hell this man had gotten past Billy Casebolt, then the drifter jerked his gun away from the woman and pointed the shaking barrel at the stranger. "Don't move, old man!" screamed the gunman.

The white-haired stranger lifted his hands. "Wouldn't think of it, son." He nodded toward the body on the floor. "Who's that?"

"A cheatin' tinhorn who deserved to die!"

"Why, he's not dead. I just saw him move."

The gunman looked down, and the stranger moved. He went to his right, his hands darting underneath his coat. Startled, the gunman jerked his Remington in that direction and triggered off a shot. At the same instant, Cole palmed out his own revolver and Hank Parker swung the sawed-off shotgun at the drifter's head. The woman struggled frantically and managed to twist out of the gunman's grip.

Cole fired as soon as she was clear. The bullet struck the drifter in the shoulder and threw him back. The short barrels of Parker's greener slammed into the side of his head, driving him off his feet. He collapsed on the floor, senseless and bleeding, the gun slipping from his fingers.

Cole leaped forward and kicked the man's gun away, sending it sliding across the sawdust-littered floor well out of reach. Then he cocked his Colt again and trained it on the fallen drifter. The man didn't show any signs of moving any time soon.

"Good move, Parker," said Cole. "I was afraid you were going to touch off that scattergun and kill both of them."

The burly saloonkeeper snorted. "And have to break in a new girl? Hell, Tyler, I get enough turnover in here without shooting the people who work for me."

Cole had to grin at that for a second, then he turned his attention to the young woman and the white-haired stranger. The man was helping her to her feet, and he said, "There you go, my dear. You're fine now."

She was shaking and crying in reaction to what had happened, though, and she didn't look fine. Some of the other women who worked in the saloon came rushing down the stairs now that the danger was over and gathered around her. They led her over to one of the tables, and one of them got a bottle from behind the bar. It wasn't the watered-down house whiskey, either, Cole noted before glaring at the stranger.

"What the hell was that about, mister?" he demanded. "What gave you the right to come barging in here like that?"

The stranger still had an ivory-handled Colt in one hand. Not in any hurry to answer Cole's questions, he returned the gun to its holster, a shoulder rig that hung underneath his coat. There was a matching holster and pistol on the other side, Cole saw while the stranger's coat was open.

"I heard there was trouble and came to lend a hand, Marshal," the man said blandly. "Lawmen have to stick together, you know."

"You're the law?" Cole asked, frowning.

"Deputy U.S. Marshal Dan Boyd." The man took a small, black leather folder from his pocket. "Here are my credentials, if you want to look at them."

"Hang on a minute," Cole said as Billy Casebolt came hurrying into the saloon. Cole gestured at the unconscious killer and went on, "Billy, get some men and take this fella over to the jail. You'd better fetch Dr. Kent to take a look at his shoulder, too. Kent ought to be finished patching up that other gambler by now."

"Sure, Marshal," Casebolt replied with a nod of his head. He looked uncertainly at Dan Boyd. "This feller came up and said he was a federal badge, and he didn't pay no attention when I told him he ought to stay out o' here."

"No harm done, Billy," Cole assured his deputy. "At least not to anybody but that drifter who gunned down Brownie. Get him out of here."

While Casebolt was tending to that, Cole opened the folder Boyd had given him and briefly studied the documents it held and the badge pinned inside. It looked like

Boyd was what he claimed to be, all right—a federal star packer.

Cole handed the folder back and said, "You still didn't have the right to come busting in and risk all of our lives."

"I suppose you're right, Marshal," Boyd agreed mildly. "Old habits die hard, though, I reckon. When I see some trouble, I just naturally take a hand."

"Not around here, you don't. Not unless it's a matter of federal jurisdiction."

Boyd inclined his head in acknowledgment of Cole's point, but Cole saw a flicker of something in the man's blue eyes. Anger, maybe. Boyd probably wasn't used to anybody talking to him like that. Cole didn't particularly care.

"If that lady hadn't managed to get loose, she could've been hit by a bullet," Cole went on.

"I was confident you wouldn't shoot until she was out of the line of fire," Boyd said. "And that gentleman behind the bar acted wisely by using his shotgun as a club, rather than shooting."

"Luck," Cole snapped. "The whole thing was pure luck."

"Ah, but that's where you're wrong, Marshal. There's no such thing as *pure* luck. Skill and planning and experience always enter into everything."

Cole wasn't in any mood to listen to a lecture. He said, "What are you doing here in Wind River, anyway?"

"I'm here on business, Marshal, as you might assume. I would have been here a couple of days ago, but a rock slide blocked the tracks over by Wamsutter and the train had to wait until it was cleared away."

"Law business?" Cole asked.

Boyd smiled. "What other kind is there?"

Cole waited a few seconds, then when Boyd didn't go on, he said impatiently, "Well? Are you going to tell me about it or not?"

Boyd kept smiling, but that hard look was in his eyes again. "It's a matter of federal jurisdiction," he said.

And then he turned and walked out of the saloon, leaving Cole to stare after him in anger and surprise.

Jeremiah Newton was frustrated. He wrung his big hands together impatiently as he sat on a hard wooden bench that was too small for him. The bench was in the outer office of the Wind River Land Development Company, and Jeremiah was waiting to talk to Simone McKay.

Simone had another visitor at the moment, which was why the clerk had told Jeremiah to wait, but that wasn't the only reason impatience gripped him. Ever since his run-in with Hank Parker the day before, he had wanted to discuss the situation with Simone, who knew more about the business of dealing in land than anyone else in Wind River. But he couldn't talk about the matter on Sunday, of course; discussing business on the Sabbath would have violated the Third Commandment. And he had been surprisingly busy at the blacksmith shop this morning, with several customers already waiting for him when he fired up the forge. It had taken him until nearly the middle of the day to get away from there.

Then, on the way here, he had been asked by Billy

Casebolt to lend a hand with a prisoner being taken to the jail. The man had been shot and was only semi-conscious. Jeremiah had done as the deputy asked since Casebolt was his friend. The result was that it was now a little after noon and he *still* hadn't talked to Simone.

The door to Simone's private office opened, and Jeremiah looked up. Lawton Paine emerged from the room, limping a little from injuries he had received during the Civil War that would no doubt plague him the rest of his life. Paine owned Wind River's largest and best boardinghouse and had a good wife and a brood of children, but despite that there was usually a rather sour expression on his face. Today, however, he looked happy for a change and was actually almost smiling.

Simone followed Paine out of the office and shook hands with him. "Congratulations, Lawton," she said.

"Thanks, Mrs. McKay. It's been a pleasure doing business with you," responded Paine. He put a hat on his prematurely gray hair and turned to leave the office. As he did so, he even nodded pleasantly at Jeremiah, who returned the nod, then stood up and turned toward Simone.

"Hello, Jeremiah," she said. "What brings you here this morning?"

"I came to see you, ma'am," he said. "I, uh, need some advice."

"Well, I'm not sure what kind of advice I could give a man like you, but please, come in. I have a few minutes free right now."

Jeremiah motioned for her to go first, then followed her into the office. Simone shut the door and said, "Have a seat. Tell me what I can do for you."

Jeremiah settled his considerable bulk on a straight-backed chair in front of the desk and hoped it would hold him. Finding himself unexpectedly hesitant to get to the heart of the matter, he said, "Brother Paine looked mighty happy when he left just now."

Simone seated herself in the padded leather chair behind the desk. She said, "Lawton has good reason to be happy. He just gave me the final payment on the land he was buying. The boarding house, and the land it's sitting on, are his free and clear now."

"That *is* good," Jeremiah agreed. He had bought the land on which his shop sat from Durand and McKay in the early days of the settlement, and it had always pleased him to know that no one could take his place away from him. He took a deep breath and went on, "It's about buying some land that I've come to see you today, Mrs. McKay."

"The land for your church?" Simone guessed.

Jeremiah bobbed his head in a nod.

"That's wonderful," she said with a smile. "I'm so glad you've decided to go ahead with it. Where do you plan to build?"

"That little knoll with the trees on it, just south of town."

Simone's smile disappeared and was replaced with a frown. "Oh. I see," she said.

Immediately, tension gripped Jeremiah and made him lean forward in his chair. It groaned a little under him. "What's wrong?" he asked. "Don't you think it'll be a good place for the church?"

"I think it will make a fine location for the church. It's just that, I had hoped . . . when you decided where you wanted to build . . . that I could make you a present of the land. A contribution, you could call it."

Jeremiah was thunderstruck. He blinked rapidly several times and was finally able to say, "Why, Mrs. McKay, that's just about the nicest . . . the most charitable thing I ever heard of!"

"You don't understand, Jeremiah," she said seriously. "I'm sorry, but I can't give you that land."

That knocked the props out from under Jeremiah's excitement. He struggled for words for a moment before he said, "But . . . but why not?"

"I don't own it," Simone said.

Realization burst through Jeremiah. "Parker," he breathed, surprising even himself with the amount of venom he was able to put into the name. Parker must have gotten to Simone first and had already purchased the land.

She was frowning in confusion. "You mean Hank Parker? What about him?"

"He was already here, wasn't he? He bought that knoll right out from under me!" Somehow, without even knowing it, Jeremiah had stood up. He towered over the desk as he asked the question.

Simone didn't appear to be intimidated by the sheer size of the blacksmith, however. Coolly, she shook her head. "Hank Parker bought the land for his saloon from me, but that's the only dealing I've had with the man. The only one I *want* to have, I might add. Parker couldn't have bought that knoll from me, because I haven't owned it for months. Goodness, I guess it's been almost a year since I sold that parcel of land."

It was Jeremiah's turn to look confused. "Sold the land?" he repeated. "Sold it to who?"

Simone shook her head. "I wish I could tell you."

That baffled Jeremiah even more. "You don't *know* who bought the land?"

"It was purchased by a company back east. I don't recall the name right now, but I can look it up for you."

"What would some eastern company want with a piece of land all the way out here in Wyoming?" asked Jeremiah.

"I don't know, but I've heard that some eastern business syndicates have been purchasing land to use as ranches. The syndicate members act as absentee owners and hire managers to actually run the ranches. It's becoming fairly common throughout the West." Simone frowned again. "However, that can't be the case here, because the company that bought that knoll didn't purchase any other land in this area, and that one tract isn't big enough for a ranch, or even a decent farm."

"There's nothing up there," Jeremiah said. "I was there just yesterday, and the land's sitting there empty."

Simone shrugged delicately. "Someone who buys land doesn't necessarily have to *do* anything with it."

Jeremiah began to pace back and forth, even though he couldn't go very far in the relatively small office. After a moment, he asked, "Can you get me the name and address of the company that bought the land? Maybe I can write to them and explain the situation and buy the property from them."

"Of course." Simone opened one of the drawers in her desk. "That's a good idea, Jeremiah. In fact, I'll even write to them on your behalf as well, if you'd like."

"That's mighty gracious of you, Mrs. McKay. If whoever's in charge hears from both of us, maybe they'll understand how important this is."

"We can hope so," Simone said. "But if not, Jeremiah, you could always build your church somewhere else. The Wind River Land Development Company still owns a great deal of property in this area."

Jeremiah shook his head. "That's the place, ma'am. That's where it has to be. It's sort of hard to explain, but I just *know* I've got to build the church there."

"Well, we'll see what we can do." She took several papers out of the drawer, flipped through the documents, and selected the one she wanted. As she looked at it, a puzzled expression appeared on her face. She murmured, "Now, that's odd."

"What?" Jeremiah asked anxiously, able to tell from Simone's expression that something else was wrong.

"These papers don't list any of the names of the officers of that company, nor who its general manager is. My records show that the property was paid for with a Wells Fargo draft. We may be able to trace the owners of the company, but it's going to take some time, Jeremiah."

His spirits sagged for a moment, but then he told himself that the situation could have been much worse. If he couldn't get his hands on that land, neither could Hank Parker. From here on out, it was going to be a race to see who could locate the actual owners first and convince them to sell. Jeremiah felt a surge of confidence. He had Simone on his side, and she was an intelligent, competent woman. And that wasn't all.

He had the Lord on his side, too. He *had* to win.

By Wednesday, Cole was about ready to pull a gun on Dan Boyd and get some answers to his questions, one way or another. It was damned irritating to have another lawman poking around *his* town. Cole had talked to Boyd several times, and the federal man was still being tight-lipped about the job that had brought him to Wind River.

Boyd didn't seem to be doing anything with his time except wandering around town and talking to people. He chatted with Harvey Raymond at the general store while buying some extra shells for those ivory-handled Colts of his. He drank at the Pronghorn and the other saloons in town, although he seemed to spend more time talking to the bartenders, the percentage girls, and the house gamblers than he did actually drinking. He ate at the Wind River Café and most of the other hash houses and diners, and he charmed all the waitresses with his quick smile and his booming laughter. Dan Boyd was just about the most congenial son of a bitch Cole had ever seen.

But he was obviously looking for someone, and it just about drove Cole crazy not to know who the federal marshal was after and why.

Boyd had brought a horse with him on the train, the animal riding in one of the baggage cars. The horse was a white stallion, a fine-looking mount of the sort that usually had plenty of strength and stamina. Cole had seen the horse several times when Boyd rode out of town, and he couldn't help but wonder how the white stallion would match up against his golden sorrel Ulysses. Cole had never seen a horse the equal of Ulysses, but Boyd's mount probably came closer than any. Fancy looks didn't mean a thing, though, so until Cole saw the stallion run, he wasn't going to give it too much credit.

As far as Cole could tell, Boyd didn't really go anywhere when he left Wind River. The federal man just wandered around the countryside, seemingly aimlessly, much like he did when he was in town. To Cole, however, that was just one more sign that Boyd was searching for something—or somebody.

On Wednesday morning, Cole was leaning against one of the boardwalk posts in front of the jail, while Casebolt sat in a ladderback chair and leaned back so that he could prop his feet on the hitch rack along the edge of the walk. Cole saw Dan Boyd lead that white stallion out of the livery stable and swing up into the saddle. Instead of the suit he had worn when he got off the train, Boyd now wore a black shirt, denim pants, and high-topped boots, looking more like a typical range rider than the dude he had first appeared to be. He still had on that hat with that damned Montana pinch, though, Cole noted, and those ivory-handled Colts now rode in tied-down holsters attached to a black shell belt around Boyd's hips. Boyd rode east along Grenville Avenue, in the opposite direction from the jail. Cole was watching the man leave town when he noticed Dr. Judson Kent strolling toward the jail. The physician had a folded newspaper in his hand, and he held it up in greeting as he approached the two lawmen.

"Good morning, gentlemen," Kent said.

Casebolt lowered his outstretched legs so that Kent could pass by. "Howdy, Doc," he said. "How you doin' this mornin'?"

"Splendid," replied Kent. He held up the newspaper again. "I take it the two of you have already seen this week's edition of the *Sentinel*?"

"Nope," Cole said. "I haven't picked it up yet. How about you, Billy?"

"'Fraid not. Figgered I'd go over to the newspaper office and get one from Michael after while. Something interestin' in it, Doc?"

Kent smiled. "You might say that." He unfolded the paper and held it so that Cole and Casebolt could read the headlines on the front page. One in particular caught Cole's eye, just as he supposed Kent had intended.

CALL FOR ELECTIONS, it read.

Casebolt's lips moved as he scanned the words, and then he said aloud, "Eee-lections. Lordy mercy. The boy's talkin' about *politics*!"

"Let me see that," Cole said. He took the paper from Kent and with a frown began reading the boxed editorial underneath the headline. "'Our community is at a turning point. Will Wind River continue to be the rough and ready frontier hamlet it has been since its inception, or will it take the required steps to become a vital, growing, progressive city? The *Sentinel* firmly believes that Wind River should—nay, must—take those steps. Therefore, this newspaper is now calling for the first elections in the history of our fair city, for the purpose of electing a mayor and a town council for the governance of our affairs. This is not to cast any aspersions on the current, unofficial leadership of our community, but rather to assure that in the future, progress and civilization will continue to prosper here in our midst.'" Cole looked up, almost aghast. "That's just the first paragraph. He goes on like that for two or three more, saying pretty much the same thing over and over again."

Casebolt let out a whistle. "Michael can sure sling the words around, all right."

"I think it's a capital idea, myself," Kent put in.

"Well, I'm not so sure I do," Cole said. "And I'm a little surprised that you do, Doctor. After all, you're one of those unofficial leaders Michael's talking about in here. I'd rather have folks like you and Simone running things than a bunch of politicians. I saw enough of what *they* can do when I was scouting for the Army."

Kent took the paper when Cole handed it to him, then said, "You're looking at this entirely the wrong way, Marshal. Anyone who runs for office here in Wind River will be a citizen, with the same sort of stake in doing what's right for the community that any of us have. If you're afraid that this editorial will lead to some sort of political exodus of outsiders to Wind River, I think you're mistaken. The politicos in Washington— or in Cheyenne, for that matter—are quite content where they are and will have no interest in our little settlement."

"Well, you may be right about that," Cole agreed grudgingly. "I was happy to work for the little committee that asked me to take the job in the first place, though."

"Nonsense." Kent tapped the newspaper. "This will be a very good thing for the town. You'll see."

"Maybe so," Cole said dubiously. Before they could argue any more about the subject, the sound of a train whistle cut through the morning air.

Casebolt stood up. "There's the westbound. Reckon I'll amble on down to the station."

"Better be careful," advised Cole. "For some reason, trouble seems to break out just about every time one of those trains comes in lately."

Casebolt nodded and said, "I sort of noticed the same thing. Don't happen with the eastbounds, though. Wonder why that is?"

Neither Cole nor Judson Kent had an answer to that question. With a shrug, Casebolt started toward the UP depot in his jerky gait.

"I don't worry about the trains bringing in trouble near as much as I do about that editorial," Cole commented darkly to the physician.

"You're wrong about this, Marshal," Kent insisted. "You'll see. An election will be the best thing in the world for Wind River."

With a hiss of steam, the locomotive came to a stop next to the water tank beyond the depot building. That put the passenger cars alongside the platform, and people began to disembark as porters set the portable steps in place.

A dark-haired man in a light brown tweed suit climbed down from one of the cars. A thin black cheroot was clamped between even, white teeth. His narrow-brimmed hat was a little darker than his suit. When he reached the platform, he stood there and waited, his feet spread a little apart, while he looked around the station. Three more men came down the steps behind him. These men were also wearing suits, but they didn't look as comfortable in them as the first man. One of them pointed at the sign hanging over the platform with the station name painted on it and said, "This is it, Mr. Drummond. Wind River."

The man called Drummond took his cigar from his mouth and smiled thinly. "That's right, Amos. This is Wind River."

"Don't look like much, boss," said one of the other men. He was as burly as his companions, but his skin was darker and he spoke with a rich, slow drawl.

Drummond said, "I don't care what the place looks like, Lige, as long as I find what I'm after."

Clearly, Drummond was in command here. The third man asked, "You want me to see about getting our bags?" He was the oldest of the trio, with big hands, a weather-beaten face, and blond hair.

"That would be fine, Saul," Drummond replied. As he

looked around the platform some more, he felt eyes watching him and turned to see a tall, thin, roughly dressed man staring at him.

There was a deputy's star pinned to the man's shirt, right next to one of his suspender straps.

His smile widening into a grin, Drummond strolled toward the watching lawman. Amos called softly after him, "Hey, boss—", but Drummond made a smooth motion with his hand that forestalled any question or warning.

"Hello, Deputy," Drummond said as he walked right up to the lawman. "I was wondering if I could ask you a question."

"Well . . . sure," the man replied.

"What's the best place to eat in this town?"

The deputy blinked. "The best eatin' place?" he repeated. "Why, I reckon that'd be the Wind River Café, leastways as far as I'm concerned."

"And the best hotel?"

"The Territorial House." The answer came without hesitation. "Ain't no doubt about that."

"Thank you," Drummond said. "I'm pleased to hear it."

He turned and went back to the other men, who were loading the bags onto one of the wagons that usually sat outside the depot, ready to be hired for just such a task. Drummond looked back, gave the deputy a friendly wave, then stepped lithely up to the seat next to the driver. The other men climbed into the back, and the driver got the team of mules moving. The wagon rolled away.

And behind it, Billy Casebolt came to the edge of the platform, watched the wagon as it moved toward the hotel, and wondered just what the hell *that* had been all about.

8

Drummond wasn't smiling a little later as he looked across the desk at the clerk on duty in the lobby of the Territorial House.

"What do you mean they're not here?" Drummond demanded.

"I'm sorry, sir," the clerk said. He was a man in his thirties named Burt, a former gandy dancer with slicked-down hair parted in the middle, who had decided that clerking in a hotel was easier work than wrestling steel for the Union Pacific. Right now, he wasn't so sure of that, as the man who had just checked into the hotel continued to glare at him. Burt swallowed and went on, "The owner of the hotel, Mrs. McKay, felt it might be better if the two, ah, ladies in question sought accommodation elsewhere."

"You mean they weren't good enough to stay here?" snapped Drummond.

"No, sir, I didn't say that! I just do what my boss tells me to do."

Drummond controlled his anger with an effort. He said, "It might interest you—and this Mrs. McKay, whoever she is—to know that those two young women have stayed in the most elegant hotels in New Orleans, which I assure you are more than a cut above the Territorial House in Wind River, Wyoming!"

Burt's head bobbed up and down. "Yes, sir, I reckon," he said weakly.

Drummond took a deep breath and waved a well-manicured hand. "Well, that's neither here nor there, I suppose. Where *can* I find Miss Lucy and Miss Irene?"

"Last I heard, they were stayin' at Schirmer's place. It's, ah, a little hotel on the east side of town. You just go down this main street here about four blocks and turn south on Ashley Street. You'll see the sign for Schirmer's right around the corner."

"Thanks." Drummond jerked his chin at the pile of bags in front of the desk. "Have these taken up to our rooms. And have two more rooms prepared for the ladies. They'll be returning with me."

Burt began, "Well, sir, I'll have to ask—"

"Just do it," Drummond said. "Tell your Mrs. McKay to talk to me if she's got some sort of problem with it."

Burt swallowed again. "Yes, sir." Being a member of his old section gang again didn't look so unappealing right now.

Drummond went out the front door of the hotel, trailed by Amos, Lige, and Saul. He didn't like to walk, but Wind River seemed too small to justify the expense of renting a buggy. Besides, he didn't intend to be here for very long. It probably wouldn't take him more than a day or two to tend to the errand that had brought him to Wyoming Territory, and then he could go back home to

New Orleans. He started down the street toward the other hotel the clerk had mentioned.

As it turned out, Drummond and his companions didn't have to go all the way to Schirmer's place, because they had only walked a couple of blocks when a female voice called happily from the other side of the street, "John!"

Drummond turned to see Lucy and Irene on the opposite boardwalk, both of them looking as lovely as ever. Irene was waving at him, and she started across the dusty boulevard toward him without hesitation. Lucy followed more slowly. But then, Drummond reflected, Lucy had always been more reserved than Irene. She was almost too cool-headed to be a whore. But some men liked that sense of reserve in a woman.

If there was one thing Drummond knew about, it was what men liked in women.

He stepped down off the boardwalk to greet Irene. She caught his hands and leaned up to give him a quick, hard kiss on the mouth. She said excitedly, "It's so good to see you, John. Does this mean we can go back home now?"

"Soon," Drummond told her with a smile. "But not yet." Gently, he disengaged his fingers from Irene's and turned to the brunette who had come up to join them. "Hello, Lucy."

"John," she said quietly. "You must have left as soon as you got our telegram."

"I was waiting for it. I caught the first train."

"I'm a little surprised you came yourself instead of just sending someone."

Drummond frowned a little. "Of course I came. This is a personal matter, and I intend to deal with it personally."

"I would have thought it had more to do with business."

A new harshness came into Drummond's cultured tones as he said, "No one takes away what's mine. That makes it personal." He took a breath and then leaned forward to brush a kiss across Lucy's cheek. "But it *is* good to see you again, too. It seems like more than three months since the two of you left New Orleans. I was about to decide that your mission wasn't going to be successful." He paused, then said, "You're sure it's her?"

"I'm sure," Lucy said. "She still looks like the daguerreotype you showed us before we left. She's Rosemary, all right." A faint smile appeared briefly on Lucy's face. "She even calls herself Rose."

Drummond clenched a fist in satisfaction. "And she doesn't know who the two of you are?"

Irene shook her head. "She doesn't have any idea," the blonde said confidently. "We didn't come to work for you until *after* she was gone, remember?"

"Of course I remember," Drummond said a bit impatiently. "That's why I chose you and Lucy and the others I sent out looking. I didn't want her to be tipped off so that she could run again. This search has gone on long enough. Too long, in fact."

"She thinks we're her friends," Lucy said.

Drummond laughed. "That's priceless. You've done very well. I'll settle up with you later at the Territorial House."

Irene caught her lower lip between her teeth for a moment, then said, "We're not staying there. The owner wouldn't let us."

"Well, you are now," declared Drummond. "Get your things and go on up there. The clerk is expecting you, and if the old harridan who owns the place has any problems with the situation, she can speak to me."

Lucy said, "I wouldn't exactly call Mrs. McKay an old harridan—"

Drummond waved off the comment. "Whatever. Right now I have something more important to tend to."

"You're going to see her . . . now?"

"No point in putting it off. I've already waited two years for this." To the trio of silent, hard-faced men with him, he said, "Come on, boys," then turned and went in the other direction—toward the Wind River Café.

Lon Rogers stepped from the seat of the wagon to the raised porch in front of the general store. He had already set the brake and tied the reins of the team around the lever. The wagon wouldn't go anywhere.

The emporium was busy, with quite a few customers in the aisles and several standing at the long counter in the back, so Lon had to wait a while before he was able to give the cook's list to Harvey Raymond. "It's Coosie's usual list, Mr. Raymond," Lon said. "Reckon you can fill it?"

The store manager looked over the scrawled list and muttered, "Let's see . . . fifty pounds of flour, fifty pounds of salt, twenty of sugar, five of coffee, a barrel of beans . . . . Yeah, we've got all this, Lon. I'll get the boys started loading it for you."

"Thanks, Mr. Raymond. I'll sign for it when you're done."

Raymond grinned. "You Texas boys always surprise me. Damned near all of you can write your name."

Lon just smiled at the veiled insult. He knew that Texans weren't necessarily all that welcome up here in Wyoming Territory—especially since one of them, the man Lon rode for, had established the biggest, most successful ranch in the area. But it wasn't worth arguing over, especially not today.

He had something else he wanted to do while the supplies were being gathered and loaded onto the wagon.

"I'll be back in a little bit, Mr. Raymond," Lon said with a wave of his hand. The general store's manager just nodded without looking up from what he was doing, which was checking off items on the list Lon had given him with the stub of a pencil.

Lon left the emporium and walked west along Grenville Avenue. The farther he went, the more nervous he got. Rose had made it mighty clear how she really felt about him. She considered him a bother, sort of like a horsefly buzzing around a rider's head, and she had been friendly to him only out of politeness. The night she had made that plain to him, he had ridden back to the Diamond S fully intending never to bother her again.

But ever since then, he had been unable to get her out of his thoughts. Whether he was riding the range or repairing a corral or peeling a mess of spuds for Coosie, the image of Rose Foster's lovely face had always been in his brain. Maybe even more so when he was taking his turn as the cook's helper, because that made him think of all the good times he had spent in the café, talking to Rose and reveling in her company. Already, even though it had been only a few days, he missed those times so strongly that it was like an ache inside him.

So she was just going to have to listen to what he had to say, he told himself firmly as he approached the café. All right, so she didn't want any kind of romance with him. If that was how it had to be, he could live with that, even though it would be difficult. But she couldn't forbid him to be her friend. That would be just too cruel.

And when you got right down to it, Lon thought, Rose Foster didn't have a cruel bone in her body. He knew her well enough to be sure of that.

The café was one of the most popular places for breakfast in Wind River, but it was midmorning by now. Most of the customers would be gone. At least Lon hoped that would be the case. It would be easier to talk to Rose without a lot of people around.

Sure enough, when he pushed the door of the café open a moment later and stepped inside, he saw only a couple of old men sitting at one of the tables, nursing cups of coffee. Rose was nowhere in sight, and neither was Monty Riordan. A second later, though, the swinging door to the kitchen opened and Rose came out in response to the ringing of the bell over the front door. It had jingled when Lon came in.

Rose hesitated when she saw the young cowboy, but then she went behind the counter, a wary look in her eyes, and said, "Hello, Lon. What can I do for you?"

"I came into town to pick up some supplies for the ranch," Lon replied. "Mr. Raymond over at the general store is filling the order now. I thought I might get a cup of coffee while I wait."

"I see," Rose said with a nod. She seemed to relax a little. "All right, sit down. I'll get a cup."

She retreated into the kitchen again and came out a moment later with a cup of steaming coffee. She set it on the counter in front of Lon, who had taken the stool closest to the kitchen door. He laid a coin down and said, "Thank you, Rose."

"I'll get your change."

"Oh, that's all right," Lon said quickly. "You keep it."

Rose hesitated again, but she didn't argue. She swept the coin into the till and closed it.

Lon sipped the coffee. It was hot, strong, and good, and he was grateful for the bracing effect of it. He had never been much of a drinking man, but a jot of whiskey in that coffee right about now might have helped too. He swallowed another sip, then began, "You know, Rose, I've been thinking—"

"About what?" she cut in.

"Well . . . about you and me," he said, wishing she would have let him lead up to it more gradually.

Rose shook her head. "I thought I made myself plain the other night, Lon. There's not going to be anything between you and me."

Lon glanced at the two old men, knowing that they were listening despite their efforts to look casual and uncomprehending of what was going on at the counter. He took a deep breath and forced himself to say, "Not even friendship, Rose? I reckon I could be satisfied, just being your friend."

He saw a mixture of impatience and sympathy on her face, and the latter emotion gave him hope. If he could just get her to give him a chance . . .

But then her expression hardened a little, and she shook her head firmly. "No, Lon, I don't think that would be a good idea. I can't stop you from coming into the café, but I don't want you walking me home, and I don't want you hanging around outside all the time. You're just going to have to give up these ideas you've got in your head—"

She broke off as the bell over the front door jingled again. Lon saw her turn her head, saw her lift her gaze toward the newcomers.

And then, suddenly, he saw more fear, more pure horror, than he had ever seen before in the eyes of another human being.

"Hello, Rosemary," said a smooth, quiet, male voice.

Lon swiveled quickly on the stool, his hand going instinctively toward the gun on his hip. All he saw was a handsome, dark-haired man in a suit, however, followed by three other men. Lon stopped the motion before his fingers touched the butt of his gun.

"You—you can't be here!" Rose gasped after a few seconds.

The dark-haired man strolled toward the counter, trailed by his burly companions. He said, "As you can see, I *am* here, Rosemary. I'm not sure why you seem so surprised to see me. You had to know that I'd find you."

Despite the stranger's expensive clothes and cultured voice, there was something about him that set Lon's teeth on edge. Maybe it was just Rose's reaction to the man that made him feel that way, but Lon remembered the chill that had gone down his spine every time he had seen a big diamondback rattler coiled up on the trail down in Texas.

He felt just about the same way when he looked at this man.

Rose swallowed hard and said, "Lon, you'd better leave now."

He glanced back at her. Her peaches-and-cream complexion had turned ashen, and her eyes were still wide with shock and fear. He said, "But I haven't finished my coffee, Rose."

"I don't care about that. Just go."

The two old men were already doing just that, slipping out the open door behind the newcomers. The stranger in the lead smiled at Lon and said, "That's a good idea, cowboy. Why don't you do like she says?"

Lon felt nervous, but he wasn't going to let these men intimidate him, no matter how tough the three bruisers bringing up the rear looked. He said stubbornly, "I'm not going anywhere until I finish my coffee. Hell, I paid for it already."

"Oh, well, if that's all that's keeping you." The dark-haired man slipped a hand into the pocket of his expensive suit coat, brought it out, and flipped a coin through the air. It landed on the floor at Lon's feet with a rattle. "There. That's a lot more than you paid for that cup of coffee, cowboy. Take the money and get out."

Lon glanced down. The coin was a double eagle, a twenty dollar gold piece. Two-thirds of a month's salary for a puncher like him.

But all the sight of the coin did was make him angrier. He looked up at the man, scowled, and said, "Maybe you're the one who better leave, mister. I don't think the lady wants you here."

"Lady?" the handsome stranger repeated scornfully. "That's a good one, boy." He laughed.

Lon's face flushed and he stood up, but as he did Rose reached quickly across the counter and caught hold of his arm. "No, Lon!" she said urgently. "Don't do it. Just . . . just stay out of this. Please. It's none of your business."

Her words hurt him, but he could tell she was still frightened. Even though she hadn't wanted any sort of romance, hadn't even wanted to be friends with him, he couldn't abandon her now. Obviously, these men represented some sort of trouble for her, and no cowboy—no man—worth his salt ran out on a woman in trouble.

Not too roughly, Lon pulled his arm free of her grasp

and faced the four men. His hand hovered near his gun. A pulse hammered in his head. This wasn't the first time he had faced danger; he'd had a run-in with a pack of wolves the previous winter and had survived that. He didn't see how these human lobos could be any worse.

"You gents better mosey on," Lon said. "I don't care what Miss Rose says, I know she doesn't want you here. If you get out now, there won't be any trouble."

All four of the strangers stiffened, and despite the suave exterior of the leader, a look of almost feral hatred came into his eyes. He didn't like being crossed, didn't like it at all.

But after a tense moment, the man grinned cockily again—although the expression in his eyes didn't warm up any—as he said, "I think this cowboy wants us to leave, boys."

"Yeah, Mr. Drummond, I think you're right," said one of the others. "What do you want us to do?"

"Well, we could do as he says and 'mosey on'." The man laughed. "That would make him quite the hero."

Rose leaned over the counter toward Lon and hissed, "Please, Lon, don't do this! You don't understand what's going on here. You don't know what these men are . . . are capable of!"

Without looking around, he told her in a tight voice, "I reckon I've got a pretty good idea. But I'm not worried. Fellas like them are just bullies, and somebody's got to stand up to 'em." Lon lifted his voice a little. "Besides, I figure Monty's back there in the kitchen with that scatter-gun of his, just waiting to take a hand if there's trouble."

That made the strangers tense again, until Rose said bleakly, "Monty's not here, Lon. I sent him to buy supplies while we weren't busy this morning."

Lon restrained the impulse to say *Oh, hell*. He had been counting on Monty Riordan backing him up. Now he was on his own against four apparently dangerous men.

But he couldn't back down. Not with Rose watching. If he slunk out of here now like a dog with its tail between its legs, she would never respect him again. And if she lost all respect for him, there wouldn't ever be a chance that he could get her to change her mind about letting him court her, or even be her friend.

He had gotten himself into this mess. It was up to him to get both of them out of it.

"All right now," he said as he squared his shoulders. "This has gone on long enough. You fellas get out of here."

"I agree with you," the handsome, dark-haired man said.

That took Lon by surprise. "You do?"

"Yes, I certainly do. This has gone on more than long enough." Without looking over his shoulder at his companions, the man flicked his hand in a lazy gesture of command. "Throw the son of a bitch out of here."

Savage grins on their faces, the other three men started forward, stepping past their boss as they clenched their fists. Rose let out a little scream, and Lon gulped and reached for his gun.

It was like that wolf pack was closing in on him all over again.

Cole was inside the office at the jail when Casebolt came back from the Union Pacific depot. There was a puzzled look on the deputy's lean, beard-stubbled features.

"What's up, Billy?" Cole asked as he leaned back in the chair behind the desk.

Casebolt hung his battered old campaign hat on one of the nails beside the door. "I ain't sure anything is," he said. "There was just somethin' a mite strange that happened down at the depot."

"I didn't hear any gunshots this time."

"Nope, there weren't no shootin' when the westbound pulled in today. But some fellers got off that struck me wrong."

Cole straightened a little. He trusted Billy Casebolt's instincts. The old-timer wouldn't have lived as long as he had without possessing a sort of sixth sense that warned him of impending trouble. Cole had that same sense himself. He asked, "What did these men look like?"

"One of 'em was pretty handsome, 'bout medium-sized,

looked like he was used to getting whatever he wanted. The others were all big and tough-lookin'. All four of 'em was from back east. Didn't take but one look at the way they was dressed to see that."

"Lots of easterners are coming here now," Cole pointed out.

"Not like these," Casebolt said with a frown.

Cole pushed himself to his feet. If the looks of these strangers had bothered Casebolt that much, they would bear some checking out. Cole was sure of that. "Where did they go?"

"One of the big fellers put their bags on a wagon, and they started toward Miz McKay's hotel. The handsome gent, he seemed to be in charge. He asked me where the best place to stay was, and I told him the Territorial House." Casebolt's frown deepened. "Asked me to recommend an eatin' place, too, and without thinkin' I said the Wind River Café. Hope I ain't caused trouble for either Miz McKay or Miss Rose."

"I wouldn't worry about it," Cole said as he came out from behind the desk. "We'll just go take a look at these men, maybe introduce ourselves and make sure they understand we won't allow any trouble here in town."

"Yeah," Casebolt said as he reached for his hat again. "I reckon that's what we need to do, all right."

Before the two lawmen could reach the door, however, it opened and a couple of elderly men came hurrying into the office. Cole couldn't recall their names, but he knew they spent most of their time playing dominoes in front of various businesses. Both of them lived with relatives here in town, Cole thought.

"Marshal!" one of them began. "Looks like there's goin' to be—"

"Trouble!" finished the other one. Then they both began to talk at once, a jumble of voices that made no sense.

Cole held up his hands to stop them. "Hold it, hold it!" he snapped. "One at a time, damn it! Now, where's this trouble you're talking about?"

"Down at the café," one of the men said.

Cole felt a tingle of alarm and exchanged a quick, worried glance with Billy Casebolt. "Which café?" he asked.

"Miss Rose's," the other old man said. "The Wind River Café. Looks like there's goin' to be a fight."

"Blast it, Marshal!" exclaimed Casebolt. "I knew I should've kept an eye on them fellers!"

"We don't know it was them, Billy," Cole said as he started quickly toward the door. "Come on, we'll take a look."

Even as he spoke, however, all of Cole's instincts were telling him that the four strangers Casebolt had seen and talked to at the railroad station were indeed responsible for the disturbance—whatever it was—at Rose Foster's café. But no lawman could anticipate every problem, and those who tried could just about drive themselves loco. Casebolt had sensed there might be something wrong about the newcomers.

It was just that no one would have expected the trouble to break out so soon.

And break out it had, because as Cole and Casebolt started toward the café, the sound of a gunshot suddenly shattered the air.

Lon jerked his gun out of its holster as the three men lunged at him. Before he even had a chance to bring it up, however, he was forced to duck under a looping punch that could have torn his head off. Another man grabbed his right wrist, forcing it down and twisting it brutally. Lon's finger clenched on the trigger of the revolver, and the weapon's blast was deafening even in the big, open room of the café. The bullet thudded harmlessly into the floor at Lon's feet.

The next instant, a fist crashed into Lon's belly and doubled him over. He staggered forward, into a bear hug that crushed the air from his lungs. His feet came up off the floor and he dangled there in the grip of one of the big men, helpless.

Not quite helpless, he realized a second later as he desperately brought a knee up into his opponent's groin. For all the man's size, it didn't protect him from the force of Lon's blow. The man let out a howl of pain, and his grip loosened enough for Lon to twist out of it. The pistol was still in the young cowboy's hand, so he lashed out with it, slamming the barrel into the side of the man's head. The impact of the blow slewed the big man half-around, and he went to one knee, out of the fight for the moment.

Unfortunately, there were still two more of the bruisers. One of them laced his fingers together and clubbed his hands against the back of Lon's neck. Lon was driven forward by the blow, and the gun slipped from his fingers to fall to the floor. His boots hit the revolver and sent it skidding away. Lon struggled to keep his balance and turn to meet the new threat, but as he did so the third man slammed a punch into his lower back. Lon straightened and cried out from the pain that shot through him. He'd be passing blood for the next few days from that blow to the kidneys, he thought—if they didn't just beat him to death right here.

Lon was vaguely aware that Rose was still screaming and shouting. He had hoped she would take advantage of the chance to slip out the back while he occupied the attention of these men who frightened her so. But evidently she wasn't any more inclined to abandon him than he had been to run out on her. But her fear had rooted her behind the counter, and she wasn't taking part in the struggle going on. Lon was glad of that much, at least.

He threw punches wildly, so many that some of them had to connect. But none of the blows were solid enough to do more than slow down his adversaries temporarily, and he took a flurry of punches that staggered him in return. His entire body seemed to be filled with pain as hard, knobby fists thudded into him, rocking him back and forth.

Abruptly, arms looped around him from behind, holding him tightly again. One of the other men began slamming blows into his midsection. Lon's stomach was already in turmoil from the first punch he had taken there, and now the coffee he had drunk earlier came spewing back up. The man in front of him cursed, stepped to the side, backhanded him viciously. Lon felt consciousness trying to slip away from him.

But still he was aware of the handsome, dark-haired leader of these men, who was standing and observing calmly the brutal beating he had ordered. His arms were crossed, and there was a satisfied smile on his face.

"Oh, my God, John!" cried Rose. "Make them stop, please make them stop!"

"For you, my dear Rosemary, anything," the dark-haired man murmured. He spoke to his men in a sharper tone. "That's enough. Throw the cowboy out in the gutter with the rest of the trash."

Lon's head lolled forward loosely on his chest. He knew the men had stopped hitting him, but he wasn't aware of much else. His boots scraped on the floor as he was dragged to the door. A couple of seconds later, he was flying through the air—

Then he hit something softer than the ground, something that went, "Ooof!" Lon sprawled on the boardwalk with the thing he had hit now underneath him, poking him painfully.

"Dadblast it, get off o' me, boy! I can't breathe with you layin' on me!"

Lon's brain cleared enough for him to recognize Billy Casebolt's voice. The deputy sounded mighty irritated.

Then there was another sound that Lon recognized, a sound full of unmistakable menace.

It was the distinctive metallic click of a Colt revolver's hammer being pulled back to full cock.

Cole felt a surge of anger go through him as he watched Lon Rogers struggling to get up off of Casebolt. Lon's face was bloody and swollen, and his shirt was ripped and also blood-stained. The youngster from Texas had obviously had the hell beaten out of him by someone, most likely the men who stood just inside the open door of the café.

It had taken Cole and Casebolt both by surprise when the door opened and Lon came flying out. Casebolt had been unlucky enough to be in the young cowboy's path, and they had come together in a tooth-jarring, bone-rattling crash that sent them sprawling to the boardwalk. Now Casebolt had hold of Lon's arm and was helping him climb unsteadily back to his feet.

"Back off, damn it!" Cole barked at the three men as he covered them with his pistol. He saw one of the men edge a hand underneath the lapel of his coat. "Don't try it, mister!"

Suddenly, one of the other men stepped aside to let a smaller, well-dressed man stroll through the door. This man had his hands casually tucked into the pockets of his trousers. "What seems to be the trouble here, Marshal?" he asked.

"That's what I want to know," Cole said. "Take your hands out of your pockets, mister—*slow*!"

The man raised his eyebrows in surprise and carefully withdrew his hands from his pockets, just as Cole had ordered. "What's wrong, Marshal, did you think I was clutching some sort of . . . hogleg? Isn't that what you call them out here?"

"I just don't want any surprises that'll make me pull this trigger," Cole said. "Billy, are you all right?"

"Yep, just got the wind knocked out of me a mite," Casebolt replied. "I got my breath back now, and I'm in a heck of a lot better shape than this waddy here."

"Take Rogers down to Doc Kent's," Cole said. "I'll handle these gents."

As soon as Lon heard that, he twisted away from Casebolt's hand on his arm. "No!" he said thickly, his voice coming roughly through swollen lips. "Rose is in there! Somebody's got to . . . to help her, Marshal!"

Cole's eyes narrowed as he regarded the handsome, dark-haired man. "Where's Miss Foster?" he asked. "What've you done to her?"

"Not a thing, Marshal," the man said smoothly. He looked back over his shoulder. "Rosemary, my dear, there's a man out here who wishes to speak with you."

A second later, Rose pushed past him, a look of hatred on her face. She hurried over to Lon and caught up one of his hands, saying, "Oh! Oh, Lon, are you all right?"

"I reckon I will be . . . long as I know you are, Miss Rose. The marshal won't let those sidewinders . . . do anything to you . . . "

"The marshal has no say in this matter," the dark-haired man said coldly.

Cole's jaw tightened. "How the hell do you figure that?" he grated. "You have your boys beat the living daylights out of a fella, then throw him out of a building and knock down my deputy—"

"I'm sorry about your deputy," the man said. "That was an accident. But as for that man there—" He pointed at Lon. "He's in the wrong, and my assistants were just defending themselves when he pulled a gun on them. Surely you heard the weapon go off."

"I heard the shot," Cole said grimly. "That's why we came galloping down here."

"That's not the way it was," Rose said, her voice shaking with emotion. "Lon was just trying to help me. He was defending me."

"Defending you from what?" the dark-haired man asked. "All I want to do is talk with you."

"Then why did you have these men throw Lon out of the café?"

"He was interfering with me," the man said coldly. "He had no right to do that."

Cole frowned. He still hadn't lowered his gun. "How the hell do you figure Lon didn't have a right to stand up for Miss Rose?"

The man looked straight at Cole and said, "That cowboy had no right to interfere between me and my wife."

"Wife?" The startled exclamation came from Cole, Lon, and Casebolt at the same time.

Cole turned in amazement to Rose. She caught her lower lip between her teeth and lowered her gaze, refusing to meet his stare.

Lon looked at Rose with pain on his face that didn't come wholly from the beating he had received. He asked, "Is . . . is that fella telling the truth, Miss Rose?"

She hesitated, and before she could answer, the dark-haired man stepped forward and said, "My name is John Drummond, Marshal, and this woman is my wife Rosemary. I have documents to prove that if you want to examine them, but you can see for yourself that she's not denying it."

"Yes," Rose said bitterly. "It's true. I'm married to him."

Billy Casebolt let out a low whistle of surprise.

"How . . . why didn't you ever . . . you could have told me!" Lon stammered. "I would have understood—"

"There's nothing to understand, cowboy," Drummond said sharply. "Rosemary is my wife, and I intend to speak with her. Neither you nor these lawmen can legally stop me."

"I reckon that's right," Cole said, "but there's still the matter of that fight between your men and Lon."

Drummond shrugged. "As I told you, he pulled a gun on us. My men had no choice but to defend themselves."

"They were about to attack him anyway!" accused Rose.

"Only because he was unlawfully keeping me from talking to my own wife," countered Drummond.

Cole didn't like this, didn't like it a bit. But from the looks of things, this stranger called John Drummond did indeed have the law on his side. It was stretching things a bit to call beating up Lon so badly self-defense, but even that would probably be disregarded by a judge since Rose didn't deny that she was married to Drummond. Any benefit of the doubt in the law would go to him.

"All right," Cole said grudgingly. "I reckon you made your point, mister." To Casebolt, he went on, "Take Lon down to the doctor's, Billy, like I told you."

"No!" Lon protested. "You can't leave them here with her! She's afraid of them! They're going to hurt her!"

"Is that true, Rose?" asked Cole. "Are you afraid these men are going to hurt you?"

She glanced at Drummond, whose smug expression seemed to be firmly in place now, then she shook her head slightly. "No, Marshal," she said quietly. "I'll be all right. You can go on, too."

"You're sure?"

Rose nodded this time, her voice a little stronger as she replied, "I'm sure."

Cole lowered his gun and eased down the hammer, then slipped the .44 back into its holster. "All right," he said with a sigh. "Come on, you two." He motioned to Casebolt and Lon.

The young cowboy still didn't want to go. Cole and Casebolt had to get on either side of him and practically drag him down the street toward Dr. Judson Kent's office. "This isn't right," Lon said as they urged him along. "I tell you, Rose isn't safe with that man! He . . . he's no good!"

"Could be you're right, Lon," Cole said. "But even if you are, there's nothing we can do about it. She's married to him."

"The law can't mix in 'tween a man and his wife," added Casebolt. "That's just the way it is, whether we like it or not."

"I'm not the law," Lon said. "I'm just a man."

"But you're not her husband," Cole pointed out. "Drummond is. Come on, Lon. All this arguing isn't getting us anywhere. Let Dr. Kent take a look at you, and then we'll talk about what we can do for Rose, if anything."

That quieted Lon down, and he came along without any further complaint.

Cole glanced back over his shoulder, however, at the café. Rose and Drummond had disappeared inside the building, but the three bruisers were still on the boardwalk outside. That eased Cole's mind a little. Whatever was going on in there, it was now strictly between Rose and Drummond, and that was the way it ought to be, Cole supposed, since they were married.

But if anything happened to Rose, if Drummond hurt her . . .

Then, husband or not, he was going to be damned sorry.

10

Rose stalked into the café's kitchen, knowing that Drummond was following her. She had her arms crossed across her chest and was hugging herself as if she was cold, despite the warmth of the day. She turned to face him as he sauntered into the kitchen after her.

"I suppose you've come to kill me," she said to him, "just like you killed Nick."

Drummond raised an eyebrow. "You're mistaken, Rose," he said. "I've never killed anyone."

"You have it done. It's the same thing."

"You're imagining things, my dear, just like you always imagined them during the rest of our marriage."

Rose shook her head. "The only thing I ever imagined was that I loved you. The rest of it was true. All the evil things you did, all of it was true."

"I'm really sorry that you feel that way, Rosemary."

"My name is Rose," she snapped.

"You're Rosemary du Charlaine Drummond, of the

Baton Rouge du Charlaines, and my wife," he insisted. "I don't know where you got the name Foster. But if you really wanted to run away from me, you should have changed your name completely and cut off some of that gorgeous hair and dyed it a different color." Drummond shrugged. "But even if you had done all those things, I would have found you. Sooner or later, I would have found you. Even if it had taken twenty years instead of two."

Rose took a deep breath. Even though it would not have been his style to do so, she had halfway expected him to pull a gun and shoot her. But evidently, he felt like talking, and the longer she could keep him talking, the better. While he was boasting, at least he couldn't hurt her.

"How *did* you find me?" she asked.

"I sent out agents, of course. I wasn't sure which direction you'd gone, so I had people searching up the Mississippi, over across Texas, and along all the railroads. I knew it might take a long time, but I never gave up hope."

"Agents," Rose repeated. "Who was it that found me?"

"That's not important," Drummond answered with a shake of his head. "What matters is that I want you to come back to New Orleans with me."

Rose wasn't ready to let go of her last question yet, however. With realization dawning on her face, she said, "It must have been those two women, those prostitutes. They're the only strangers I've talked to lately." She laughed bitterly. "Agents, you said. I should have known you meant whores. Who else is a whoremonger going to use when he needs something done?"

Drummond's face hardened. "That's about enough of

that, Rosemary. Lucy and Irene were just doing their jobs, doing what I asked them to do. They're loyal to me . . . unlike some women I could mention."

Rose stared at him. "My God!" she exclaimed after a moment, her voice shaking. "You talk about loyalty! You're the biggest criminal in New Orleans, John. You can have just about anybody murdered with a snap of your fingers. I was too stupid to see it at first, but now I know what kind of man—what kind of *monster*—you really are. And you expect me to go back with you!"

Stoically, Drummond endured the harsh words that lashed at him. When Rose fell silent, he said, "You can believe me or not, Rosemary, but I wasn't responsible for Nick Murdoch's death."

"I *don't* believe you."

"Let me finish. I didn't have anything to do with Nick's death. He worked for me, true, but he was a friend of mine as well. I wouldn't have hurt him—not even after I found out you'd betrayed me with him."

Rose looked down at the floor and said softly, "Nick was . . . kind to me. He never hurt me."

"He used you," Drummond snapped. "He was ambitious. He wanted to take my place in more than your bed. He wanted to take over everything that I'd built up!" Drummond's hands clenched into fists, but he controlled himself with a visible effort. "You think it was easy, keeping everything together through the chaos of the Civil War? And then Reconstruction was worse. It's still difficult enough without having to cope with the betrayal of my wife and my best friend."

"But you always managed to hold on to your power," Rose said. "You made deals with the smugglers and the blockade runners, and then when the city fell you were right there with your arms open to welcome every corrupt Yankee officer you could find."

"I'm a survivor," murmured Drummond. "I do what I have to. You should appreciate that. My efforts saved you and your family a great deal of distress and provided a luxurious life for you when most of the old aristocrats were suffering terribly."

"Yes, but at what price?" Rose demanded. "All you took was my happiness . . . my soul!"

Slowly, Drummond shook his head. "You were always a bit overdramatic, my dear. The fact of the matter is that your little adventure is over. I still love you, despite what you've done, and I want you to come back to New Orleans with me."

"Love?" Rose asked in amazement. "You don't know the meaning of the word, John!"

Drummond's mouth drew down into a thin, angry line. "We're wasting time," he snapped. "Pack your things, Rosemary. You're coming back with me to the hotel tonight, and tomorrow when the eastbound train comes through, we'll be on it. I won't allow any more argument."

"I don't give a damn what you'll allow! I won't go with you, and you can't force me to!"

A humorless smile touched Drummond's face. "Ah, but that's where you're wrong, my dear. I'm your husband, and you have to do as I say. The law can't interfere, and you've already seen what happened to your young knight of the range when he tried to step in."

Rose's chest heaved with emotion, and she suddenly hissed, "You son of a bitch!" Her fingers crooked into claws, and she threw herself at him, reaching for his eyes.

Drummond caught her wrists easily and jerked her against him. Rose felt a wave of repulsion go through her as her breasts flattened against his chest. His mouth came down on hers. She gagged and tried to twist her face away from him, but he was holding her too tightly. His fingers were locked around her wrists like iron, his grip so strong that she winced from the pain. A shudder of horror went through her as he thrust his tongue between her lips and invaded her mouth with it.

That was when someone yelled in the front room of the café, and a split-second later, a pair of gunshots boomed.

Drummond let go of her and jerked around, his hand darting underneath his coat and reappearing with a small, silver-plated pistol clutched in his fingers. He strode to the door and pushed it open, stepping into the main room. Rose was right behind him, afraid that Lon Rogers had come back and started a gunfight with the other three men, a fight he would have been bound to lose.

Instead, though, when Rose looked past Drummond's shoulder, she saw a man she had never seen before standing just inside the front door of the café, covering Drummond's three men with a pair of ivory-handled Colts.

No, on second thought she *had* seen this man before, she realized, recognizing the white hair, the high-crowned black hat, and the keen blue eyes. He had eaten in the café a time or two, Rose recalled, but she didn't know his name. His hearty voice was familiar, though, as he said, "Hello, Drummond. Better put that gun away before it gives your boys ideas. I promise, I'll shoot you first."

"Boyd!" Drummond spat, and Rose had never heard so much venom in his voice, not even when he was talking about Nick Murdoch.

"Nice to see you, too," the man called Boyd said dryly. He glanced past Drummond at Rose and went on, "We haven't been formally introduced, ma'am, although I've sampled your excellent food a couple of times. My name's Dan Boyd. I'm a deputy United States marshal."

A surge of hope went through Rose, but it faded quickly. It had already been established that the law could do little or nothing to help her. If Cole Tyler was unable to step in legally on her behalf, she couldn't expect anything more from this pleasant-faced, middle-aged man, even if he *was* a United States marshal.

After all, terrorizing your wife wasn't a federal crime, now was it? Rose thought . . .

"What are you doing here, Boyd?" Drummond demanded. "What gives you the right to wave those guns around and threaten my men?"

"I was just trying to persuade them not to reach for anything under their coats," Boyd said, a hard edge creeping into his voice. "Sorry, Miss Foster, but I had to put a couple of bulletholes in your floor. I'll pay to have them patched."

"That's all right," Rose said with a weary sigh. She was just grateful that Boyd didn't seem to be backing down before Drummond's threats. Maybe he would hold Drummond and the others here long enough for her to get to her room at the boardinghouse, pack a few things and rent a horse. Then she could run again.

But suddenly, the whole idea of flight seemed futile to her. Drummond had found her here in Wind River, where she had finally come to believe that she was safe. He would find her no matter where she hid. She was becoming convinced of that now. Besides, it was ludicrous to think that she could set out across the Wyoming frontier on horseback, on her own, and survive. She wouldn't last out the week, she thought.

"I got a tip you were on your way up here to Wind River, Drummond," Boyd was saying. "I figured I'd get here before you did and be waiting when you arrived. I guess that organization of yours isn't quite as trustworthy as you thought it was, eh?"

Drummond's jaw clenched angrily, but he didn't say anything. The look in his eyes boded ill for whoever had tipped off Boyd about his plans, however. Rose knew what that meant. Somebody would wind up floating face-down in the bayous.

"I've been watching for you, but I didn't know you were in town yet," Boyd went on. "When I saw these big fellas who work for you coming into the café, I knew you had to be here, too. That would make you Rosemary du Charlaine, wouldn't it, ma'am?"

Before Rose could answer, Drummond snapped, "She's Rosemary Drummond, Boyd, and you know it. She's my wife."

"Sure." To Rose, the federal man said, "I never saw a photograph of you, ma'am, more's the pity. But I pretty well had Rose Foster pegged as the lady Drummond's been looking for. Forgive me for being so plain-spoken about it, but you and Mrs. McKay are the only ladies in Wind River attractive enough for a man like Drummond to marry, and I knew it wasn't Mrs. McKay he was looking for."

"Please," Rose said, "I don't know what your connection with my husband is, Marshal, but can't you arrest him? Can't you take him back to New Orleans?"

"That's what I'm here for," Boyd said bluntly.

Drummond gave a short laugh. "Don't be ridiculous,

Boyd. You know there's no solid evidence against me, and not one single witness has come forward to testify against me."

Boyd snorted in contempt. "Of course not. You've had all the ones who had any guts killed already."

"Prove it," Drummond dared him.

"One of these days, I will," Boyd replied grimly.

"One of these days! Hah! Give it up, Boyd. You and that special prosecutor President Grant appointed have been trying for six months now. You haven't turned up a shred of proof."

"I'm through arguing with you, Drummond," snapped Boyd. "You want these men out of here, ma'am?"

"Yes," Rose said. "Please."

"You heard the lady, Drummond."

"That designation is still questionable," Drummond said with a shrug. "But I suppose we have no choice except to leave. Your superiors will hear about this high-handed, illegal treatment, though, Marshal Boyd. You can count on it."

"I'll do that," grunted Boyd. "Now git!"

He backed away, still covering Drummond and the other men with his guns as they started toward the door. Rose moved behind the counter, and Boyd put his back against it. His gun barrels tracked Drummond right out the door.

Boyd waited until the New Orleans crime lord and his henchmen were out of sight before smoothly holstering his guns. Then he turned to Rose and said, "I've been looking for you for quite a while, Miss Foster. Or do you prefer Mrs. Drummond?"

Rose shuddered. "Please. Anything but that."

"All right. Do you mind answering a few questions?"

Instantly, out of long habit, Rose was wary. She didn't like questions of the sort that Boyd was bound to ask. She had carefully avoided discussing her past for two years now.

"I guess I'm beholden to you," she said slowly. "You protected me from John and his men when our local marshal wouldn't."

"Now, I wouldn't go feeling badly toward Marshal Tyler for that," Boyd said. "His powers don't extend as far as a federal lawman's do. And he doesn't have a personal stake in this case, either, so he's not as likely to bend the law."

"What's your personal stake, Marshal?" Rose asked, curious.

"More than six months of hard work trying to get something solid on Drummond," Boyd replied. "Miss Foster . . . why did you run off after he had Nick Murdoch killed? I'd have thought you'd want to stay and nail Drummond. Your testimony could convict him."

"Stay in New Orleans?" Rose said bitterly. "Stay there so that Amos or Saul or Lige could put a knife in me and dump me in the river, like they did with Nick? I don't think so, Marshal Boyd."

"You had to know there was talk of a special prosecutor being appointed," Boyd insisted. "You would have been protected."

"That prosecutor wasn't appointed until earlier this year." Rose shook her head. "I would have been dead long before that."

"Well, you're safe now," Boyd said confidently. "I'll get us some train tickets, and in less than a week, you'll be home and Drummond will be behind bars where he belongs."

For a long moment, Rose just stared at the federal lawman as if he had grown a third eye, then she shook her head. "I'm not going back," she said.

Boyd frowned. "What? You've got to go back and testify."

"No. I don't. And I'm not going to."

"Wait just a minute," Boyd said, growing angry. "I've devoted a lot of time and trouble to finding a way to convict Drummond, and you're it, Miss Foster."

Rose took a deep breath. "I came to Wind River to put my past behind me, and that's just what I intend to do."

"You can't be serious."

"I'm very serious."

Boyd brought his palm down sharply on the counter. "Blast it, ma'am, if you stay here, Drummond will try to have you killed! You know that!"

Rose lifted her chin stubbornly and said, "I'll take my chances."

In the back of her mind, though, she knew that Boyd was at least partially correct. Wind River would never be completely safe for her again, now that John Drummond knew she was here. She would have to leave, go on the run again, find a place to start a new life. Maybe it would be safer than the one she had thought she had here.

But only if Drummond didn't have her killed first.

"What's going on here?" Cole Tyler asked from the doorway.

Rose looked up, startled by his arrival. He must have come to investigate the two shots Boyd had fired to keep Drummond's men at bay, she thought. If there was something surprising, it was that he hadn't shown up earlier.

"It . . . it's nothing, Marshal," Rose said.

"What happened to that fella Drummond? And what are you doing here, Boyd?"

"Just came in for a cup of coffee and a piece of pie, Marshal," Boyd answered easily. "This café's got the best eats in town. But I reckon you know that already."

Rose wasn't sure why he was lying to Cole, but she didn't want to involve the local lawman in her dilemma any more than he already was, either. So she said, "That's right, Marshal. And my husband and his friends already left. There wasn't any more trouble."

Cole was frowning suspiciously. "Somebody told me they heard some shots coming from down here. I'd have been here sooner to investigate, but Billy and I had to bust up a fight in the Pronghorn. Parker's place is getting worse again. It's almost as bad as when the railhead was here."

"Oh, I don't think it's that bad," Rose forced herself to say calmly. She saw the glance Boyd gave her as she picked up a rag and began to wipe the counter. He realized she was playing along with him. "I didn't hear any shots. Did you, Mr. Boyd?"

"No, ma'am, not a one. Either the fella who told you about them was mistaken, Marshal Tyler, or they came from somewhere else."

For a moment, Cole didn't reply, then he nodded slowly. "Right," he said, not sounding too convinced. His gaze went to the floor, rested there a moment, then lifted to Rose again. "If Drummond gives you any more trouble, let me know," he said. "I don't care if he's your husband or not, he's not going to hurt you."

"Thank you, Cole," Rose said. "I . . . don't think he's going to bother me anymore." She wished that was true.

Cole turned toward the door. "You coming, Boyd?"

"I never got that coffee and pie," the federal lawman said.

"I need to brew up some fresh coffee," Rose said quickly, "and the only pies I've got are still baking. You'd better come back later."

Boyd's blue eyes hardened as he looked at her. "I'll do that," he said.

"Now, if you gentlemen will excuse me, the lunch rush will be starting soon, and my cook's not back with our supplies yet."

"He's on his way," Cole said, looking out the window. "Here he comes now."

Rose looked past him and saw Monty Riordan coming toward the café, trundling the wheelbarrow he had taken to the general store. It was loaded with sacks of flour, sugar, and salt.

Cole glanced back at Rose. "You're sure you're going to be all right?"

She nodded. "Of course."

And it was true for the time being. With Monty here, and with the crowd of customers that would be arriving as noontime approached, Drummond wouldn't try anything.

"Well, come on, Marshal," Cole said to Boyd. "Let's let the lady get busy."

"Sure." Boyd lifted a finger to the brim of his hat as he nodded to Rose. She read the unspoken message in his eyes and knew that he would be back. She hadn't seen the last of him, just as she knew Drummond wouldn't go away and leave her alone, either. Boyd wouldn't give up until she had agreed to go back to New Orleans, and Drummond had to be aware of that.

Which meant that he wouldn't be satisfied until she was no longer a threat to him.

In other words, until she was dead.

The flames of the campfire crackled merrily, but that was
the only thing merry about the camp nestled in a bowl in
the foothills. The men who sat around the blaze were
long-faced and glum for the most part. Some of them
were angry, and that was evident from the way they took
quick pulls at the bottle of whiskey they passed around.

Lew Stanton stood a little apart from the others,
watching his men, and he could almost smell the tension
in the air. He could have pointed to this man and that
one and known that when the trouble came, it would
come from them.

That 'breed from down in Arizona, Alejandro Reyes, was
the worst, Stanton thought. Reyes had been complaining
ever since Stanton had decided to hit that westbound train
between Rawlins and Wind River.

"Nobody robs trains," Reyes had said, "not even Frank
and Jesse James. The only ones who have tried are the
hermanos Reno, and look where it got them."

"I know John Reno and his brothers got lynched,"

Stanton had snapped in reply. "We just have to be smarter than they were. The key is in the organizing and the planning."

So Stanton had organized and he had planned, and he had been sure that the gang's first train hold-up would be successful. It wouldn't be the last one, either. He had foreseen a long, lucrative run in which he and his men would prey on the trains of the Union Pacific.

Instead, nearly half the men had been killed, and the loot they had gotten away with from the passengers added up to less than two hundred dollars. He had even been nicked with a bullet himself, a wound that was healing well but still a little painful. The job had been an ignominious failure.

But that didn't mean Stanton was going to allow this one setback to defeat him. If nothing else, his military service had taught him that one battle didn't make a whole war. The important thing was living to fight another day.

Now, though, Reyes and that hillbilly from Arkansas, Turner, and the Garn brothers, Matt and Josh, and tall, hatchet-faced Ben Lannigan, were all muttering among themselves and getting drunker and drunker. It would be all right with Stanton if they all drank themselves into a stupor. Then they wouldn't be able to give him any trouble when he told the gang about the next job he had planned, and when they woke up in the morning, their heads would hurt too much to complain too loudly.

All of them seemed to be holding their liquor well, however, and it wasn't very likely they would pass out anytime soon. Stanton knew he could only postpone revealing his plans for so long, and he sensed that time was just about up. The men were getting anxious, eager to find out what their next target would be. Stanton hunkered beside the fire, filled a cup with coffee from the pot that sat at the edge of the flames, and drank it slowly. Postponing this discussion any longer would just make things worse, he decided.

He threw the dregs of his coffee into the fire, liking the sizzling sound they made when they hit the flames. "Reckon it's time to talk about the next job," he said.

"Another train, *mi general*?" asked Reyes mockingly. Turner and the Garns grinned broadly, but Lannigan just watched Stanton to see what his reaction would be. Lannigan was the most dangerous of the bunch, the fastest on the draw, Stanton knew.

Stanton would be sure to kill him first, if it came to that.

For now, though, the outlaw leader just shook his head. "No more trains for a while. They're liable to be expecting that."

"Then what *are* we gonna rob?" Josh Garn asked. He and his brother were twins, bearded men who had been farmers in Pennsylvania before the war. It wasn't easy to tell them apart as long as they kept their mouths shut, but once they started talking the difference between them was obvious: Josh still had a relatively full set of teeth, while Matt's mouth was just about empty. Matt didn't talk much because of that.

"You boys know I've had agents check out every good-sized town around here," Stanton said, making an effort to keep his temper under control despite the attitude of Reyes and his cohorts. "During the war we always used spies to find out what the enemy was up to."

Turner said, "Whenever we caught one o' them pecker-woods, we always strung him up from a tree limb. Ain't nothin' like watchin' a fella kick hisself to death at the end of a rope." The man cackled with laughter.

Stanton glanced at Turner with distaste, then went on. "The man I sent to Wind River reports that they have a brand-new bank there, the first bank in this part of the territory. I'd say it's just waiting for us to pay it a visit, gentlemen."

Reyes frowned darkly. "A bank? I don't know, Stanton. Some of them safes are mighty hard to crack."

"That's why we make somebody open it for us," Stanton said. "Why don't you listen to the whole plan before you start criticizing it, Reyes?"

The 'breed shrugged. "Sure. I just don't want to wind up dead like our *compadres* we had to leave behind at the train."

"Nobody's winding up dead this time," snapped Stanton, "not unless some of those townies are stupid enough to try to stop us. And they'll be the ones dying."

"Tell us what you've got in mind," Lannigan said quietly. "And if this bank is new, how do you know it's got enough money in it to make the risk worthwhile?"

"There's plenty of money in it. A lot of those settlers are from back east, and they're used to having a bank where they can put their money. Now that one has opened up, I reckon just about everybody in Wind River is putting money in it." Stanton grinned, sensing that the lure of wealth had hooked the men. There wouldn't be too many objections from them, not even from Reyes and his bunch. They were just as greedy as the next man, and in this outfit, that was pretty greedy. Stanton went on, "It's going to be up to us to take all that money *out*, and anybody who gets in our way dies. Now, here's the way I've got it figured . . ."

* * *

Jeremiah Newton put the canvas bag down on the counter and said, "I'd like to deposit this in the church's account, Brother Smollett."

Nathan Smollett, the bank manager, returned the smile the big blacksmith gave him. Smollett was a man in his forties, a lifelong bachelor, mild-looking with thinning hair. He wore a pince-nez and looked like he would have been more at home in New England, which was, in fact, where he had come from. Pittsfield, Massachusetts, to be precise, which Nathan Smollett usually was.

But despite his appearance, he liked to think he had an adventurous streak in him. Otherwise, he would have stayed where he was and been head cashier in the bank in Pittsfield until his retirement. But instead he had answered the lure of the frontier—and the advertisement placed in eastern newspapers by Mrs. Simone McKay—and journeyed all the way out here to Wind River to become the manager, vice-president, and cashier of the town's first and so far only bank. That he was also the only employee didn't bother him. Smollett found the West to be quite invigorating, both for its wildly beautiful landscapes and for its colorful characters . . . such as the man facing him across the counter.

"Certainly, Mr. Newton," Smollett said as he untied the cord that held the neck of the bag closed.

"Call me Brother Jeremiah."

"All right." Smollett upended the bag, pouring out the coins, gold nuggets, and wads of greenbacks it held. He began separating the money so that he could count it. "This week's collection?"

"That's right," rumbled Jeremiah.

There were no other customers in the bank at the moment, so Smollett took his time sorting and counting the money. The nuggets had to be weighed on the little scale he kept underneath the counter so that he would know how much they were worth. As he set each nugget aside, he used a quill pen to make a notation of its value. Finally, Smollett was able to add up the coins, the currency, and the gold and announce to Jeremiah, "You have a hundred and eighty-seven dollars and thirty-nine cents here, Mr. Newton—I mean Brother Jeremiah."

"Put it with the other funds I've deposited," Jeremiah said.

"Storing up treasures on earth rather than in Heaven, eh?" Smollett asked with a smile.

He wasn't prepared for the thunderous frown that appeared on Jeremiah's face. "That's the church's money, not mine," the big blacksmith said.

"Certainly, sir, I know that," Smollett said hastily. "And I meant no offense, Brother Jeremiah. I just thought . . . perhaps a little Biblical humor . . . "

"The Bible isn't meant to be humorous, Brother Smollett."

"No, of course not." Smollett swallowed hard and dipped the quill pen in the inkwell again. "If you have your deposit book with you, I'll just enter this amount."

"Sure." Jeremiah took a small black folder from his coat pocket, dwarfing the little book with his huge hands. He looked a bit sheepish as he laid the deposit book on the counter in front of Smollett. "I apologize for nearly losing my temper with you, brother. I've been upset because of a problem concerning the land where I want to build the new church."

"Hank Parker," Smollett said.

Jeremiah looked surprised. "How did you know?"

"Mrs. McKay mentioned the matter to me. We confer

quite frequently, you know, since she's the owner and president of the bank. She said that you and Mr. Parker were both interested in the same piece of property."

"That's right. And we don't even know for certain yet who owns the land."

Smollett looked past Jeremiah and out the big plate glass window in the front wall of the bank, his attention drawn by movement on the boardwalk in front of the solid-looking brick building. "Speak of Beelzebub," muttered the banker.

Jeremiah glanced around and saw Hank Parker pass the window. A second later, the front door of the bank opened and the saloonkeeper came inside. Parker was whistling, an unusually cheery display for him, but he fell silent and stopped short as he saw Jeremiah standing in front of the counter. Parker's habitual frown creased his forehead.

"What are you doing here, Newton?" he asked.

"That's none of your business," Jeremiah said curtly. It was un-Christian of him to be impolite to anyone, even Hank Parker, but he couldn't help himself where the burly, one-armed saloon owner was concerned. To Jeremiah, Parker seemed to be the living embodiment of so much of the evil that infested certain sections of Wind River, the evil that Jeremiah was pledged to combat. It had grown even more difficult for him to tolerate Parker since the clash they had had over the knoll south of town.

"Looks to me like you're putting money in the bank," Parker said as he jerked his thumb at the pile of coins and bills and nuggets that still lay on the counter. He had a bag of his own clutched in his hand, and it clinked when he made the gesture. He went on, "Hurry it up.

That's what I'm here for, and I want to get back to the Pronghorn before my bartenders steal me blind."

Jeremiah wanted to ask Parker why he hired men he couldn't trust, but he didn't waste his time or breath. A man like Parker could never fully trust anyone, because he himself wasn't trustworthy and he knew that deep down. Jeremiah turned back to Smollett and indicated the deposit book with a long, blunt finger. "You said you were going to enter this transaction."

"Yes, of course," the banker said. He had to dip the pen again before it would write, but then with a series of quick strokes, he put down the deposit, added it to the balance, and said, "You now have almost two thousand dollars in your account, Brother Jeremiah."

"Not me," Jeremiah said firmly. "This money belongs to the church, which means it belongs to God, not to me."

"Well, give it to God and get the hell out of the way," Parker said impatiently.

With a deep breath, Jeremiah restrained his temper. He waited until Smollett had given him a receipt and placed the money and gold in the cash drawer underneath the counter. Then he turned and walked out of the bank, moving with solemn dignity past Hank Parker.

When Jeremiah was gone, Parker came up to the counter and set his bag down with a thump. It seemed to be considerably heavier than the blacksmith's. "Touchy son of a bitch, ain't he?" commented Parker.

Smollett instinctively liked Jeremiah Newton more than he did the crass saloonkeeper, but Parker was one of the bank's customers, too, and his money was just as important as the church's. Not to mention the fact that the saloon generated at least twice as many deposits in one night as did the collection held each week at Jeremiah's services.

Without making any reply to Parker's comment, Smollett said, "I'll be glad to count this and deposit it for you, Mr. Parker."

"I know how much is there: six hundred and seventy dollars."

"Well, I'll just make sure. All deposits have to be counted by the cashier, you know. That's a banking rule."

Parker scowled. "You saying you don't trust me?"

"Oh, no, sir, not at all. It's just . . . a rule," Smollett finished limply.

"Well, hurry it up."

Five minutes later, Parker walked out of the bank, a receipt in his pocket. He took out a cigar and put it in his mouth, but he didn't bother to light it. He glanced up and down Grenville Avenue, looking for anything interesting. Despite what he had said about his bartenders robbing him, he didn't figure there was really much chance of that happening. They would be too afraid of what would happen if he found out to even risk it.

It was the middle of the day, and there were quite a few people on the boardwalks. Parker suddenly spotted somebody he wanted to talk to, and he strode out into the street, crossing toward the opposite walk. As he went, he called, "Hey, Hatfield! Hold on there!"

Michael Hatfield, who had been hurrying along the boardwalk, stopped and turned to see who was hailing him. A worried expression appeared on his face when he saw it was Hank Parker.

Good, Parker thought. The little piss-ant ought to be scared of him.

Parker's long legs carried him quickly across the

street. As he stepped up onto the boardwalk, Michael asked, "What can I do for you, Mr. Parker?"

"I didn't much like what you had to say in the newspaper last week, Hatfield," Parker said. "That editorial you wrote made it sound like Wind River was some sort of backwoods hellhole!"

"Well, I certainly didn't mean that," Michael replied. "I just thought that by holding an election, the town would be taking the first step toward some real progress."

"Yeah? What's the second step? Running honest businessmen like me out of town?"

Michael's eyes widened. "I never suggested—"

"Well, I've seen it happen before," Parker said angrily. "First it's law and order, then it's politics, then people start wanting to get rid of everybody who doesn't think just like they do."

"Nobody ever said—"

Parker stopped Michael by poking him hard in the chest. Michael gasped in pain and took an involuntary step back. "I know how it works. You're just a mouthpiece for Simone McKay. She's the one in back of this. She was quick enough to take my money when I bought that land, but now she's decided that my place and the other saloons aren't good enough for Wind River. She wants to get rid of all of us. Hell, maybe she wants to get her hands on that land so she can sell it again to some other poor bastards!"

"That'll be enough of that," a voice said behind Parker.

The words were spoken quietly, but there was an unmistakable edge of menace in them. Parker turned his head to look over his shoulder and saw Cole Tyler standing there tensely. The marshal's face was calm, but anger swirled in his gray-green eyes.

"Stop harassing Michael," Cole went on. "He was just doing his job when he wrote that editorial in the paper. He's got a right to his opinion."

"Well, I don't like his opinion," Parker snapped. "Besides, he was just repeating what the McKay woman told him to say. What's the matter, Marshal? Don't want to hear the truth about her because you're sweet on her?"

For an instant, Parker thought he had gone too far. He had confronted Michael Hatfield and then baited the marshal just for the entertainment of it, but the look that flashed across Cole's face made Parker think he had made a bad mistake. Cole wanted to pull that .44 on his hip and put a slug through him, no doubt about it. And there was no way Parker could pull the belly gun from its holster under his vest in time to get off the first shot. But the marshal didn't reach for his gun. Instead he said, "You'd better go on back to the Pronghorn, Parker. We've all got business to tend to."

"Yeah," Parker grunted, "just don't try to stick your nose too far into mine." He pushed past Michael, leaving the young newspaperman staggering a little.

When they could no longer see his face, Parker grinned. Since he hadn't gotten killed, that had been fun after all. He relished the sudden feeling of anticipation that had gripped the street when the onlookers had believed they were about to witness a shoot-out. The whole confrontation had been a good way of spicing up a lazy afternoon.

But now he had other things on his mind, and his heavy features grew solemn again. Seeing Jeremiah Newton in the bank reminded him that he hadn't found out yet just who owned that land he wanted to buy. A wire to a former associate of his in the territorial capital of Cheyenne had turned up the name of the outfit back east that had bought the property from the Wind River Land Development Company. Such transactions were public records, on file at the capital. The buyers called themselves the B and D Investment Corporation. But who the hell were B and D?

That was exactly what Parker intended to find out, and the sooner the better.

12

Rose sighed and leaned back as hands fell lightly on her shoulders. Late afternoon sunlight slanted through the French windows of the second-floor apartment that led onto a balcony surrounded by black wrought-iron railings. The sun warmed her skin through the thin robe she wore. A man's hard-muscled body pressed against her as he put his arms around her. She closed her eyes and sighed again when he brought his hands up and cupped her breasts. His touch was so strong, so compelling, and yet so gentle at the same time. She lived for moments like this. They made her life worthwhile. They were *all* that made her want to continue living. If he was ever taken away from her . . . if anything ever happened to Nick Murdoch . . . she didn't know what she would do.

But with any luck she would never have to find out. Soon she and Nick would leave New Orleans and go somewhere far, far away, a place where they could start over and live their own lives and be happy. The thought of that made Rose almost purr in contentment like a cat as Nick caressed her. She felt his warm breath on the side of her neck as he nuzzled her ear, and she turned her head and opened her eyes, intending to kiss him.

Instead she found herself staring into the eyes of John Drummond.

Her husband.

The man who wanted to kill her.

Rose screamed. And screamed and screamed . . .

It was morning again, and the long night was over, along with the dreams that had catapulted her from sleep time and time again, drenched with sweat and shivering. Rose was grateful for that, and for the fact that evidently she hadn't actually screamed out loud. That would have disturbed the other boarders and brought someone to her room to find out what was wrong. She had gotten up and left the boardinghouse early, as was her habit, so that she could arrive at the café well before first light. Today she had risen a little earlier than usual, in fact, since not even Abigail Paine had been up yet, and like Rose, Abigail awoke before dawn to get started preparing breakfast for her husband, their children, and their boarders.

Rose had been nervous as she walked through the darkened streets toward the café. The only lights and sounds in town came from the saloons on the eastern side of the settlement. Those places never closed. The west side of town was quiet and dark, however, and Rose thought that if Drummond and his men wanted to kill her with no witnesses around to ruin things, they would never have a better opportunity than now.

That was why as she walked she had her fingers wrapped around the butt of the little pistol hidden in her bag. If Drummond and his henchmen wanted her dead, she was sure she couldn't stop them from accomplishing their mission.

But she would take at least one of them—preferably John Drummond—to hell with her.

But everything had seemed peaceful and no one had bothered her. Now she was at the café and the breakfast rush was in full swing. Half the stools at the counter were occupied, and so were most of the tables. Rose waited on tables and worked behind the counter while Monty Riordan stayed busy in the kitchen frying bacon, sausage, ham, and steaks, as well as cooking eggs and flipping hotcakes. The familiar, somehow comforting smells of hot coffee and good food filled the room. Her old life in New Orleans, and the dangers that had followed her here to Wyoming Territory, were far from her mind.

That was the way she wanted it. As long as she didn't think about the threat, she wouldn't have to deal with it.

Sooner or later, though, it would come calling again. She was sure of that.

Dan Boyd walked in the front door of the café just as Rose was coming out of the kitchen with a platter of food for some men who were sitting at one of the tables. She stopped short at the sight of the federal lawman, who smiled at her. Rose took a deep breath and went on with what she was doing, pointedly paying no attention to Boyd as he sauntered over to the counter and sat down on one of the empty stools.

She couldn't continue ignoring him, however. That would look bad to her other customers, who didn't know who the man really was or what he was doing in Wind River. So after taking the tray back to the kitchen, she pushed through the swinging door again and came down the counter to face him across its polished surface.

"What can I get you?" she asked, her voice clipped. She had to serve him, but she didn't have to be friendly toward him.

"Coffee and a stack of flapjacks will do me just fine, Miss Foster," Boyd replied. "Maybe with some bacon on the side."

Rose nodded. "Sure." She turned to call the order through the window to Monty, then started to move along behind the counter without looking at Boyd again.

He stopped her by saying, "Miss Foster."

Rose turned her head. "What is it?"

"Do you always get here so early every morning?"

Rose stiffened. He had been watching her. She'd had no idea that Boyd was keeping an eye on her, but now that she thought about it, the idea made sense. Boyd still wanted her to go back to New Orleans and testify against Drummond. He had a stake in keeping her alive, just like Drummond had a reason to want her dead.

At the same time, she resented the fact that Boyd was spying on her. He seemed like a competent, dedicated lawman, but there was only one of him. Drummond had his three bruisers with him, and for that matter, Drummond himself was a dangerous man when he had to be. If Boyd had really wanted to protect her and take her back to New Orleans, he should have brought a whole posse of deputy marshals with him, Rose thought bitterly. By himself, he was no match for John Drummond and his men.

Boyd was still waiting for an answer to his question.

Coolly, Rose said, "I don't think my schedule is any of your business, Mr. Boyd."

"That's where you're wrong, ma'am. I intend to make it my business."

There were two empty stools to Boyd's left, another empty place to his right. He had his voice pitched low so that the conversation with Rose would be difficult to overhear inside the café, which was fairly noisy with customers talking and laughing and Monty Riordan singing an old song with his cracked voice in the kitchen. Rose looked around, saw that no one was paying any attention to what she and Boyd were saying, and pressed her lips together tightly. She wanted to tell him to go to hell and throw him out of the café, but that would attract too much notice. She had lived a quiet life here in Wind River, and she didn't want to become an object of gossip.

Leaning over the counter toward Boyd, Rose said quietly, "You can come in here to eat, and I can't stop you from doing that. But please stay out of the rest of my life, Mr. Boyd."

"You'll change your mind sooner or later," he said, a hint of smugness in his voice.

Rose swallowed the irritation she felt toward him and said instead, "I'll get you your coffee."

Boyd dawdled over his breakfast, just as she expected him to do, but finally he paid for his meal and left. She figured he was hanging around outside, though, somewhere close by. He might not even let the place out of his sight all day long, she thought.

She was halfway dreading that Drummond and his men would show up again during one of the slack times, but there was no sign of them during the day. Rose was grateful for that. She didn't know if her nerves could stand the sight of her husband and his lackeys sitting in the café and pretending to be harmless, when all along the only thing they wanted was to see her dead.

Cole Tyler and Billy Casebolt each put in an appearance, however. Both of them wanted to know if Drummond had been around bothering her again, and Rose was able to tell them honestly, "I haven't seen him or his men all day."

"They haven't left town," Cole told her during his visit to the café. "Billy and I have been checking at the hotel. They seem to be staying in their rooms." Cole hesitated, then added, "Them and those two women, Lucy and Irene."

Rose just nodded, trying not to show the hurt she felt. She had actually believed that the prostitutes were her friends. She should have known better. The fact that they were whores should have been an immediate warning signal that they might have something to do with John Drummond. After all, Drummond had amassed a good portion of his livelihood from women just like them . . .

Not that he was a cheap pimp, Rose reflected as she wiped the counter with a rag after Cole left. There had been much more to Drummond's criminal activities than just prostitution. He had a finger in every illegal pie in southern Louisiana. Over the years he had built up a fortune, a fortune which Rose had been more than happy to help him spend—until she realized where all the money was coming from. By that time it was too late.

Nick Murdoch had offered her a way out. He wanted to break from Drummond just as much as Rose did. It was only natural that the two of them had gotten together.

But someone had betrayed them. Somehow, Drummond had found out about them. And John Drummond could not allow anyone to take anything from him, could not allow a chink in his armor to continue to exist. Nick Murdoch had died, and Rose was sure she would have, too, if she hadn't run.

And kept running, until she reached Wind River.

It hadn't been far enough after all.

Darkness eased down over the settlement, and Dan Boyd was grateful for the shadows as he moved closer to the trunk of the tree where he waited, watching the front door of the Wind River Café. He had moved around several times during the day, but this spot was the best one yet, on the other side of the street and about half a block from the café. From here he could not only see the front door of the place, but he also had a good view down the narrow alley that ran alongside the building. He wished there was some way to keep an eye on both the front and the back doors, but that was impossible for one man unless he was on high ground. The highest ground in Wind River was the second story of the Territorial House, and that just wasn't high enough.

Unless, Boyd mused, he climbed onto the roof. Then he might be able to see both doors . . .

He discarded that idea after only a moment of consideration. He was getting too old to go clambering around on rooftops. That would be a good way to fall and break some of his fool bones. Then he wouldn't be any good at all to Rose Foster—or Rosemary Drummond, as she was really.

Boyd had the makin's in the breast pocket of his shirt

and felt like building a smoke, but he resisted the urge. The telltale red glow of the ash at the end of a quirly would give away his presence here in the thick shadows underneath the tree. He didn't want anyone besides Rose to know that he was watching her. Drummond might suspect, but he couldn't know for sure.

And Drummond, despite his natural caution, couldn't wait forever. The crime lord from New Orleans had to make a move sometime to remove Rose as a danger to him, which she was and always would be as long as she continued to draw breath.

Boyd intended to be waiting when Drummond struck.

"Hello, Marshal," a voice said quietly behind him.

Boyd's breath caught in his throat and he started to whirl around, his hand darting toward his gun. Strong fingers wrapped around his wrist, stopping the draw before it could be completed.

"No need for that," Cole Tyler said.

Cole let go of Boyd's wrist, and the federal lawman glared at the local star packer. In these shadows, Cole was nothing but a deeper patch of darkness. Boyd could barely make him out. "You shouldn't go slipping up on a man like that," Boyd said harshly. "That's a good way to get yourself killed."

"So's skulking around in the dark," Cole replied. "Besides, I figured I could stop you before you shot me."

And that was exactly what he had done, Boyd thought. He cursed himself silently. Not only had Cole managed to come up behind him unheard, but the younger man had also been fast enough to stop Boyd from even drawing his gun. If this had been a shoot-out, Boyd would be dead now, and he knew it. The knowledge didn't make him happy. Maybe he really *was* getting too old for this job.

"What do you want, Tyler?" Boyd asked.

"Just wondered what you were doing."

"You must have good eyes, or you'd never have seen me here."

Cole shrugged. "I've sat up a few nights when the Sioux and the Arapaho and the Pawnee were trying to slip up on me, back in the days when I was scouting for the Army. A man learns to look sharp if he wants to live."

"That's the truth," Boyd agreed fervently. "But I wasn't doing anything, Marshal, except getting a little night air."

"You wouldn't be keeping an eye on the café over there?" asked Cole. "I talked to some folks around town, and they tell me you took all three meals there today."

Damn! Cole was smarter than Boyd would have given him credit for, knowing that the man had no background in law enforcement but had instead been a trapper, scout, and buffalo hunter before pinning on the badge here in Wind River. Cole had figured out there was some connection between Rose Foster, her husband John Drummond, and Boyd's presence in town.

"Might as well tell me the truth," Cole went on when Boyd didn't say anything. "You ever see a kid poking a stick in a hole until he prods up whatever's down there? That's me, Boyd. I'm going to poke with that stick until you tell me what's going on in my town."

Boyd sighed wearily. There was no point in concealing the truth from Cole Tyler any longer. There had been no real reason to keep his job here a secret in the first place, Boyd reflected, other than his habit of working alone and his reluctance to rely on small-town lawmen to give him a hand. Cole seemed to be a little different than most local badge-toters, however. He struck Boyd as more intelligent, not to mention quiet and quick on his feet, and fast with his gunhand. Maybe he could put Cole Tyler's insistent curiosity to some good use.

"All right," Boyd said. "I don't want to talk about it out here where somebody could overhear us, though."

"We can go over to my office," Cole suggested.

Boyd glanced at the café. It was still brightly lit, the warm yellow glow of lanterns shining through its windows, and customers were still hitching horses and buggy teams outside. Boyd watched several townsmen go into the café before he made his decision. As long as Rose was over there surrounded by witnesses, it was unlikely Drummond would try anything. She would probably be safe enough for a while.

"All right, Marshal," he said to Cole. "Let's go."

"Dadgummit!" said Monty Riordan. "This bag o' flour's full o' some damned weevils!"

Rose heard the cook's angry exclamation through the opening between the café's dining room and the kitchen. She turned and hissed, "Quiet, Monty. You don't want the customers to hear something like that."

Riordan came to the window and showed Rose a handful of flour that he had taken from a bag he had obviously just opened. Sure enough, too many small insects to count were crawling through the white powder. "Look at that," he said in disgust.

"Things like that happen," Rose said, trying to be reasonable. "Just take the bag back over to the general store tomorrow and show the flour to Mr. Raymond. I'm sure he'll replace it."

"Yeah, I reckon," Monty agreed. "But now I got to go

out to the shed and get another bag. I've done used up all I got in here."

Rose glanced over her shoulder. The stools along the counter were all empty, and only a few of the tables were still occupied. Everyone in the place already had food, and it was late enough now that Rose doubted any more customers would be coming in. She said to Riordan, "Let it wait until the morning. I think you can put out the fire in the stove and call it a night."

"Nope, I ain't goin' to do it. Don't want to start off first thing in the mornin' by havin' to lug a bag o' flour in here. I'll go get it right now."

There was no point in arguing with him, Rose thought. Besides, it wouldn't take him but a minute to step out the back door, open the storage shed that was built on the rear of the building, and carry in a fresh bag of flour. She watched him with a faint smile on her face as he went to the back door, opened it, and stepped out into the night. The door swung shut behind him.

Rose topped off a couple of cups of coffee for some of the late diners, then went into the kitchen and set the pot back on the stove. Something thumped against the back door. Rose smiled again.

Monty hadn't meant to let the door shut behind him, she thought, and he was standing out there now with a bag of flour in his arms, kicking the door so that she would come and open it for him. She went over to it, calling softly, "All right, Monty, I'll get the door."

She grasped the latch, tugged on it, and pushed out. The door swung smoothly on its hinges.

But Monty Riordan wasn't out there, with or without a bag of flour. Rose frowned. She was sure she had heard something. She stepped just outside the door, lifting her voice a little as she said, "Monty? Are you all right?"

That was when flame and noise split the night as a gun exploded in the darkness behind the café.

13

"Coffee?" Cole asked as he gestured at the pot on the stove in the corner of the marshal's office. "It's been simmering all day, so I reckon it's old enough to've grown legs by now."

Boyd shook his head. "No, thanks." He patted his stomach. "I've already had more than my share of Arbuckle's today. Doesn't do my belly much good."

Cole went behind the desk and sat down. "You're making the right decision, then," he said. "My deputy brewed that pot, and Billy likes the stuff potent enough to peel paint off a door. Have a chair."

The federal lawman picked up one of the ladderback chairs in front of the desk, reversed it, and straddled it. He thumbed his broad-brimmed hat back on the thatch of white hair, then rested his arms on the back of the chair. "So you want to know about Rose Foster and John Drummond, do you?"

"That's why you're here, isn't it?" asked Cole. "Too

many things are happening all of a sudden for them to be coincidences."

"You're right," Boyd admitted. "You know that Rose Foster isn't really the lady's name, don't you?"

"I know that Drummond claims to be her husband, and Rose didn't deny it. I reckon that'd make her Rose Drummond, if you want to get right down to it."

"Her maiden name was Rosemary du Charlaine," said Boyd. "Her father owned a plantation upriver from New Orleans. The place made it through the war—which is more than can be said for some of those plantations down south—but the effect was still devastating. You hear much about Reconstruction out here in the West?"

"Enough," Cole said, a faintly grim tone coming into his voice. "The Yankees said they were rebuilding the South. Seemed to me it was more like taking revenge on the Confederacy."

Boyd waved a hand. "No need for us to argue politics, Marshal. Whether the North's actions have been right or not, they've had a tremendous effect on the South. The planters who survived the war itself were ruined by the aftermath, including the du Charlaines."

"Rose's family," Cole said.

"That's right. So when a rich man like John Drummond came courting her, it was like throwing a rope to a drowning man. Even if Rosemary hadn't been taken with him—and by all accounts, she was—her loyalty to her family would have forced her to marry him in hopes of restoring the du Charlaines to some sort of stability."

Cole frowned. "How do you know all this?" he asked.

"I was assigned to Drummond's case earlier this year, when President Grant appointed a special prosecutor to look into the crime and corruption down in New Orleans.

My investigation turned up quite a bit. The brigands who have called New Orleans home, all the way back to old Jean Lafitte, have always lived out their lives in public view for the most part. I just couldn't come up with any evidence of illegal activity against Drummond that would stand up in court. I'm convinced he's behind a great deal of the mischief down there, though."

Cole mulled that over for a moment, then said, "You were talking about Rose marrying him."

"That's right, she did. And for several months she seemed quite happy about it. But then somehow she found out what Drummond really did for a living—"

"She didn't know when she married him?" Cole cut in.

"She didn't seem to," Boyd said. "At least, judging from what happened over the next few months, she didn't. She began having an affair with a dissatisfied lieutenant of Drummond's, a man named Nick Murdoch."

"That doesn't sound like Rose," objected Cole.

Boyd shrugged his shoulders and said, "Maybe you don't know the lady as well as you think you do, Marshal. At any rate, I can't be certain just what the relationship between Mrs. Drummond and Murdoch was; I can only speculate based on the information I dug up about them. I think that the two of them planned to run away together, and they may have gathered some evidence against Drummond to use for protection if he ever came after them. But Murdoch wound up dead before that could happen."

"Drummond had him killed?"

"He was found floating in a bayou with a knife wound in his back," Boyd said. "That big Cajun who's always with Drummond, the one they called Lige, he's supposed to be good with a knife."

"You can't prove Drummond's behind Murdoch's murder, though."

"Not yet. But I will."

Boyd sounded awfully confident. Cole scraped back his chair, stood up, and began to pace back and forth. "What happened to Rose after Murdoch turned up dead?"

"She disappeared. For a while, she was rumored to be dead, too, but I knew that couldn't be the case because Drummond was still looking for her. He wouldn't be going to that much trouble if he had already disposed of her." Boyd's grip on the back of the chair tightened. "No, she ran for her life, and she kept running until she wound up here. I guess she thought Drummond would never find her in Wind River. But she was wrong."

"Why don't you just arrest this fella Drummond and take him back to New Orleans?"

"And charge him with what? I told you, there's no solid evidence against him, only rumor and hearsay. *Unless* I can convince his wife to testify against him. I'm sure she knows enough that she'd be able to put him behind bars, if not at the end of a hangrope."

Cole let out a low whistle. "So that's why you've been hanging around town and bird-dogging Rose."

"I was tipped off by an informant that Drummond had purchased train tickets for the Wyoming Territory. There was no good reason for him to come all the way out here—unless he thought he'd find his wife here. I managed to get ahead of him and made it to Wind River first. But I knew it was just a matter of time before Drummond showed up and confirmed the theory I'd already formed: that Rose Foster was really Rosemary Drummond."

Cole swung around to face Boyd, his rugged features

taut. He said, "If everything you've told me is true, Drummond can't afford to let Rose live. As long as she's alive, he has to worry that someday she'll go into court and tell the truth about him."

Boyd nodded gravely. "That's about the size of it, all right."

"And the fact that you're here in Wind River has to have spooked Drummond even more. He'll figure that you've come to take Rose back to New Orleans with you."

"That's exactly what I plan to do," Boyd confirmed.

"Then, damn it, why didn't you bring more men with you?" Cole exclaimed. "Probably all you've done is make Drummond even more anxious to kill Rose!"

"I can handle Drummond and his men," Boyd said sharply. "And I can protect the young lady. That is, if I can ever convince her to return to Louisiana with me."

"She won't go?" Cole asked, somewhat surprised.

"So far she's refused," Boyd replied, "and I can't force her to go with me. To tell you the truth, Marshal, I believe she's thinking about running again."

Cole frowned. He didn't like that idea at all. If Rose lit a shuck out of Wind River, Drummond would just hunt her down again. The crime boss had already demonstrated just how determined and resourceful he was. And when he caught up to Rose next time, there might not be anybody around to take her side and protect her.

"Seems to me you're playing mighty fast and loose with the lady's life, Boyd," Cole said to the federal lawman.

Boyd shrugged. "All she has to do is testify against Drummond. He'll wind up in jail or dead, and he won't be able to hurt her anymore. If you really want to help Miss Foster, Marshal, what you ought to do is try to convince her to cooperate with me."

Cole wasn't so sure about that. At the same time, he knew Rose didn't have too many options, either. She faced danger no matter what she decided to do.

He was pondering that when he heard the sudden wicked crack of a gunshot from down the street. A Winchester, from the sound of it.

"Rose!" Cole exclaimed, his instincts sending him lunging toward the door of the office. Dan Boyd was right behind him as the two of them raced out into the night.

Lon Rogers kept his horse moving at a brisk trot as he rode through the night toward Wind River. He could already see the lights of the town up ahead, and they were a beacon to him, drawing him on.

He ignored the twinges of pain that shot through his bruised body with every step of his horse. The beating he had suffered at the hands of John Drummond's men had left Lon in a great deal of pain, but he was enduring it stoically. He had gone about his work on the ranch without complaint, and at supper tonight he had been able to laugh off the good-natured gibes of the other members of the crew.

Not everybody on the Diamond S took the incident so lightly, however. It had been all Lon could do to talk his boss, Kermit Sawyer, and the foreman, Frenchy LeDoux, out of going into Wind River and teaching the men who had jumped him a lesson. If one Diamond S rider was attacked, they all were. That was how Sawyer and Frenchy saw it, and to tell the truth, the other men did too, although they covered up their anger with humor. Any man on the ranch would have gladly ridden into town with Lon tonight, no matter what the odds.

It had taken some arguing, but Lon had finally convinced them that he wasn't looking for another fight. He just wanted to make sure Rose Foster was all right. If more trouble came his way, though, Lon had insisted it was his right to handle it without involving anybody else. His pride was at stake here.

Sawyer and Frenchy could understand that. They had agreed grudgingly to let Lon ride into the settlement alone.

"But if anything else happens, we ain't goin' to let it pass," Sawyer had said. "Texans stick up for their own, by God, even if we *are* way the hell up and gone in Wyoming Territory."

Lon couldn't argue with that.

He still wondered, however, about the startling revelation that John Drummond was really Rose's husband. She had never said anything to him about being married, and they'd had some lengthy conversations in the past . . . before Rose had decided that she didn't want him around anymore.

Maybe that was because she had been afraid her husband would show up, Lon speculated now as he neared the town. Could be she was afraid that if he was courting her, he might wind up getting hurt. And that was exactly what had happened, of course.

She hadn't been trying to run him off because she didn't like him, he realized. She had just been worried about him.

A warm glow filled Lon at that thought. Maybe there was some hope for him and Rose after all, once this problem with her husband was solved.

Trouble was, he didn't have the slightest idea what the solution to that problem might be.

The trail turned into a road that intersected Grenville Avenue. Lon turned west along Wind River's main street, ignoring the piano music and laughter that came from the saloons behind him. He was more interested in the lights of the café, which he saw shining through the front windows of the building ahead of him. He had pulled his horse down to a walk when he reached Grenville Avenue, but now he heeled it into a trot again.

Lon had just reached the hitch rack in front of the café when he thought he heard Rose's voice. He reined in, frowning. It sounded like she was out back, and he thought she was calling Monty Riordan.

Then, in the next instant, a gunshot slammed through the night, and it came from the rear of the building, too.

Without even thinking, Lon jammed his spurs into the flanks of his mount, yelled, "Rose!", and sent the horse plunging down the darkened alley alongside the café.

Splinters stung Rose's cheek as the bullet chewed a hole in the open door beside her. For an instant she froze, barely even feeling the pain of the wood slivers that had gouged into her flesh. The sound of the shot rang in her ears and the muzzle flash had dazzled her so that she couldn't see.

All her instincts were screaming at her to move, though, so without any real thought she flung herself forward, falling to the ground just outside the rear door of the café. As she did so, the rifle roared again, and this time the slug whined over her head.

Then, before the rifleman hidden in the trees behind the café could fire again, a man on horseback burst around the corner of the building. Rose heard someone shouting her name, the voice faint and muffled as if its owner was far away. More crashes filled the night, and as Rose glanced up she saw Lon Rogers, his face lit up garishly by the backflash of the gun in his hand as he triggered off several shots. His features were grim, a mixture of fear and anger.

Lon threw himself out of the saddle and landed on his feet, stumbling a little as he regained his balance. He fired toward the trees again as he raced to Rose's side. Using his free hand, he bent over and grasped her arm, pulling her roughly to her feet. Rose was too stunned to struggle with him, and that was for the best. As Lon snapped another shot toward the bushwhacker's hiding place, he was able to shove Rose back through the door into the café.

Instead of darting inside after her, Lon kicked the door shut behind her. He had no idea how many men he was facing, but he was going to give them something to shoot at besides Rose.

Unfortunately, he couldn't do much fighting back.

His gun was empty, all five chambers that had been loaded having been fired toward the trees.

As he stood there, his pulse hammering wildly in his head, he was surprised that no more shots exploded in the night. Maybe there had been only one rifleman hidden in the trees, and Lon's shots might have scared him off. Might have even killed him, Lon thought suddenly.

He swallowed hard. He hadn't killed all that many men. Just a couple, in fact, and those in the heat of battle with rustlers. But if the rifleman was lying out there dead, then the son of a bitch had deserved it, Lon told himself. After all, the man had been trying to kill Rose.

Rose! Lon swung around toward the door. He didn't

know if she had been hit or not. She had been lying on the ground when he first saw her, and she might have been wounded, even though he didn't recall seeing any blood on her dress. Lon reached for the door latch, convinced now that the bushwhacker was no longer a threat.

"Hold it!" a voice barked at him. He heard the sound of a revolver being cocked.

"Wait a minute, damn it!" That was Marshal Cole Tyler. "Lon, is that you?"

"It's me, all right, Marshal," Lon called back. "You'd better be careful. Somebody hidden in those trees just took a couple of shots at Miss Rose."

"Blast it!" the other man said. He hurried toward Lon. "Where is she?"

The back door of the café opened and Rose said, "I'm right here. Lon, are you all right?"

"I'm not hit," he told her, "but don't worry about me. What about you?"

Before she could answer, the man who had come running with Cole in response to the shooting bulled his way past Lon. The young cowboy didn't recognize the man, who was middle-aged, white-haired, and wore dark clothing. Lon could see that much in the light that spilled out through the open door.

He could also see that Rose appeared to be uninjured, although she was pale and shaken. Lon glanced over at Cole and said, "Marshal, I reckon we ought to stop standing around in front of this door, just in case."

"Good idea, Lon," Cole replied. "You and Rose and Marshal Boyd go on inside. I'll take a look around out here."

Marshal Boyd? Then the white-haired man was a lawman, too, Lon thought.

Rose wasn't agreeable to the idea of going inside, however. She said, "Monty came out here just before the shooting started, and I haven't seen him since. He may be hurt."

"I'll find him," Cole said.

A groan sounded, making all of them jump a little, and Monty Riordan came unsteadily around the corner of the storage shed, a hand pressed to his head. "Ain't nobody goin' to have to find me," he said irritably. "I'm right here, damn it. Some jackass clouted me over the head. I just come to, 'round there on the other side of the shed."

Rose hurried to his side and clutched his arm, and Cole said, "Let me take a look at your head." All five of them moved inside, and Lon shut the door while Cole sent the customers who had come into the kitchen back into the dining room. "Nothing to see back here, folks," he told them sternly.

Billy Casebolt came through the front door of the café while Cole was examining the lump on Riordan's head. The deputy had a shotgun clutched in his hands, and when Cole saw him, he jerked a thumb toward the rear of the place and said, "Take a look around out back, Billy. You might find a dead or wounded bushwhacker, so be careful."

"Might not find anybody," Lon put in. "The jasper could have run."

Cole nodded. "I know that. We can hope otherwise, though."

Casebolt hurried out, and Cole resumed his examination of the old cook's injury. "You may need Doc Kent to take a couple of stitches in your hide, Monty," he said. "And I imagine he'll tell you to take it easy for a few days, too."

"Take it easy, hell," growled Riordan. "I want to find the skalleyhooter who did this to me."

"Leave that to Billy and me."

Boyd said, "There's not much doubt about who's to blame, if you ask me." He looked at Rose. "We both know who's responsible, don't we . . . Mrs. Drummond."

Lon wasn't sure what was going on, but he didn't like the tone of Boyd's voice or the way Rose's lips pressed together tightly when the man called her by that name. Lon put a hand on Boyd's arm and said, "That'll be about enough of that, mister."

Boyd smiled, but there wasn't much humor in the expression, or in his cold blue eyes. "Better be careful, boy. You don't know what's going on here. Judging by those bruises you're sporting, you'd be the Galahad who came to Miss Foster's defense yesterday. I heard about that little scuffle."

"I'll do it again, too, if I have to," Lon said stubbornly.

"That's enough from both of you," Cole snapped. "If you want to act proddy, go somewhere else to do it." He turned back to Rose. "The doctor had better take a look at you, too. You've got a little blood on your cheek."

Rose lifted her hand to her face, and when she took her fingers away, there was a faint smear of red on their tips. "It's from the splinters that hit me when that first bullet struck the door, I think. I'm getting it all sorted out in my mind now."

Billy Casebolt came in the back door, the greener tucked under his arm. "Nobody back there now, Marshal," he reported. "I lit a match and looked around in them trees, and I found tracks where somebody was standin' just a little while ago."

"One man?" asked Cole.

"Looked like it," Casebolt said.

Boyd spoke up. "Was he wearing shoes or boots?"

"Shoot, I couldn't tell that," replied Casebolt. "If I had to guess, I'd say shoes, but they might've been boots."

"One of Drummond's men," Boyd said with a nod.

"I reckon it's time we paid a visit to Mr. Drummond," Cole said. "Billy, take Miss Rose and Monty down to Doc Kent's. Keep an eye peeled for trouble along the way."

"You bet," Casebolt said.

Lon looked at Rose. "I'm going with you."

She started to object, but Cole said, "That's probably a good idea. Having another gun around won't hurt anything. But you be careful, too, Lon."

The young cowboy drew his empty gun and started reloading it. "I intend to be, Marshal," he said grimly. "But if anybody tries to bother Miss Rose, then they're the ones who'd better look out!"

Cole wasn't sure who Dan Boyd was angrier at, John Drummond—or himself, for leaving the café unwatched when the attempt on Rose's life had been made. But one thing was certain: the federal lawman looked mad enough to chew nails as he and Cole came through the front door of the Territorial House.

To Cole's surprise, Simone McKay was there, standing behind the desk along with the clerk who was on duty. The door behind the counter that led to the hotel office was open, and Cole supposed that Simone had been in there, going over the place's books or some such chore. The flurry of shooting would have brought her out, though, just as it had aroused the curiosity of the entire town. Cole and Boyd had already brushed past quite a few people wanting to know what was going on while they were walking up the street to the hotel.

"What is it, Cole?" Simone asked. "We heard some shots a little while ago."

"Somebody tried to kill Rose Foster," Cole replied. The answer brought a gasp of surprise from Simone.

"Is Rose all right?" she asked anxiously.

Cole nodded. Boyd obviously wanted to get upstairs and confront Drummond, but Simone had a right to know what was about to happen. The hotel belonged to her, after all, and if there was going to be a shoot-out on the second floor, well . . .

"Is Drummond upstairs?" Boyd asked curtly.

"I believe so," Simone said. "Is he involved? I wouldn't be surprised, what with those two women he has staying with him."

Cole recalled that Simone hadn't liked Lucy and Irene, but evidently she had relented and allowed them to stay in the Territorial House after all.

"Drummond's involved, all right, ma'am," Boyd said. "That's why we're going up to see him."

"We don't know for sure he had anything to do with it," Cole said.

Boyd gave him a withering look. "Of course he did. We both know that, Marshal. Now come on, if you're going with me."

Cole bit back the angry retort that sprang to his lips at Boyd's sharp tone. He nodded and said to Simone, "There may be trouble. Just stay down here and you ought to be out of the line of fire."

Her eyes widened. "The line of fire," she repeated. "Just what do you intend to do, kick down Mr. Drummond's door and go in with your guns blazing?"

"I've heard worse plans," said Boyd.

Simone marched out from behind the desk. "Not in my hotel, gentlemen. Wind River is a civilized town. At least I'm trying to make it so." She stood at the foot of the stairs and crossed her arms over her chest, glaring stubbornly at the two lawmen.

Boyd glowered right back at her. "You're interfering with a federal officer in the performance of his duties, Mrs. McKay. That's against the law right there. If you're serious about civilizing this settlement, then step aside and let us go on about our business."

Simone sighed, then lifted her shoulders in a shrug. "I suppose you're right, Marshal Boyd," she said. She moved to one side. "All right, go ahead. But try not to shoot up the place too badly."

Cole said, "Maybe there won't be any shooting at all."

Boyd made a sound of disbelief, and to tell the truth, Cole wasn't expecting things to go that smoothly, either. Drummond wasn't the type to come along peacefully.

The two men started up the stairs, but they hadn't even reached the halfway point when several people appeared on the second floor landing. Cole stopped in surprise, as did Boyd. John Drummond stood there at the head of the stairs, flanked by Lucy and Irene, and the other three men were behind him. Drummond smiled pleasantly and nodded to Cole and Boyd.

"Good evening, gentlemen," Drummond said smoothly. "What are the representatives of law and order doing out and about tonight?"

"You know damned well what we're doing," growled Boyd. "We came looking for you, Drummond. One of your men just tried to kill your wife. That is, unless you decided to do the job yourself this time."

Drummond frowned. "Someone tried to kill Rosemary? I assure you, Marshal, my associates and I know nothing about it. Do we, boys?"

The three men behind Drummond all shook their heads in unison.

Boyd laughed, but instead of the usual hearty sound, this laughter was thin and humorless. "You don't expect us to believe that, do you? Whoever tried to ambush Miss Foster, they've had plenty of time to get back here to the hotel."

Drummond looked past Cole and Boyd at Simone and the desk clerk. "I ask you, Mrs. McKay," he said, "did you or your man there see any of us come in through the lobby in the past few minutes?"

"No," Simone said slowly. "I didn't. What about you, Jimmy?"

The clerk shook his head. "No, ma'am, I sure didn't."

Drummond grinned cockily at Boyd. "There, you see? We're innocent of these wild accusations."

"This hotel's got a back door, doesn't it, ma'am?" Boyd asked Simone.

"Yes, it does, and some outside stairs that lead up to the second floor as well."

Boyd turned back to Drummond. "Still looks to me like you're guilty as hell."

Cole was getting tired of standing there and looking up at Drummond and the others. His neck was beginning to stiffen. He said, "Let's take a look at your boots, Drummond, and those of your men."

"Boots?" Drummond asked with a frown.

"The bushwhacker hid in some trees out back of the café," Cole explained. "My deputy found his tracks. Whoever tried to kill Rose likely has some dust on his boots or shoes."

"Feel free to examine our footwear, Marshal Tyler," Drummond said with an expansive wave of his hand.

"Search our rooms as well. Perhaps you can find the weapon that was used in this so-called bushwhacking."

As soon as the man said that, Cole's spirits dropped. Drummond wouldn't have made such an offer if there was anything incriminating to be found in their rooms. The ambusher must have hidden his rifle somewhere else, and for that matter, the man had had time to change boots, too, maybe even to clean the ones he had been wearing earlier in the evening.

Cole and Boyd exchanged a glance. The federal man knew the same things Cole had already figured out. Boyd's eyes were bleak as he said, "We might as well go through with it. Maybe one of them made a mistake."

That turned out not to be the case, however. They climbed the stairs, examined the feet of Drummond and his men, and discovered nothing except that all four of them wore shoes instead of boots. A search of the rooms that Drummond had taken for his party didn't turn up anything, either, except some pistols that obviously hadn't been fired for quite some time. Cole could tell that by sniffing the barrels. It was to be expected that travelers here on the frontier would be armed, so there was nothing unusual about Drummond's men having guns in their rooms. Each of the three men was carrying a pistol, as well, but none of them had been fired, either.

There was no sign of a Winchester or any other rifle.

"Satisfied now, gentlemen?" Drummond asked as Cole and Boyd concluded their search. Cole thought he heard a faint edge of mockery in the man's voice.

"All right, so you're slick enough to have covered up all the evidence," snapped Boyd. "I already knew you were slick, Drummond. But that doesn't mean you're not guilty."

"Yes, but there's still that inconvenient matter of proof," Drummond said. "Now, if you gentlemen are through delaying us, my friends and I were on our way out for an evening's entertainment. I hear the Pronghorn Saloon is the best place in town for a little excitement."

Boyd was seething. Cole put a hand on his arm and said, "Come on, Marshal."

"This isn't over, Drummond," Boyd said. "Sooner or later, you're going to make a mistake. I won't let you kill your wife like you did Nick Murdoch."

"I had nothing to do with poor Nick's death." Drummond linked arms with the two women. "Come along, ladies."

Cole watched them as they left the hotel, and for a change he concentrated his attention on Lucy and Irene. The blonde appeared to be pretty much uncaring about what was going on, but Cole thought he saw a flicker of something in Lucy's eyes. She had been disturbed by this confrontation for some reason.

That might be something worth remembering, Cole thought.

When Drummond and his companions had left the hotel lobby and turned toward the eastern side of town, Simone said, "I don't like this, Cole. That man and his friends frighten me."

"I don't think you've got anything to worry about. Drummond's not interested in anything except what brought him here to start with, and that's Rose Foster."

"He's a danger to anybody who gets in his way, though," Boyd said. "I've got to figure out some way to persuade Miss Foster to go back to New Orleans with me and testify against him."

"Perhaps I could speak to Rose," offered Simone.

"That might help, ma'am. And right now, I'll take all the help I can get."

Cole and Boyd left the hotel and walked toward Judson Kent's office. When they got there, the doctor was stitching up the gash on Monty Riordan's scalp. Monty was cussing a blue streak. There was no sign of Rose, Lon, or Billy Casebolt.

"Where's everybody else, Judson?" Cole asked the British physician.

"Gone back down to the café, I assume," replied Kent. "I daresay Miss Foster will be safe enough with Deputy Casebolt and young Rogers watching over her."

"She wasn't hurt, was she?" asked Boyd.

"Only some slight scratches on her face from some splinters. I removed the ones that were still embedded and cleaned the wounds. She's certainly in no danger from them."

"Well, that's good," Boyd said. "I suppose it could have been a lot worse." He looked at Cole, his expression bleak. "And before it's over, I'm afraid it will be."

Cole didn't like to admit it, but he shared that same fear.

To Cole's surprise, the next couple of days passed quietly. There had been so much trouble that he just naturally expected more to break out without any warning. Cole and Billy Casebolt tried to keep an eye on Rose most of the time, but it was impossible to watch her twenty-four hours a day. Lon Rogers was also in town a great deal, and Cole wondered if Kermit Sawyer was getting tired of one of his hands spending his time like that, instead of working on the Diamond S.

John Drummond, his men, and the two prostitutes were still staying at the Territorial House, and Cole knew that as long as they were in town, the threat wasn't over. Drummond was probably just waiting for another opportunity to strike at Rose.

Cole was bound and determined not to give him that chance.

Dan Boyd had spoken to Rose several times, and Simone had talked to her as well. So far, neither of them had had any luck in convincing her to leave Wind River and go back to New Orleans with Boyd. Cole wasn't sure he could blame Rose for that. Once they were on board an eastbound train, there would be nothing stopping Drummond and his men from taking the same train. Then, Rose would have only Boyd to watch over her. Chances are she would never reach New Orleans alive.

Three days after the attempt on Rose's life, some thick gray clouds moved in, and a late summer storm sent lightning flickering across the sky. A fine mist began to fall on Wind River. Cole figured it would turn into rain later in the day. As he walked toward the café, he pulled his hat from its usual position—hanging down his back from its chin strap—and settled it on his head to keep the moisture out of his eyes.

He ran into Rose before he even reached the café. Billy Casebolt was with her, carrying the shotgun that he was seldom without these days. He said, "Howdy, Marshal. Miss Rose here was just on her way down to the bank, and I said I'd go with her."

"That's a good idea, Billy." Cole looked at Rose. "Got some banking business to do?"

"Receipts to deposit," she replied. Her face had a haunted look about it these days, with dark circles under her eyes. Cole figured she wasn't sleeping much. She was making a game attempt to bear up under the strain, but she couldn't keep it up forever, he thought. Sooner or later, this stalemate had to break.

Thunder rumbled in the distance. Cole nodded to Rose and said, "I won't keep you." To Casebolt, he added unnecessarily, "Be careful, Billy."

Casebolt just nodded and moved on down the board-walk with Rose. Cole watched them for a moment. Since Rose wasn't at the café, there was no point in him going down there, he decided. His only reason for making the visit had been to make sure Rose was all right, and he'd seen that for himself now.

Instead, he ambled along the boardwalk to the office of the *Wind River Sentinel*. There was a new edition out today, Cole recalled, and he figured he would pick it up to see what Michael Hatfield was editorializing about this week.

The press was silent when Cole entered the newspaper office. Michael was seated at his desk, but his chair was turned so that he could stretch his legs out in front of him. The young editor's shoulders slumped wearily. Michael always looked like that on the mornings the paper came out, Cole recalled. Printing the sheets and getting them ready to distribute was a process that took most of the night, and although Michael had a couple of helpers to give him a hand with the press, he still had to do much of the work himself. When Michael joked that he did everything from editing the paper to sweeping out the place, he wasn't far from the truth.

He was able to summon up a smile of greeting for Cole, however. "Good morning, Marshal," he said.

"Howdy, Michael," Cole replied as he pushed through the gate in the railing that divided the front room of the office. He took a coin from the pocket of his denim trousers and tossed it onto the desk. "Thought I'd pick up a paper."

Michael took one of the papers from a stack on the desk and held it out toward Cole. "Here you go. Hot off the press, as they say."

Cole took the paper and unfolded it to scan the front page. Another boxed editorial jumped out at him. It took him only a moment to see that it was another call for elections, pretty much the same thing that Michael had said in the previous week's editorial.

"Still beating the same drum, I see," commented Cole.

"You mean about the elections? It's important enough to bear repeating. Don't you like the idea of having a vote to elect a mayor and town council?"

Cole shrugged. "Doesn't matter that much to me, one way or the other."

"It could, though."

"How's that?"

"What if the people who were elected decided to hire a new marshal?"

Cole looked up from the newspaper, a surprised frown on his face. Michael was right, of course. A newly elected mayor and town council could hire whoever they damn well pleased as marshal. He might be out of a job.

A grin suddenly tugged at Cole's mouth as he thought about the implications. "That'd be a shame," he said dryly. "If that happened, I'd have to go back to what I was doing before you folks talked me into pinning on a badge in the first place."

"That might be more difficult than you think it would

be, Marshal. After all, by this time you've gotten used to being the law around here."

That was true, Cole supposed. He thought of Wind River as his town now, his responsibility. But with that responsibility came problems like the one concerning Rose Foster, problems with no good answers. If it came down to it, Cole thought he could walk away from the badge and the job that went with it without ever looking back.

"We'll see," he said. "You've got to get that election set up first. Might be worrying about nothing."

"Oh, there'll be an election," Michael said confidently. "All that's necessary is for the people to realize they want one."

"And how's that going to happen?"

Michael smiled despite his weariness. "I run a newspaper, Marshal. I'm going to tell them what they want."

Rose Foster and Billy Casebolt left the bank a little later. Rose had deposited several days worth of receipts from the café. She was glad that Wind River had a bank now; it had been worrisome, keeping her savings hidden in her room at the Paines' boardinghouse. The bank was just one more sign that the town was growing.

Nathan Smollett had had the current edition of the *Sentinel* lying on the counter, folded so that Rose could see the editorial by Michael Hatfield. Michael was still trying to get some local elections called, and Rose was sure that he would be successful sooner or later. Wind River was well on its way to being a real town. She hated to think about leaving here. She had grown accustomed to her life in this settlement, more so than she had ever thought she would be. It was a far cry from the elegant lifestyle she had enjoyed in New Orleans.

But that elegance had turned to ugliness, once she discovered just what sort of man John Drummond really was. Now she much preferred the simple, quiet existence she led here—or had led until Drummond had once again come into her life to ruin it.

He had no right, she told herself bitterly. He had no right to have done the things he had to her.

Rose took a deep breath and tried to calm her raging emotions. Simple chores, those were the things she had to concentrate on. Like picking up a few things at the general store. She had made a list the night before of what she needed, personal items such as some new needles and a spool of thread. Several of her dresses needed mending, and long gone were the days when she could afford to discard a dress because of a little rip or tear. The café was fairly successful, but she still had to watch her pennies.

She and Casebolt were about to pass the emporium, so Rose put her hand in her bag to see if she had brought along the list she'd made. The list was there, but Rose came to a stop as she realized something else was missing.

"What's wrong, Miss Rose?" asked Casebolt, also stopping beside her on the boardwalk.

"I don't think Mr. Smollett returned my deposit book," she said. Quickly, she felt around inside the bag, moving aside the little pistol she still carried in order to do so. She looked up at Casebolt. "No, I definitely don't have it."

"Reckon he just forgot to give it back after he wrote down the money you deposited today. We'll just run back down to the bank. He's probably found it by now."

Rose thought rapidly. She had already been away from the café longer than she had intended, since the bank had been fairly busy. "Why don't you go to the bank and get the deposit book, Billy?" she suggested. "I need to do some shopping here at the general store. I'll do that while you're at the bank."

Casebolt frowned, shifted his feet nervously, and said, "I don't know about that, ma'am. Marshal Tyler told me to keep a mighty close eye on you, and that's what I been doin'."

"And I've certainly felt safer while you were around. But Billy, I'll just be in the general store. I don't think anything's going to happen to me there, especially not in the middle of the day like this. You go ahead. I'll be fine."

Casebolt hesitated a second longer, then nodded. "I reckon you're right. I'll be back quicker'n you can spit—beggin' your pardon, Miss Rose. Didn't mean to be so crude."

She smiled and said, "Don't worry about it, Billy. I'll be inside the store."

He nodded again, then hurried off toward the bank.

Rose walked the few steps to the emporium's entrance and opened one of the double doors. She stepped inside. All the lamps were lit because of the overcast day, but some of the aisles were still shadowy. Rose gave a little shudder. She had never feared the shadows before—but she did now. She took a deep breath, shook her head, and started toward the rear of the store.

That was when two women came around the corner of a display case and started toward her, and she recognized them as Lucy and Irene.

Rose stopped short, facing the two soiled doves at a distance of about a dozen feet. Lucy and Irene came to a halt as well. The blonde met Rose's angry glare squarely, and a smile spread slowly across her face. Lucy, on the other hand, looked away, seemingly unwilling to look at Rose.

"Well," Rose said after a moment, "I haven't seen the two of you around much lately. I suppose you've been staying in the hotel with Drummond. Or have you been *working*?" Scorn dripped from her voice as she asked the question.

Rose's anger didn't seem to bother Irene. Still smiling, she said, "Why would you care, dearie? After all, you used to be in the same line of work."

Rose's breath caught in her throat. "I never—"

"Sure you did," Irene cut in. "What do you think marrying John was? He's told us all about you. Sweet little Rosemary from the poor but proud family. Sweet little Rosemary who married him so that she could have money again. What would you call it, honey? There may have been a marriage license involved, but you were doing the same thing for your money that we do for ours."

Rose felt her heart pounding heavily in her chest. "That's a lie," she said, her voice shaking with outrage. "You've got it all wrong."

"Have I?"

Lucy caught hold of Irene's arm. "Leave her alone," she said. "There's no point in arguing with her."

The blonde shook off Lucy's hand. "I'm just tired of the way women like her think they can lord it over us! They think they're so much better than we are, when really they're all the same. Take away the part that's just for show, and they're not any different. She was just as much a whore as us!"

With an effort, Rose controlled her anger. She wanted

nothing now but to go on with the errand that had brought her here and ignore the two women. She turned to go down a different aisle, but she couldn't resist adding bitterly, "And to think I believed that you two were my friends!"

Irene laughed stridently. "Friends with a stupid bitch like you? You actually thought you could do what you did to John and get away with it! You never even thought about the rest of your family!"

"Irene, no!" Lucy hissed.

It was too late. Rose stopped in her tracks again and looked in horror at the blonde. "What are you talking about?" she asked in a hollow voice.

"You mean it never occurred to you that John would start settling the score with your parents? He foreclosed on that plantation over a year ago. Your parents had to get off the land. They found work in the fields on another plantation that was bought by one of the carpet-baggers who came in after the war." Irene smirked. "I guess at their age it was just too much for them. They both died within a few months."

Lucy closed her eyes, clenched her teeth, and shook her head. "You didn't have to do that," she grated.

Rose stood there, stunned. It was almost impossible to believe what she had just heard. And yet, she had had no contact with her mother and father since fleeing New Orleans. She had thought that would be safer for them. But Irene was right—she had been stupid. Stupid enough to think that John Drummond wouldn't take out his hatred for her on the two people who mattered most to her.

Irene laughed again. "If you ask me, they got what was coming to them for raising you. They deserved to die."

The words ripped at Rose's soul. She lifted her head slowly, her lips drawing back from her teeth in a grimace. Anger and sorrow and hate welled up inside her.

And burst out in a scream as she dropped her bag and threw herself at Irene, clawing at the eyes of the startled blonde.

Lew Stanton walked across Grenville Avenue, the tails of his duster swirling around the tops of his boots. The mist was still too light to be called rain, but Stanton could feel the moisture against his face. It was a pleasant sensation after the heat and dust of the trail these past few days. He glanced at the clouds in the sky, hoping there was some good rain in them.

A gullywasher was just what he and his men needed to wipe out their tracks after they robbed the bank and galloped out of Wind River.

Without looking behind him, Stanton knew that Turner, Matt Garn, and two more members of the gang were coming out of the hardware store right about now. Josh Garn and another man were at a saddle shop a couple of doors down from the bank, talking to the owner about a non-existent saddle that needed repairing. Reyes, Lannigan, and the other men were in a nearby saloon, watching for his signal. Stanton lifted his hand

and tugged on the brim of his hat. Within a couple of minutes, the others would begin to filter out of the saloon and start ambling down the street toward the bank.

They had ridden into town in small groups of three or less. Nothing put a small-town lawdog on the alert quicker than a whole passel of strangers riding in together. Stanton was alone, and he had gone to the apothecary right across the street from the bank. For an hour, he had lingered over a wide selection of patent medicines, trying to decide which of the remedies would be the best for a condition he didn't even have. During that time, he had engaged the druggist in a lengthy, friendly conversation—and kept his eye on the bank at the same time.

The place was busy, busier than he had expected, in fact. But by keeping mental track of who went in and who came out, Stanton was able to be pretty sure when the bank was empty. He might have missed a customer or two, but that wasn't enough to worry about. If anybody else was in there besides the banker, they would just have to behave themselves.

If they didn't, Stanton was sure Reyes would be glad to slit their throats for them.

Stanton stepped up onto the boardwalk in front of the bank. A glance up and down the street told him that nobody was paying any attention to him. A few minutes earlier, a pretty young woman with strawberry-blond hair under her bonnet and a skinny old geezer with a shotgun had left the bank. The old man had worried Stanton; carrying a greener like that, he was likely some sort of lawman. But the old-timer was several blocks away now, talking to the young woman in front of what appeared to be a big general store.

Stanton opened the door and went into the bank. Without trying to be too obvious about it, he looked around the room and saw that he had been right in his estimate. There was no one in the place except the dude behind the counter. The man looked up, greeted Stanton by smiling and saying, "Good day to you, sir. What can I do for you?"

Stanton returned the smile. He knew that he might look a little rough, but he had enough education and charm that he could keep this gent from suspecting anything until it was too late. "I'd like to see about opening an account."

"Certainly, sir. How much did you wish to deposit?"

"I've got a little over a hundred dollars here." Stanton took a small canvas bag from underneath his duster. Inside the poke was most of the take from the aborted train robbery. The members of the gang had pooled their shares once Stanton had explained the plan, although some of them—Reyes and his cronies—had been a little reluctant to give up even a penny once they got their hands on it. The situation was just temporary, though, Stanton had assured them.

The banker said, "That'll be a fine opening deposit. I'll have to count it, of course."

"Sure," Stanton said. He untied the drawstring at the top of the bag and carefully removed the bills and the stacks of coins, placing them on the counter between him and the banker. "Go right ahead."

As the banker began counting the money, Stanton heard the door of the bank open behind him. He didn't look around, but the other man glanced up and said, "I'll be right with you, gentlemen."

"Take your time, mister. We're in no hurry."

That was Turner, Stanton knew. A moment later he heard the door open again and more booted feet entered the bank. The banker glanced up from his counting, chuckled, and said, "My, this has been a busy day so far."

"I guess a lot of people want to do business here," Stanton said.

"Well, that's not surprising. It's more than a hundred miles to the nearest bank." The man adjusted his pince-nez, looked up at Stanton, and went on, "You were absolutely correct, sir. I make the amount one hundred and three dollars and eighty-nine cents. Does that sound correct to you?"

"Close enough," Stanton agreed. "Right on the money, I guess you could say."

The banker chuckled at Stanton's comment. He took a deposit book from a shelf underneath the counter and opened it, then reached for the quill pen in the inkwell at his elbow. "You wish to deposit the entire amount?"

"Sure, why not?" Stanton answered.

"And what will the name on the account be?"

"Colt. Samuel Colt." Metal whispered against leather as Stanton's revolver slid out of its holster. He cocked it as the barrel came up above the level of the counter and went on, "And I've changed my mind. I think this'll be a withdrawal instead of a deposit."

The banker blinked rapidly as he stared at the mouth of the gun barrel. He took several quick, sharp breaths. "Oh, my God," he said in hushed tones. "This is a robbery, isn't it?"

"You catch on real quick, mister," said Stanton. "What's your name?"

"N-Nathan. Nathan Smollett."

"Well, Nathan, you just go ahead and take however much cash you've got in that drawer and put it in this bag. One of my friends back there has got a bigger bag for what's in the safe."

Smollett finally tore his eyes away from the muzzle of Stanton's gun and looked past the leader of the gang. His eyes widened even more in fear, and Stanton knew he had seen the guns the rest of the men had drawn.

"No need to lose your head, Nathan," Stanton said, "and no need for anybody to get hurt. Just get on with what I told you to do."

Smollett nodded jerkily and began taking money from the drawer and stuffing it into the bag.

Stanton glanced over his shoulder, confident that the mousy little banker wasn't going to try anything. His men had spread out around the room, guns drawn and ready. He looked at Josh Garn and said, "You be the lookout. Anybody looks like they're headed here, sing out." When Josh hesitated, Stanton snapped, "Go on, blast it!"

Garn shrugged and moved over by the window, standing to one side so that nobody looking in would be able to see his gun. Stanton turned his attention back to the banker.

"That's it, Nathan. You're doing just fine. Now, don't forget to put that hundred I brought in back into the bag."

"All right," Smollett said. "That . . . that's the last of the money here in the drawer."

"Now for the safe," Stanton said. "You *can* open the safe, can't you, Nathan?"

The question seemed to offend the banker. He drew himself up to his full height and said, "Of course I can open the safe."

"Well, then, let's do it." Stanton gestured with his gun, motioning Smollett toward the heavy iron safe that sat in the rear corner, behind the counter. He had to grin as he moved around the end of the counter to join the banker. So far, everything had gone smoothly and quickly, just like he had planned.

Smollett was crouched in front of the safe, turning the dial of the combination lock back and forth until the door opened. Stanton motioned to Turner, who took a large, folded-up canvas bag from underneath his duster and brought it around the counter. Turner held the bag open while Nathan Smollett took stacks and stacks of greenbacks from the safe and placed them inside the bag. Stanton's grin widened as he watched the money disappearing into the sack. It took only a few minutes to empty the safe. Yes sir, the outlaw leader thought, this job was going just fine.

"Fit! Fumboys fummin!"

Stanton's head snapped around at the yell from Josh Garn. "What?" he demanded.

"He said somebody's comin', Goddamn it!" shouted the other Garn, and Stanton knew with a sinking feeling that he had appointed the wrong brother as lookout. He had mistaken Matt for Josh.

And that moment's confusion had given the old man with the shotgun time to reach the door of the bank, because it swung open just then and the man stepped inside, his eyes widening and the barrels of the shotgun starting to rise as he looked around and saw the armed outlaws scattered around the room.

Stanton jerked his revolver up and fired.

*   *   *

Rose's attack took Irene completely by surprise. Rose crashed into the blond prostitute, staggering both of them. The fingernails of her right hand found Irene's cheek and raked down the painted flesh, leaving behind furrows where blood welled up. Irene shrieked in pain and rage. She swung the bag in her hand at Rose's head.

"Stop it!" Lucy cried. "Stop it, both of you!"

Neither woman paid any attention to her. Rose threw up an arm to block the blows Irene was aiming at her head, and then she bulled into the soiled dove once more. This time both of them lost their balance and went down, sprawling on the floor of the aisle. Rose landed on top, knocking the breath out of Irene and stunning her. She stopped trying to claw the blonde's eyes out and clenched her hands into fists instead. She gave a little, inarticulate cry each time she lashed out at Irene.

Vaguely, Rose was aware of Harvey Raymond yelling, "Hey! Hey, stop that!" She ignored the storekeeper. Two years worth of grief, anger, and fear had exploded inside Rose, and she wasn't thinking anymore. She was just striking out at the woman who had become a symbol of everything that had gone wrong with her life.

Strong hands suddenly grabbed hold of Rose's shoulders and jerked her roughly to the side, toppling her off the fallen Irene. Rose twisted and kicked, her foot catching Lucy on the leg. Lucy was the one who had interfered, and all of Rose's rage was redirected toward the brunette, who hobbled back a couple of steps and held up her hands.

"Listen!" Lucy said urgently. "We don't have to do this, Rose!"

Rose got to one knee and glared at the brunette. "The

hell we don't," she grated as she lunged to her feet and threw herself at Lucy.

Lucy tried to ward off the charge, but Rose was too angry, too out of control. She tackled Lucy, driving her back against one of the glass-topped display cases. Harvey Raymond let out a howl of dismay as the case swayed under the impact and almost fell over. Rose held Lucy pinned there, grabbing her hair with one hand and using the other to slap back and forth across Lucy's face. The blows jolted Lucy's head from side to side.

Then something landed on Rose's back and fingers jerked savagely on her own hair. Irene wrapped her arms and legs around Rose and screamed curses at her. The added weight of the blonde sent the display case toppling over with a crash of glass. Harvey Raymond shouted again. The small part of Rose's brain that was beginning to function rationally again heard him frantically telling someone to go find the marshal.

She rolled over on the floor of the emporium, ignoring the shards of glass from the shattered display case. The thought that Cole Tyler might find her here like this, thrashing around with a pair of trollops, sickened her. She put her hands on the floor, pushed herself to her knees, then climbed shakily to her feet. She started toward the front door of the general store, still paying no attention to Raymond's anguished protests.

Rose had just reached the doorway when Irene shouted, "Bitch!" and crashed into her from behind again. Both women stumbled across the raised porch. Suddenly there was nothing but air underneath Rose's feet. She plummeted off the porch to land heavily in the rain-dampened street. Irene came down on top of her, and this time it was Rose who gasped for breath.

She was too stunned to fight back as Irene rolled her over, sat on her midsection, and began slapping her. Rose's head was jolted from side to side each time Irene's hand cracked against her face. All the rage that had fueled her attack on the prostitutes had fled, leaving her a husk with no will to stop the pummeling. Rose was barely aware that Lucy had come out of the store and was tugging at Irene's shoulders.

"Stop it!" Lucy screamed. "You're going to kill her!"

Might as well, Rose found herself thinking. She had nothing left to live for, nothing left in her future but more running and eventually death at the hands of John Drummond. Thunder rumbled and boomed, and Rose's face was wet from the rain that poured down from the sky.

But not all the explosions were thunder, she realized foggily. There were too many of them for that.

Some of them were gunfire.

Billy Casebolt's eyes took in the scene inside the bank immediately. He was about to open his mouth to call out a greeting to the manager, Nathan Smollett, when he saw the dozen or so hard-faced men standing around the bank lobby with guns in their hands. A fella didn't have to be a genius to know what was going on. Casebolt didn't see Smollett and wondered fleetingly if the bandits had already killed him. At the same time he was jerking his shotgun level, intending to fire both barrels as he went back out the door.

Then the tall owlhoot behind the counter shot him.

The bullet took Casebolt in the left arm, midway between the shoulder and the elbow. It missed the bone but punched through the meat of the deputy's arm. The impact was enough to slew Casebolt halfway around. He was still able to trigger the shotgun one-handed, but the recoil as both barrels blasted tore the weapon out of his grip. His aim was off, too. He had meant to go for the man behind the counter, who had been right in front of Casebolt. Instead, the charge caught one of the men who was off to the right of the door and considerably closer. At that range, the buckshot blew the outlaw practically in half. He didn't even have time to scream.

More guns crashed as Casebolt spun back through the doorway, clutching his bullet-torn arm with his other hand. He didn't know if any of them hit him or not, but he managed to stay on his feet and throw himself toward the edge of the boardwalk. He sailed off the walk, landing in the street and rolling desperately to the side as he grabbed at the revolver holstered on his hip. His wounded arm dragged limply behind him.

Inside the bank, Lew Stanton cursed luridly. He stepped over to Nathan Smollett and slashed at the banker's head with the barrel of his gun. Smollett cried out and flung up his hands, trying to protect himself from the blow, but the barrel of the Colt slammed into the side of his head anyway. The gun's sight raked a gash in his temple. He sprawled senseless on the floor in front of the open safe.

"Come on!" Stanton shouted to his men. "We've got to get out of here!"

Their horses were tied up in various places along the street, all of them close to the bank but not right in front. Any getaway they made would have to be a quick one, before the shooting roused the entire town. Stanton didn't waste time going around the counter. He put his free hand down and vaulted over it, the tails of his duster flying out behind him. He paused, turned around, and called to Turner, "Throw me the bag!"

The hillbilly tossed the canvas bag full of money over the counter. Stanton caught it, then spun toward the door again. Lannigan had already burst out through the entrance, triggering his gun wildly. Alejandro Reyes followed him, also firing as fast as his finger could pull the trigger. One of the Garns was down, lying in a pool of blood with his belly blown apart by that old man's shotgun blast. The other one knelt beside his dead brother, his face twisted with grief and anger.

"Move, damn it!" Stanton snapped at the man, who looked up at him and mouthed incoherent curses. Had to be Matt, thought Stanton, then he didn't waste any more time worrying about it. He dashed past the Garns, the sack of loot held tightly in his arm, and his boots pounded on the boardwalk as he darted through the entrance.

Lightning flashed, thunder boomed, and a downpour slashed at Stanton's face. He didn't mind a bit. The sudden storm would make it more difficult for any of the townspeople to get a clear shot at him. A gun boomed to his right, and he twisted his head in that direction to see the old-timer who had started this ball. The old man was crouched at the corner of the bank, using the building for cover while he threw shots at the fleeing outlaws. Stanton snapped a shot of his own that made the old man duck back hurriedly.

Stanton's horse was tied up in front of the next building. He wheeled toward it and broke into a run, his boots splashing water from the puddles that were already forming. He jammed his gun into its holster, jerked the horse's reins loose from the rack, and swung up into the saddle. It seemed like more slugs were whining past his ears, but he couldn't be sure with all the thunder and lightning going on.

As soon as he hit leather, he hauled the horse around and raked his spurs across its flanks. The animal lunged forward in a gallop that carried it back past the bank. Stanton handled the reins as best he could with the hand that also held the bag of loot. With his other hand he fired twice at the old man as he passed. He couldn't tell if either shot hit its target, however.

The other members of the gang were all mounted by now, and Stanton caught glimpses of them through the driving rain as they pounded along the street with him. The storm was going to give them a chance to get away, but this wasn't how Stanton had wanted to leave Wind River. His plan had called for them to slip out of town before the robbery was ever discovered, so they could get a big enough lead that no one would be able to catch them. As it had turned out, though, they might get out of the settlement safely, but there would be a posse on their trail right away. The last thing Stanton wanted was a running fight between his men and a group of angry, vengeful townspeople. What they needed was an edge, something to discourage pursuit.

And suddenly, up ahead, rolling around in the mud, he saw just what he needed.

Rose stumbled to her feet as Lucy pulled Irene off of her. The thunder of gunshots had turned into the pounding of hooves, and a huge shape abruptly loomed up in front of her. A man she had never seen before barely slowed his galloping horse as he leaned over, looped an arm around her, and jerked her off her feet. She felt herself lifted, then she slammed down on her stomach across the horse's back, in front of the saddle. She was too shocked to fight back.

"Get 'em!" shouted the man who had snatched her off the street. "Get those other two women!"

Rose heard someone screaming, heard more gunfire. Lightning flared, but there was nothing for her to see except the muddy street sweeping past underneath the flashing hooves of the horse she was on. She had no idea what was going on—

But once again Fate had grabbed her up and was carrying her along. She fought against the crazy impulse to laugh. Surely John Drummond hadn't had anything to do with this, but judging from the bullets that seemed to be flying around, someone else might take care of his problem for him. If one of the stray slugs hit her, she could die without even knowing the reason why.

Cole Tyler had been at his desk in the marshal's office a few minutes earlier when one of the townspeople came in. The man seemed to be in a hurry, but he was chuckling and didn't appear to be alarmed. He jerked a thumb over his shoulder and said, "You ought to go on down to the general store, Marshal. It's a sight to see."

"What is?" Cole asked as he pushed aside the reward dodgers he had been studying. It was something to do on a day that had turned rainy.

"Miss Rose, you know, from down at the café, is in a sure-enough cat fight with a couple of whores."

Cole bolted up out of his chair. "What the hell did you say?" he demanded.

The townie frowned and took a step backward, obviously surprised by the marshal's reaction. "I said Rose Foster's down at the general store fightin' with a couple of whores."

"Damn it!" Cole grated. He came out from behind his desk and brushed past the startled townie.

A finger of lightning crackled across the sky as Cole emerged from the jail. At the same instant he heard the boom of a shotgun, although it took him a second to realize he wasn't hearing thunder. He looked through the rain at the emporium and saw three bedraggled figures struggling in the muddy street in front of the building. A second later, there were more crashes of gunfire.

Cole asked himself what in blazes was going on as he pulled his gun from its holster and started toward the center of town at a run.

Before he could get there, he spotted Billy Casebolt scrambling out of the street toward the corner of the bank building. Casebolt had lost his hat somehow and the rain had plastered his thin hair to his head, but there was no mistaking the deputy's tall, spare figure. He had his revolver in his hand and started firing toward the men who burst out the front door of the bank a second later. Their return fire forced Casebolt to seek cover.

Cole bit back a curse as he ran. Obviously, Casebolt had stumbled onto a bank robbery in progress. That was the only explanation that made any sense. Cole wanted to join the fight with his deputy, but he was still too far away for a handgun to do any good. Besides, the three women were still struggling in front of the general store, and they were in his line of fire.

Several of the outlaws had reached their horses. A couple of them raced down the street toward Cole. He dropped to one knee behind a water trough and squeezed off a shot at them. One of the owlhoots jerked in his saddle but managed to stay on his horse. The other man sprayed slugs at Cole and forced him to sprawl full-length on the ground behind the water trough.

The outlaws pounded past. Cole lifted himself to look down the street again and saw more of the gang galloping toward him. He started to scramble to his feet when suddenly one of the men veered toward the three women in front of the general store. Cole's eyes widened in surprise as he realized what was about to happen.

"Rose, look out!" he shouted, but he didn't know if she heard him or not. A moment later, the outlaw scooped her up deftly and kept riding. Rose's dress was covered with mud, but Cole could tell it was her because her bonnet had slipped down, revealing that unmistakable strawberry-blond hair.

Cole lifted his gun, instinct crying out for him to take a shot at the desperado who had just grabbed Rose. There was too much of a chance of hitting her accidentally, though, so he forced his finger off the trigger. The other two women were still stumbling around, but a second later two of the outlaws repeated their companion's maneuver, grabbing the women, hauling them onto the horses, and kicking the mounts into a gallop again.

The sound of rapid footsteps on the boardwalk made Cole look around. He saw several townsmen emerging from buildings in response to the fusillade of shots. Some of them were carrying pistols, but before they could open up, Cole shouted, "Hold your fire! Hold your fire, damn it!" As long as the outlaws had those three women as hostages, it was too risky to sling lead at them.

The outlaws didn't have to worry about being careful, though. They emptied their revolvers as they galloped along Grenville Avenue, forcing Cole and the other townspeople to dive for cover again. In a matter of moments, the gang was gone, disappearing into the rain as they headed west out of town.

And Rose Foster, along with the other two women, vanished with them.

Cole got to his feet hurriedly, stared with a bleak expression after the fleeing outlaws for a second, then turned and ran toward the bank. Billy Casebolt came down the street to meet him. The deputy's left sleeve was streaked with bloodstains and that arm hung limply at his side. Other than that, he didn't seem to be hurt.

"Billy, you all right?" Cole asked anxiously.

"One o' them hydrophobia skunks ventilated me!" Casebolt exclaimed. "I'm a mite shaky right now, but I reckon I'll be all right."

"Did they rob the bank?"

"That's sure as shootin' what it looked like to me. When I went in there, they was all standin' around with their guns out. I didn't see Nathan Smollett anywhere."

The outlaws might have killed the banker before Billy walked in on them, Cole thought grimly. He went to the door of the bank, ignoring the questions shouted at him by the onlookers who had come running up. The door was still open. Cole went through it with his gun ready, just in case there were any wounded bandits still inside the bank.

The gang had left one of its members behind, all right, but the man would never be a threat to anyone again. From the looks of it, he had caught a shotgun blast in the belly at close range. He was crumpled on the floor, surrounded by the blood that had leaked from his ruined body.

"Smollett!" the marshal called urgently. "Nathan Smollett! Are you in here?"

An answering groan came from behind the counter. Cole hurried around it and holstered his gun when he saw the banker trying to climb to his feet. There was a smear of blood down the side of Smollett's face from an ugly gash on his temple. He looked like he had been pistol-whipped.

Cole caught hold of the man's arm and steadied him. "You'll be all right, Mr. Smollett," he said. A glance showed him the safe with its door standing open. As far as Cole could tell, the safe was empty. "They cleaned you out?"

"They got everything!" wailed Smollett. "The bank is ruined!"

"Maybe not. We'll get that money back."

Smollett looked up at him, blinking rapidly. "You're going after them?"

"Damn right." Cole didn't say anything about the three women who had been taken prisoner by the gang. They were an even better reason to form a posse and pursue the outlaws.

Casebolt came into the bank. He had found his hat in the street outside and crammed it back on his head, despite the fact that it was bent out of shape and covered with mud. He asked Cole, "You want me to start roundin' up some men to go after them no-good thieves?"

"No, I want you to go down to Doc Kent's and get that arm patched up," Cole told him. "And take Mr. Smollett here with you. Looks like he got clouted pretty good before they busted out of here."

"Shoot, I'm all right—" Casebolt began.

Cole stopped him. "Just do what I told you, Billy. I'll round up the posse. If Judson says you can ride, you can come with us."

Casebolt grimaced but nodded his agreement. "Come on, Mr. Smollett," he said. "I reckon we're both a mite bunged up."

The two men left the bank and headed for the doctor's office, while Cole stared for a moment at the empty safe. What he was really seeing, though, was Rose Foster's face. To have gone through all she had over the past few days, only to be grabbed up by some fleeing bank robbers and used as a hostage . . . Life was sure cruel at times, Cole reflected.

He wondered why she had been fighting with those other two women, and then he realized they must have been Lucy and Irene, the soiled doves who had betrayed her to John Drummond. Obviously, Rose had had some sort of confrontation with them, and it had led to a struggle that had been interrupted by the flight of the bank robbers. Now he had to get after them before too much time elapsed and the outlaws got too big a lead to overcome.

Cole had just turned toward the doorway, ready to leave the bank, when a huge figure appeared there. "Did they get all the money from the safe?" Jeremiah Newton asked, his broad, florid face looking stricken.

Cole nodded. "Every bit."

"No!" The word boomed out from Jeremiah and seemed to almost shake the walls. "All the money I collected for the new church was here, every penny!"

"Well, it's gone now. I'm sorry, Jeremiah. But I'm going after them, and I plan to get back everything they took." The image of Rose flashed through Cole's mind again, and he repeated emphatically, "Everything."

Jeremiah's huge hands clenched into fists. "I'm going with you," he declared.

"Glad to have you. Better get down to the stable and get a horse saddled up. We'll be riding as soon as I can get a few more men. We can gather in front of your shop."

"You won't have any trouble getting volunteers, Marshal," Jeremiah said. "Nearly everybody in town had money in this bank."

That was true. There was more than just the safety of the three women riding on this pursuit.

If that money wasn't recovered, the settlement of Wind River might be ruined.

The next fifteen minutes were a whirlwind of activity. As soon as Cole stepped out of the bank, he was surrounded by anxious townspeople wanting to know what had happened and what he was going to do about it. Among them was Michael Hatfield, who was practically bursting with excitement. This was the first time such a crime had been committed right here in town, and Cole figured the young newspaperman might even put out an extra edition for this story.

Simone was there, too, her face pale under the umbrella that shielded her from the rain. The crowd parted for her, and she came up to Cole and put a hand on his arm. "Is it true?" she asked. "Those men got all the money in the bank?"

He nodded. "From what I can tell, that's right. And they took Rose Foster and a couple of other women with them when they rode out."

"Rose!" exclaimed Simone. "But how—?"

"She was unlucky enough to be on the street. One of the robbers grabbed her. They took a couple of other women with them, too."

Simone's pallor deepened. She had been held hostage by outlaws in the past, and Cole knew she must be thinking about what Rose was going through. Simone's captivity had ended with her rescue, and she hadn't been harmed.

Rose might not be that lucky.

Simone's fingers tightened on the marshal's arm. "Go after her, Cole," she said.

"I intend to." He raised his voice so the crowd could hear him over the drumming of the steady rain. "Anybody who wants to ride with me, get your guns, saddle up, and be ready to go in ten minutes, down at the blacksmith shop."

Quite a few of the men scattered, heading for home to get their rifles and horses. Cole tried to smile reassuringly at Simone. "I've got to go check on Billy," he told her. "He caught a slug during the getaway."

"Was he hurt badly?"

Cole shook his head. "I don't think so. I sent him down to Dr. Kent's with Nathan Smollett."

"Was Nathan hurt, too?"

"He had a cut on his head, looked like one of the outlaws hit him with a gun barrel. You can come with me if you want."

"I certainly do," Simone said. She fell in step beside him as he headed for the building that housed Dr. Judson Kent's practice.

Before they got there, Dan Boyd strode up to meet them, rain dripping from the brim of his black hat. The federal man's face was grim as he said, "Is what I heard true, Marshal? There was a bank robbery, and the outlaws took Rose Foster with them when they rode out?"

"That's right," Cole said. "They grabbed those two women of Drummond's, too."

"Damn!" The heartfelt curse exploded from Boyd.

"Begging your pardon, Mrs. McKay. Are you forming a posse, Marshal?"

"The men are rounding up their guns and horses right now. We'll be riding in just a few minutes." Cole looked shrewdly at Boyd. "I reckon you'll be coming along?"

"Of course I am! I can't let anything happen to Miss Foster."

No, Rose was still too important to the case Boyd was trying to build against Drummond. But to give the man his due, Cole figured Boyd would have ridden with the posse anyway. Boyd was a lawman, after all, and he wouldn't stand by while bandits robbed a bank and carried off women as hostages, no matter who they were.

"Get your horse and meet us down there in front of Jeremiah's blacksmith shop," Cole told him. "I'll be there in a few minutes."

Boyd nodded and hurried off, while Cole and Simone went on to Dr. Kent's office. As they entered the front room where Kent saw patients, Billy Casebolt was just shrugging back into his bloody, bullet-torn shirt. Nathan Smollett sat on the examining table while Kent wrapped a bandage around his head.

"You'd better take it easy for a few days, Nathan," Kent was advising the banker. "Lie in a dark room. Have someone with you to keep an eye on you. A head injury such as this is nothing to take lightly."

Smollett nodded, wincing as he did so. "All right, Doctor."

Casebolt buttoned his shirt and announced, "I'm ready to ride, Marshal. I'll go get my horse saddled."

Cole held up a hand. "Wait just a minute." To Kent, he said, "What about it, Judson? Is Billy up to going along with the posse?"

"I'd recommend against it," Kent said solemnly. "It's true that the bullet passed through Deputy Casebolt's arm quite cleanly and did a minimum of damage, but he still lost some blood and there's the matter of the shock to deal with. I've disinfected the wound and bandaged it, but I think a day or two of rest, plus a close watch on the injury, are in order now."

"You heard the man, Billy," said Cole. "Besides, I need somebody to keep an eye on things here. No telling how long it'll take us to run down those bank robbers. Could be several days before we're back."

"Jeremiah can watch over the town while we're gone," Casebolt argued.

Cole shook his head. "Jeremiah's going with me. He lost all the money for the church in this robbery."

Simone put her hand to her mouth and said, "My goodness, I didn't think about that. A lot of the other people in town had most of their money in the bank. Oh dear, Cole, this could be bad, very bad."

"That's why I intend to catch up to those—" Cole stopped himself before he could say what he was thinking. His description of the bank robbers wasn't anything that a lady needed to hear.

He pointed a finger at Casebolt and said, "Billy, you do what the doctor tells you. I've got to go."

Casebolt nodded reluctantly, and Cole left the office. He headed for the jail. He wanted to get his Sharps and his Winchester before he took off after the robbers.

The rain had begun to taper off, and it stopped entirely as Cole was leaving the jail a few minutes later with his long guns wrapped in oilcloth to protect them. That was good, he thought. If the rain had continued, it would have made it difficult, if not impossible, to pick up the trail of the bank robbers. The sky was still thickly overcast, though, and another shower could come along at any time.

There was a large group of men gathered in front of the blacksmith shop. Jeremiah was there, sitting taller in the saddle than most of his companions, and his horse was bigger to start with because it took a sturdy mount to support his weight. The overall effect really made him stand out in the crowd. He was holding the reins of Cole's golden sorrel, and Cole was glad to see that. Jeremiah's quick thinking had saved them a few minutes.

"I knew you'd want Ulysses saddled up," the blacksmith said as he handed the reins to Cole.

"Thanks, Jeremiah." Cole took the reins and swung up into the saddle. He was about to call out to the posse and tell them to get underway when he heard a startled exclamation from Dan Boyd.

"What the devil are *you* doing here?" Boyd demanded of someone.

Cole twisted in the saddle to see what was going on. His own eyes widened in surprise when he saw John Drummond and the three men called Amos, Lige, and Saul. They were all mounted on rented horses and had come up to join the group.

"Going along with this posse, of course," Drummond replied to Boyd's angry question. "I'm told that those bandits took my two friends Lucy and Irene with them. I intend to help rescue the women."

"That's a load of bull and you know it," Boyd shot back. "You know those owlhoots got Rose Foster, too, and you're hoping they'll kill her and do your dirty work for you. You're going along just in case they don't."

Drummond smiled arrogantly at Boyd. "You can accuse me of whatever you want, Marshal, but that doesn't make it true. Let's ask Marshal Tyler here if he minds having four more men along to help track down those robbers."

Cole hesitated before saying, "Four extra guns might come in handy. I reckon all of you are armed?"

Drummond's smile gave him the answer to that.

At the same time, Cole suspected Boyd was right. Drummond wasn't joining this posse out of the goodness of his heart or even out of concern for the two prostitutes who had come to Wind River on his behalf in the first place. The crime boss from New Orleans undoubtedly saw this raid on the bank as a blessing, since it had put Rose in mortal danger.

If that was the case, Drummond was in for a disappointment, Cole told himself. Because Rose Foster was coming back unharmed. He made that vow to himself.

Lifting his right arm, Cole waved toward the west, where the bandits had fled. "Let's ride!" he called, his voice ringing in the still-damp air.

Rose couldn't remember the last time she had hurt this much. Her stomach was badly bruised from lying across the back of the galloping horse, and it hadn't helped matters much when Stanton called a halt a few miles outside Wind River and paused long enough to let Rose, Lucy, and Irene climb aboard the horses in the normal manner. More hard riding had followed, and now Rose hurt in places that a lady didn't even think about, much less mention.

But she wouldn't have complained about the pain she was in anyway. She wouldn't give Lew Stanton that much satisfaction.

She knew now that was his name. He had introduced himself and the others, saying that if she was going to be riding in front of him like that, with his arm around her waist, that she ought to at least know who he was. He had chuckled as he brought his hand up over her sore midsection and let his thumb brush along the undersides of her breasts. Rose didn't have any illusions about the fate that was in store for her, as well as for Lucy and Irene, if they remained prisoners of these men for very long.

The rain had stopped not long after they left Wind River, and Rose was grateful for that. The sun even came out for a while, late in the afternoon, and helped dry her hair and her dress. She still felt clammy and uncomfortable, but she was going to have to get used to it. Stanton had already announced that they would ride most of the night.

"Got to put some distance between us and anybody who's chasing us," he explained. "That posse won't be able to track us at night. They'll have to stop, but we can make a lot of miles in the dark."

Rose wasn't sure how much more she could stand. She was already aching and exhausted, and as night fell and the gang pushed on, her weariness grew.

Finally, long after dark, Stanton held up a hand and called out to the others. "Hold on, boys. We'd better spell these horses for a while. Don't want them giving out on us tomorrow."

The man called Lannigan, who had Irene perched in front of him on his horse, said, "How about a fire and some coffee?"

Stanton shook his head. "I want a cold camp. We'll only be here an hour or so."

"An hour?" repeated the swarthy half-breed, Reyes. He let out a string of Spanish that sounded like cursing. "We're about played out, Stanton, men and horses both. We got to have more rest than that."

In a cold voice, Stanton replied, "Rest as long as you want, Alejandro. We'll go on, and you can try to catch up to us. Just don't expect us to leave your share of the money with you so that posse can get it when they come up and shoot you."

Reyes muttered some more in Spanish, but he shrugged his wide shoulders and said, "All right, an hour." His arm tightened around Lucy, who was riding with him. "I can think of some good ways to pass an hour, eh? How about you, *senorita*?"

Lucy didn't say anything, but Stanton snapped, "There's no time for that now. Tomorrow, maybe, when we can tell how far ahead of that posse we really are."

"How do you know there *is* a posse, Lew?" asked one of the other men.

Stanton swung down from the saddle and said, "They're bound to be coming after us. We cleaned out their bank, and we got these women. Those settlers aren't going to stand for either one of those things without at least trying to catch up to us. But they'll turn back."

"You sound mighty sure of that," commented Lannigan as he dismounted.

"I am," Stanton said confidently, but he didn't offer to explain any farther. Instead he reached up to Rose and went on, "Let me give you a hand."

She hated to touch him, but she was so stiff and sore she knew she might have to have help to dismount. She grasped his hand and gingerly climbed down from the back of the horse. Lucy and Irene were doing the same thing, and the blonde didn't make any secret of her discomfort. She cursed and complained as she limped away from the horse to sit down on a good-sized rock.

Now that she had a chance, Rose sat down on another rock and studied her surroundings. The thick clouds that had brought rain during the day had all broken up now, leaving only thin wisps in the sky that did little to interfere with the silver light from the moon and stars as it washed down over the Wyoming Territory landscape. Rose had never been farther west than the tree on the edge of town where Jeremiah Newton held his church services in good weather, so she had no real idea where she was. She could tell, though, that the rolling country-side was littered with rocks, and some rugged hills rose to both north and south. It all looked pretty inhos-pitable, especially to someone who had been raised in the luxury and gentility of plantation life before the war.

Stanton came up beside her and put a hand on her shoulder. She tried hard not to flinch, not wanting to anger him. He said, "I told you who I am, pretty lady. Don't you think you ought to tell me your name?"

She didn't see how being stubborn on the matter would do her any good, so she said, "It's Rose. Rose Foster." She didn't add that she had been born Rosemary du Charlaine, or that for a while she had been Rosemary Drummond. She supposed she still was, legally, but not once since leaving New Orleans had she thought of herself that way. Nor was she going to start now.

"Well, Rose Foster, I'm mighty glad to meet you. A pretty name for a pretty lady." Stanton's hand tightened on her shoulder, rubbing a little in a caressing motion. "I reckon we're going to be good friends."

Rose managed not to shudder—somehow.

Stanton sounded like an intelligent man, an educated man. She knew not to deceive herself where he was con-cerned, though. He was a cold-blooded killer. He would have to be to lead this band of ruthless desperadoes. She wasn't sure if anyone had died back there in Wind River—other than the brother of the outlaw who had been sobbing quietly to himself all day—but she knew that none of them would hesitate when it came to murder. Just the fact that Stanton had been so free with the names of the gang members convinced Rose that she and Lucy and Irene weren't intended to survive this ordeal.

"You hungry?" Stanton asked. "I've got some jerky and hardtack. You can have some, if you've got good teeth."

Rose wasn't the least bit hungry, but she wanted to keep her strength up, just in case an opportunity to escape presented itself. It would be terrible to have freedom almost in her hands, only to lose it because she was too faint from hunger. She turned to Stanton and said, "My teeth are fine. And I'd appreciate some food."

"Coming right up," he said with that cocky grin of his, his teeth shining in the moonlight. Under different circumstances, Rose thought, Lew Stanton might be a handsome, charming man. She wondered briefly what had led him to become an outlaw instead.

Not that it mattered. He was what he was—dangerous, ruthless, a killer.

Just like her husband.

That thought made a new question pop into her mind. Stanton was convinced a posse would pursue them from Wind River. Would John Drummond join it?

Before she could figure out the most likely answer to that riddle, Stanton returned with the food he had fetched from his saddlebags. "Here you go," he said, pressing a strip of jerky and a hardtack biscuit into her hand. "You'll need some water, too." He placed a canteen beside her.

"Thank you," Rose said. She opened the canteen first, took a swallow of the water, then tore off a bite of jerky with her teeth. She had to chew it for a long time, but she was finally able to get it down. She followed it with a piece of almost equally tough biscuit. She understood what Stanton had meant about having good teeth.

The other two women were eating, too, as they sat together about a dozen feet from Rose. Just like whores to be practical about things, she thought, then felt ashamed of herself. Lucy and Irene were just doing the same thing she was, trying to keep their strength up. She couldn't blame them for that, no matter how much she despised them for their association with Drummond.

Stanton said to one of the men, "Matt, come over here and keep an eye on these ladies." The outlaw did as he was told, and Stanton and the other men gathered around several yards away to discuss something, keeping their voices pitched low enough so that Rose couldn't make out what they were saying. Probably talking about how and when to murder her and the two soiled doves, she thought bitterly.

The owlhoot who had been appointed to stand guard over them was the one who had been crying earlier. She kept eating, concentrating her energy on the tough jerky and hardtack.

When Irene finished, she stood up and brushed her hands off, then took a step away from Lucy. The guard said sharply, "Moan move."

Irene pointed and said, "I'm just going over there to those bushes, mush mouth. A lady's got to have *some* privacy every now and then, you know."

The outlaw repeated, "Moan move." He turned to the others. "Woo?"

Stanton came over to see what was wrong. The guard, who obviously had no teeth and probably had a bad case of gum disease as well, judging by his distorted voice, explained what Irene wanted. Stanton nodded and said, "All right. Go with her, Matt."

"He most certainly will not!" Irene exclaimed.

Stanton shrugged. "You want to go to the bushes, Matt goes with you. Same for the other ladies. Take it or leave it."

Irene lifted her chin and glared at the outlaw called Matt. "Well, you'd better just behave yourself, that's all I've got to say." She marched toward the scrub brush with offended dignity.

She was amazing, Rose thought. Here they were, their remaining hours of life obviously numbered, lucky that they weren't being raped senseless at this very moment, and Irene was worried about her privacy! Rose might have admired the woman—under other circumstances.

Lucy and Rose visited the bushes in turn, enduring the same humiliation. At least Matt turned his back, although he stood only a couple of feet away from them. While she was there, Rose thought about looking around for a rock that she could snatch up and use to bash in the guard's head, but she discarded that plan. Even if she managed to get her hands on Matt's gun, the other outlaws would just go ahead and shoot her. They would still have Lucy and Irene to use as hostages if the posse caught up to them—and to just plain use if they gave the pursuers the slip.

When they were all done, Rose found herself standing with the two prostitutes. They looked ridiculous, she decided, in their fancy gowns covered with mud, the matching hats long since lost during the struggle in the general store. But they didn't look any more ludicrous than she did, she supposed, since she had shared the same mud bath in the street. Maybe under the circumstances, it was time she did something about the enmity between them.

"Look," she said in a low voice, "I'm sorry about the things I said to you back there in Wind River. And I'm sorry about that fight in the store."

"It wasn't your fault," Lucy said. "Irene started it."

Irene protested, "Hey! I was just saying what I thought."

"Well, you were wrong to do it!" snapped Lucy. "We'd already hurt Rose enough by telling John where to find her. You didn't have to break the news to her about her parents like that."

"No, it's all right," Rose said quickly. "I . . . I'm glad to know what happened to them. I feel like it's . . . like it's all my fault."

Lucy put a hand on her arm. "Honey, don't ever blame yourself for anything John Drummond does. He's a law unto himself, like . . . like a force of nature or something. An evil force."

Irene sniffed and said, "When we get back, I'm going to tell John what you said about him, Lucy. I don't think he'll like it, either."

Rose and Lucy traded a glance in the moonlight. Lucy shrugged and nodded, indicating that, yes, it was indeed possible for Irene to be that dense. After a moment, she said, "We're the ones who ought to be sorry, Rose. We did try to make you think we were your friends. That was how we got close to you so that we could make sure you were the one we were looking for. You don't know how long we'd been searching—" She stopped and shook her head. "No, that's no excuse. We still shouldn't have betrayed you."

"Are you crazy?" demanded Irene. "If John ever found out we'd found her and didn't tell him, how long do you think we'd be around then?"

"You mean he would have—" Rose began, then stopped herself. "What am I saying? Of course he would have killed you. Or had you killed, if he didn't happen to feel like dirtying his own hands."

"You don't have anybody to blame but yourself," Irene said. "You had everything a girl could want—a handsome husband, plenty of money, a fine place to live." She sounded genuinely interested as she went on, "What made you give all that up?"

Rose looked at her in wonderment. "Don't you understand even now? *John Drummond is a monster.* He kills people, or has them killed. He's a smuggler, a whoremonger, a thief . . . I don't know what else I can say about him to make you understand."

Lucy looked at her for a long moment, then asked, "Did you know what he was when you married him?"

Rose shook her head vehemently. "I knew he was a businessman from New Orleans, that's all. I met him through an acquaintance of my father's. I . . . I was taken with him right away. Like you said, Irene, he is handsome, and he can be so charming when he wants to be."

"You're not telling me anything I don't already know, dearie," Irene said. "You don't think he lets any of us work for him without trying us out first, do you?"

Rose gave a little humorless laugh. "That's another thing. In addition to all his other faults, he was unfaithful to me."

"You did the same thing," Lucy pointed out. "We weren't around then, but we heard the stories about you and Nick Murdoch."

Slowly, Rose nodded. "It's true. But I only turned to Nick when I found out what kind of man John really was. It was such a shock . . . and then when I got to know Nick and he said he wanted to get away from John, too . . . well, it was just so natural for us to get together."

"Natural," Irene repeated. "You could call it that."

Lucy made a shushing gesture at her. "How did you find out about John?" she asked.

Rose wasn't sure why she was opening up so much of her past to these women, but she knew it felt good to finally explain how things had really been. Besides, what did it matter? Before the sun set on another day, they'd probably all be dead anyway.

"After we were first married, I went along with everything John wanted. I was the perfect wife for him. I spent his money hand over fist, and he never seemed to mind. But then one day . . . " She took a deep breath, and even now, after two years, a shudder went through her as the memory came flooding back vividly. "We were in the parlor of the mansion there in New Orleans, and we were about to go up to bed when a messenger arrived. John talked to him for a minute, then told me to go on up without him. He . . . he said he would be up in just a few minutes and that I should get ready for him. I knew what he meant."

Rose ignored the smirk that appeared on Irene's face. She went on, "I was going to do what he said, but then I decided that it might be nice to surprise him. I . . . I put on my nightgown and went back downstairs."

"Not a very smart thing to do," Lucy said.

"No. No, it wasn't. The parlor door was open a little, and I stopped right outside it. I could hear voices inside and thought John was still just talking to the messenger. But some of his servants had brought another man in, and I heard John accuse him of stealing. I . . . I figured out after a minute that the man ran a brothel, and I could tell that John owned the place. I was shocked, but I guess that might not have been so bad. If it hadn't been for what happened next . . . "

"You don't have to tell us," Lucy said. "I think we can figure it out for ourselves."

Rose took a deep breath. "No, I want to tell it. No one has heard exactly what happened since I told Nick about it later . . . There was a noise, the most awful noise I'd ever heard. I wanted to run away, but I couldn't stop myself from pushing the door open the rest of the way. I saw the man John had been talking to. He . . . he was on his knees, and John was standing behind him. There was a knife in John's hand . . . "

Lucy reached out, caught Rose's hand, squeezed it hard.

"The man's throat was cut," Rose went on. "There was blood all over the floor. He fell forward into it . . . " She shuddered again. "John looked up and saw me watching him. He . . . he *smiled*. I realized that he had just killed that man, and he intended to come up to our bedroom afterwards and . . . and . . . "

She couldn't go on. Suddenly, sobs were wracking her, and Lucy stepped forward to put her arms around her. Even Irene looked vaguely sympathetic.

Not Lew Stanton, however. He came striding over to the three women and said impatiently, "Here now, what's all this? I let the three of you talk and you wind up blubbering."

Lucy looked up at him as she comforted Rose. "It's all right," she said. "You can't blame poor Rose for being upset. Snatched up off the street like that, carried away by a bunch of . . . of highwaymen!"

Stanton grinned. "That's us, lady. Highwaymen." He swung around to the others. "Come on, boys, mount up. We need to be riding." He turned back to the women and grasped Rose's arm. "You're riding with me again."

"Why don't you just—" Lucy began.

"No!" Rose said. "It's all right, Lucy. I'll ride with Mr. Stanton. I don't mind, really."

"Of course you don't mind," Stanton grinned. "You know ol' Lew will take care of you."

John Drummond had promised to take care of her, too, Rose thought as she climbed onto Stanton's horse again and the outlaw settled himself in the saddle behind her. And Drummond had turned out to be one of the most evil men on the face of the earth. Stanton wasn't much better, if any.

But as she glanced over at Lucy and Irene, she felt a little better. Lucy's sympathy had seemed genuine, and even Irene appeared to have been moved a little by Rose's story. Lord knew, it had been a relief to unburden herself after all this time. Rose sensed that, given a chance, she and Lucy might have really been friends.

That chance would end, though, as soon as the outlaws had safely outdistanced any pursuit. Then the women's usefulness as hostages would be over, and Stanton and his men would be free to do whatever they wanted with them. Rose knew what that would mean. Stanton urged his horse forward and led the gang and their prisoners into the night.

If John Drummond knew somehow what was going to happen to her, she wondered abruptly, would he be happy? Or would he feel cheated that he hadn't gotten to kill her himself.

A grim smile touched Rose's lips. Maybe a little something good would come out of this, she thought, even if it was only to disappoint that vicious son of a bitch she had been foolish enough to marry.

18

Stanton called another halt not long before dawn. Rose was so exhausted by then that she actually found herself dozing off as she rode, even though that meant leaning back against the outlaw boss. When she dismounted, she stumbled a little and shook her head in an attempt to clear away some of the cobwebs.

Lucy and Irene were equally worn out, and Irene was complaining about it, as usual. Since there were no larger rocks around this spot, both women sat down on the ground to rest. Rose did the same thing.

This time, Stanton didn't offer Rose any food, although all three of the prisoners were permitted to drink from a canteen they passed around. Once again, Matt Garn was detailed to stand guard over them while Stanton and the rest of the outlaws talked quietly among themselves. As Rose watched them, she had a feeling they were hatching some kind of plan, but what it might be, she couldn't say. All she knew was that it made her uneasy. She couldn't imagine anything the outlaws could come up with that would be good.

"Ohhhh, I was never so tired in my life!" Irene said. "I could work all night without being this sore."

"I guess it's just a matter of what you're used to," Rose said.

Irene laughed. "You know, honey, I think I like you more than I thought I did. You're not too bad. And I know you've been through a lot." She hesitated, then went on, "Maybe we shouldn't have told John about you after all."

That admission had probably taken quite a bit of effort, Rose thought. She smiled in the predawn dimness and said, "The two of you were just doing what you figured you had to. I can't hold that against you."

"John *is* a dangerous man," Lucy said. "What happened with Nick Murdoch? Unless you'd rather not talk about it."

Rose shook her head. "No, I don't mind. It doesn't hurt as bad as it used to. Nick and I had a place where we met, a little apartment in the French Quarter. The lady who owned the place had been a madam at one of John's houses before she retired."

Lucy exclaimed, "You mean Tante Louisa?"

"That's right," Rose said with a nod. "She was Nick's friend, and she helped us however she could without John finding out about it. I don't think he knows to this day that we were meeting in her house."

"I'm sure he doesn't," Lucy said. "He would have done something about it if he did, and as far as I know, she's still in his good graces."

"I'm glad to hear it. I want her to stay that way." Rose looked hard at Irene as she went on, "If we should happen to get out of this, I wouldn't want anybody to tell John about Tante Louisa."

Irene held her hands up. "Don't look at me. I know how to keep my mouth shut."

"I'll see that she does," Lucy said. "Go on, Rose, if you're up to it."

Since the story had taken their minds off their current predicament, Rose continued, "I was at the apartment one evening. Nick and I were supposed to meet there, and we were planning to leave New Orleans the next day. Tante Louisa came upstairs to warn me, though, that something had gone wrong. She had her sources of information, as you can well imagine—"

"She still does," Lucy said with a smile, and Rose decided that Lucy and Tante Louisa were friends, too.

"I could tell she was very upset. She said I had to leave, that I couldn't go back to the mansion. I was to get out of New Orleans as soon as I could. She even gave me some money to buy a ticket on one of the ships leaving the city. The train wasn't safe, she said, and neither were any of the boats going up the Mississippi. I had to go to sea. Naturally, I was upset, too, and I had to know why she wanted me to do that." Rose took a deep breath. "She told me that Nick's body had just been found in one of the bayous. He had been stabbed in the back."

"And you figured that John was responsible," said Lucy.

"Of course. Tante Louisa admitted that she wanted me out of her house because she couldn't allow John to find me there, not if she wanted to stay alive, too. I couldn't put her in danger, so even though I was terribly upset by the news about Nick, I . . . I went down to the docks and managed to book a berth on a ship that was leaving in less than an hour. I didn't care where it was going, as long as it was away from New Orleans. Even at that, I was almost too late. Just as the ship was sailing, I saw a couple of John's men—Saul and Amos—coming along the docks, checking all the ships. John had sent men to the train station, as well as to cover the riverboats, figuring that I might try to get back to my parents' plantation. The seagoing ships were last on his list, and Tante Louisa must have figured that out. I hid so that Saul and Amos wouldn't see me on deck, and the ship headed on out to sea."

"Where did you wind up?" asked Irene.

"Galveston, Texas," Rose replied. "From there I went to Mexico, then around Florida to Charleston, South Carolina. I started moving west across the country from there, never staying in one place for too long, figuring that John would never be able to track me to wherever I finally stopped running." She smiled faintly and shook her head. "I thought Wind River was the place. I guess it was just bad luck that brought us together."

"I wish we'd never even stopped there," Lucy said bitterly. "You deserved a chance to start over."

"Yes, you did," Irene said, surprising Rose.

"Well, none of that matters now. John won't get to have his revenge on me, but I'll be dead anyway, so he won't have to worry about me going back to New Orleans and testifying against him."

"Why didn't you go back with that marshal?" Lucy asked with a frown. "John hates him, and I think the feeling's mutual."

Rose hesitated for a moment, then said, "I didn't trust Marshal Boyd. Oh, he's honest enough, I suppose. He's not working with John or anything like that. But he actually thought he could protect me by himself." She shook her head. "I might have considered it if Cole Tyler had been going along, but I wasn't going to put my life in Boyd's hands."

"Cole Tyler, eh?" Irene said with a grin. "You mean that lawman from Wind River, the handsome one with the long brown hair? You can pick 'em all right, Rose honey."

Rose looked down at the ground and felt the flush creeping over her face. An absurd reaction to have in a situation like this one, she thought, but there was no denying it.

"Cole's a good man," she said softly. "I never really thought about it that much, because he's a lawman and I didn't want to trust any lawmen. I didn't want to trust anybody, period, or get too close to anybody. But I think, after knowing him for more than a year, that I'd trust Cole Tyler to get me safely to New Orleans."

Lucy patted her on the shoulder. "Maybe he'll get the chance, Rose," she said. "Maybe he'll get the chance."

They all knew how unlikely that was. It became even more so a moment later as Lew Stanton came over to them and said, "Time to mount up, ladies. We'll be riding again."

Rose pushed herself wearily to her feet. Somehow, she had to find the energy to endure. There was still a chance the posse from Wind River would catch up to them. She was going to cling to that hope as long as she could.

Rose, Lucy, and Irene climbed onto the horses they had been riding, and Stanton, Lannigan, and Reyes took their places as well. The other men mounted up, too, but when

Stanton, Lannigan, and Reyes sent their horses west, the others unexpectedly turned north, toward a ridge that rose sharply about a hundred yards away. Rose frowned as she watched the outlaws veer in that direction.

"Where are they going?" She couldn't stop herself from asking the question.

"Oh, they're going to take care of a little chore for me," Stanton said. "I reckon that posse's still back there somewhere, and I'm tired of worrying about them. Figured I'd leave a little welcoming party behind to say howdy to them."

Rose felt her insides turn icy, and it wasn't from the early morning chill in the air. Stanton was talking about an ambush. The rest of the outlaws were going to hide on that ridge, and when Cole and the other men from Wind River came along, the bandits would open fire on them. Without thinking, she tried to twist around and look back, and she exclaimed, "No!"

Stanton's arm just tightened around her waist. "You're a smart one, aren't you? Figured out what I was up to right away. But it won't do you any good, Rose, and neither will that posse. Those townies'll turn back once my boys shoot 'em up a little."

Rose's shoulders slumped in defeat. She knew he was right. She hadn't held out much hope of being rescued, but any hope was better than none. Now it was over, and there was nothing left to do but play out the hand.

With death waiting at the end.

There was nothing more frustrating, Cole Tyler thought, than waiting for the sun to rise so that a posse could get back on the trail of some vicious owlhoots.

Of course, there probably *were* things that were worse, he mused as he downed the last of a cup of coffee, but at the moment he sure couldn't think of them.

The rain of the day before had not returned, and Cole had been able to pick up the tracks of the bank robbers' horses about a mile out of Wind River. The trail had been pretty easy to follow, and Cole had even pushed the posse on after nightfall, tracking by moonlight.

Once the moon had set, however, he'd had no choice but to call a halt. There just wasn't enough starlight to be sure of not losing the trail, and doing that could have cost them more time in the long run than making camp and getting a few hours sleep. The rest would be good for both men and horses, because Cole had set a brutal pace since leaving Wind River.

Already there had been complaints from some of the townsmen. That was the way it was always was, Cole reflected. Folks get caught up in the excitement of forming a posse and forget that it meant lots of long, hard hours in the saddle, followed by—if they were lucky— the chance to get shot at when they finally caught up to the outlaws.

Jeremiah Newton wasn't complaining, though, and neither was Dan Boyd. In fact, both of them were ready to go this morning, even though the eastern sky was just barely turning pink on the fringes with the approach of dawn.

"We'd better pull out, Marshal," Boyd said as he came up to Cole. "Those bandits are likely putting some more miles between us right now."

"I agree with Brother Boyd," Jeremiah put in as he came up to stand beside the federal lawman. His bulk seemed to loom even larger than normal in the early morning shadows.

Cole put his hands on his knees and pushed himself to his feet. "I reckon you're right. Jeremiah, tell everybody to get saddled up. We ride in five minutes."

Jeremiah nodded, and Boyd made an impatient sound as if even five minutes was too long to wait. But he turned and hurried after the blacksmith, who was heading for where the horses were tied up and passing the order to get ready to ride as he went along.

Cole went over to John Drummond and the other three men from New Orleans. They were camped a little apart from the townsmen. The three bruisers were moaning and groaning and limping as they walked around this morning; obviously, riding a horse was something completely foreign to them. Drummond seemed rested and unbothered by the long ride the previous day, however. Maybe he kept a horse at one of the stables in New Orleans and rode regularly, Cole thought.

"With any luck, we'll catch up to that bunch today, Drummond," Cole said without any preamble. "If we do, I want you and your boys to be careful."

"We're always careful, Marshal," Drummond replied with a smile.

"What I mean is," Cole went on, "I don't want any 'accidental' shots coming toward me or Marshal Boyd. I see any so-called stray bullets coming from your direction, mister, I'm liable to just throw down on you and get it over with."

Drummond spread his hands and shook his head. "You have nothing to worry about, Marshal," he assured Cole. "All we want is to help you and these other good men rescue those women."

"Including your wife?"

For a second, Drummond's handsome features grew taut. "What's between Rosemary and myself is a personal matter, Marshal Tyler. I have no interest in seeing her come to any harm at the hands of those desperadoes."

Somewhat to his surprise, Cole found himself believing the man. Drummond wanted to settle the score with Rose himself.

Cole didn't let on that he had figured that out. Instead he said, "See that you and your boys remember that, Drummond. Now get mounted up. We're fixing to ride."

All the men were ready a few minutes later when Cole swung up into the golden sorrel's saddle and waved them forward. There was enough of a glow in the eastern sky now for him to be able to make out the tracks left by the outlaws. Once again, Cole set a fast pace.

They were riding through terrain that was by turns gently rolling prairie and stretches of rocky, more rugged landscape. Instead of due west, the trail tended to meander to the south a little, so that the rails of the Union Pacific ran several miles to the north. There were mountains in the distance to both north and south. Cole had been over this ground quite a few times before. It would continue to get rougher the farther west they went, so he hoped they would catch up to the outlaws before much longer. The tracks seemed to be getting a little fresher, as did the droppings left behind by the owlhoots' horses.

By midmorning, when the sun was high in the sky and the air was growing considerably warmer, Cole felt his anticipation growing. He was sure the outlaws weren't more than a couple of hours in front of them now. With some hard riding all day, the posse might be able to catch up to them before nightfall. Some of the men might not like it, but there would not be any breaks from now on except short ones to rest the horses—and those only when they were absolutely necessary.

Suddenly, as his eyes scanned the ground ahead of the easily loping Ulysses, Cole spotted something that made him frown and hold up his hand in the signal to halt. As he reined in, the others followed suit, and Jeremiah and Boyd edged their horses up alongside Cole's mount.

"What is it, Brother Cole?" asked Jeremiah. "You look troubled."

"I am," Cole said curtly. "Take a look at those tracks."

He pointed to the ground. The tracks of three horses—probably carrying double, judging from the depth of the markings—continued on straight ahead. But there was a welter of other tracks, probably made by at least half a dozen horses, and that trail headed north. Cole grimaced. He hadn't counted on the outlaws splitting up. He lifted his head, following the tracks that led north with his eyes—

That was when he saw the ridge, as well as the telltale flash of sunlight reflecting on metal . . .

"Everybody down!" Cole shouted as he ripped his Winchester from its saddleboot. "Get off your horses and hunt some cover!"

The warning came too late. Distant cracks of rifle fire split the air, and bullets began whining through the air around the heads of the posse.

Cole flung himself out of the saddle and landed hard on the ground, but he managed to hang on to his senses and the Winchester. He rolled to the side as a slug kicked up dust where he had been an instant earlier. He wound up sprawled behind a rock that was barely big enough to give him any cover. When he lifted his head a little, a bullet whined off the rock and made him duck back down. His lips pulled back in a grimace as he hissed a curse.

Once before he had led a posse into an ambush. He hadn't liked the feeling then, and he didn't like it how. He felt like ten kinds of fool, even though he realized logically that there was no way he could have known the outlaws would bushwhack them. There had been no indication that they had anything in mind other than pure, flat-out flight.

That knowledge didn't do the men who had been cut down by owlhoot lead a damned bit of good, Cole reflected bitterly. He twisted his head to see what the situation was. A couple of men were lying motionless on the ground, their shirts stained with blood. Gall rose in Cole's mouth at the sight of them, because he knew they were either dead or critically wounded. All the other posse members had managed to dismount and had followed his example, seeking cover behind the rocks that littered the ground on both sides of the trail.

Gunfire still crackled from the ridge, and Cole could see a haze of powdersmoke floating in the air above it. Over the din, Jeremiah called to him, "Brother Cole! Are you all right?"

Cole lifted a hand a little and waved to let the big blacksmith know he wasn't hurt. He shouted back, "How about you?"

Jeremiah nodded. He had had to find a big rock to give him some shelter from the outlaw bullets, but the boulder behind which he crouched seemed to be stopping all the slugs. Cole looked beyond Jeremiah and saw that Dan Boyd also appeared to be unhurt. The federal man was crouched behind a jumble of smaller rocks and was firing toward the ridge with those ivory-handled Colts. Boyd seemed to be the only one putting up a fight so far, and his actions were pretty much futile, Cole thought. A handgun was almost completely ineffective at that range.

Not so a Winchester. Cole waited for the inevitable lull in the firing from the ridge, and when it came he slid the barrel of the rifle over the rock and began pumping shots toward the distant height. Some of the other members of the posse who had managed to grab their rifles joined in.

When Cole had emptied the Winchester, he rolled onto his side and began to reload it with rounds from the loops on his belt. The rifle was a .44, like his revolver, so the cartridges would fit either weapon. He didn't have an endless supply of them, though. In fact, once the rifle was empty again, he wouldn't have enough shells to completely reload it.

While he was doing that, his hands moving with an automatic, practiced ease, he glanced around and noticed something else. There was no sign of Drummond or the three men who had accompanied them. Nor were their horses among the group of spooked mounts that had galloped off several hundred yards before stopping to mill around nervously. Cole wondered what had happened to the men from New Orleans. Maybe they had cut and run when the shooting started. He looked back along the trail, which curved out of sight around a bluff several hundred yards away. If Drummond and the others had fled, they were long gone by now. For all Cole knew, they had been picked off by the bushwhackers as they ran, although he didn't see their bodies anywhere.

He couldn't worry about them now. He had his own problems.

Like staying alive.

One of the possemen called, "Marshal, can we rush 'em?"

Cole shook his head. "That'd just get us killed that much quicker," he shouted back. "Stay put and try to pick them off."

That was easier said than done. He and his companions were the ones who were pinned down, not the outlaws. The ambushers had the high ground, had all the advantages. It didn't look good.

Suddenly, a fresh flurry of shots rang out from the ridge. A man appeared up there, silhouetted against the skyline for a second before he fell and tumbled loosely down the steep slope. Cole blinked in surprise. He was pretty sure none of his men had brought down that outlaw.

The firing continued, more furious than before, and Cole could tell now that some of the shots were coming from pistols instead of rifles. It sounded like the outlaws had suddenly turned on each other for some unfathomable reason and were killing themselves instead of the posse members.

"Hold your fire!" Cole shouted to his men. "Hold your fire!"

Sure enough, he could tell now that no more bullets were coming their way. No slugs were ricocheting off rocks or kicking up dust around them. All the fighting was concentrated on the ridge.

It couldn't be, Cole thought, as an unlikely possibility suggested itself to him. It just couldn't.

But a minute later, as the gunfire on the ridge died away, a familiar voice shouted down, "Tyler! Marshal Tyler! Can you hear me?"

"I hear you!" Cole shouted back. He lifted himself cautiously to his feet and called to his companions, "Don't shoot."

"It's all right!" The call came floating down. "They're all dead!"

"My God!" exclaimed Dan Boyd. "That sounds like Drummond!"

"It is Drummond," Cole said grimly as he came out from behind the rocks. The other members of the posse slowly emerged from cover as well.

Four figures appeared on top of the ridge, leading their horses. Cole, Jeremiah, and Boyd strode out to meet them as they came down the slope. Drummond and the man called Saul appeared to be unhurt. Amos and Lige were both sporting bullet creases, but nothing serious.

Cole met them at the bottom of the ridge. "The four of you circled around and got behind them, didn't you?" he asked.

Drummond shrugged. "It seemed like a tactic that might be successful. I don't think they were expecting anything quite so audacious. At least, they certainly looked surprised when we opened fire on them from behind."

"You shot them in the back?" snapped Boyd.

"Don't get self-righteous, Marshal," Drummond said. "They were outlaws and kidnappers, and they were trying to kill us. I'm not going to waste any sympathy on them."

"Neither am I," said Cole. "It pains me to say it, Drummond, but . . . thanks."

"Don't bother feeling grateful, Marshal. I just don't like anyone getting in my way when I want something. Not anyone."

Cole could believe that, just as he could believe that it wouldn't have been difficult for Drummond and his men to cut down the robbers from behind. Some of the outlaws had managed to put up a fight, obviously, but the element of surprise had been enough to swing the odds onto Drummond's side.

"Jeremiah, go back and check on the men," Cole told the blacksmith. "Boyd, we'd better go up there and make sure all those men are dead."

Drummond said, "They are, Marshal. You can take my word for it."

"I'd rather see for myself," Cole said. He trudged up the slope, the Winchester held ready in his hands in case there was any life left in the bandits.

There wasn't. Cole and Boyd checked each of the men who were sprawled lifelessly on the hard ground. The outlaws' horses were tied up on the other side of the ridge. Cole nodded toward the animals and said, "We can tie the bodies over their saddles, and some of the men can take them back to Wind River."

"Sure," Boyd grunted. "We've got a couple of dead men of our own, and some wounded who'll need to go back."

"But there are only three of those outlaws left now," Cole pointed out. "We won't have to be at full strength to handle them."

"Don't forget, they still have those women with them," Boyd pointed out.

Cole shook his head and said, "Don't worry, Marshal, I haven't forgotten. I haven't forgotten at all."

19

As it turned out, the ambush had taken a heavier toll than Cole had thought. Three members of the posse were dead, and another half a dozen were seriously wounded, leaving only five townsmen who hadn't taken at least one bullet. Once Cole had taken in the situation, he said to the five men who were uninjured, "I want all of you to head back to Wind River."

"But what about you, Marshal?" asked one of the townies. "You can't go after the rest of them outlaws by yourself."

"I won't be by myself. I'll have Jeremiah and Marshal Boyd with me, as well as Mr. Drummond and his friends. And judging by the tracks, there are only three of those owlhoots left alive." Cole clapped a hand on the townsman's shoulder. "No, you and the other boys will have your hands full enough, Roy, just getting the wounded men and all those bodies back to town. Think you can do it?"

"Well, sure, Marshal. We can take care of it for you."

"Good. Better get ready to ride, then."

The wounded men had been patched up as best he and Jeremiah could manage, and Cole felt like all of them would survive the trip back to Wind River, where Judson Kent could take charge of them. In the meantime, he and Boyd and Jeremiah would continue tracking the remaining outlaws.

And Drummond. Couldn't forget Drummond and his men, Cole thought.

It was galling to think he might owe his life to the crime boss from New Orleans, and when Cole looked at Dan Boyd, he could tell that the other lawman was even more disturbed. Boyd had dedicated months of work to bringing down Drummond, and now he had to feel grateful to the man.

They all had to forget about those concerns until the hostages were safe again, Cole told himself. And he would say the same thing to Boyd if the federal man gave any trouble. Boyd was unusually quiet, though, as they gathered up their horses and got ready to ride again.

In fact, the only thing that Boyd said to Cole came as they were leading their mounts back to where the others waited. He looked over at Cole and said, "Don't trust him. Don't ever trust him."

Cole didn't have to ask who Boyd was talking about. He just nodded and said, "I didn't intend to."

Stanton wasn't setting as fast a pace today, Rose decided. No doubt he didn't want to get too far ahead of the men he had left behind, so they wouldn't have as much trouble catching up after they had ambushed the posse from Wind River. Also, Stanton probably wanted to take it easier on the horses following the long hard run of the night before.

Rose found her thoughts going back to that ambush Stanton had set up. She was worried about Cole Tyler, knowing that he would be in the forefront of any pursuit. She didn't like to think that anything had happened to Cole, yet she knew he would be one of the primary targets of the bushwhackers.

She had never been much of one for praying, but today she was getting plenty of practice.

Around the middle of the day, Stanton called a halt and allowed Reyes and Lannigan to build a fire so that they could heat some coffee. As he stood and stared back the way they had come, he muttered, "I thought they'd've caught up to us by now."

Rose was moving around nearby, rolling her shoulders and trying to ease some of the stiffness in her muscles. She looked at Stanton and said, "Maybe the ambush didn't work."

He glared at her. "What do you mean by that?"

"Maybe the posse wiped out your men, rather than the other way around. You and your friends may be on your own now."

"Impossible," Stanton snapped. "The boys wouldn't let any bunch of townies turn the tables on them. Those men from Wind River are either dead or running back home with their tails between their legs by now, just like I planned."

Rose just smiled, knowing that would annoy Stanton even more. It did, as his deepening frown proved.

There was no point in staying on his good side, she

told herself. No matter what she or Lucy or Irene did, they would wind up being raped and murdered anyway. The more Rose thought about it, the angrier she became. She had always let someone else make all the decisions for her. First her parents, then Drummond, and even when she had found out what sort of man he was, her only reaction had been to find someone else to take care of her.

Well, Nick Murdoch hadn't been able to take care of himself, let alone her. But even her flight following his death had been controlled by her fear of Drummond. She had never really done anything for *herself*, not until she had reached Wind River and opened the café. Despite everything, she had been happy there, genuinely happy.

And then this son of a bitch Lew Stanton had taken her away from that happiness.

Of course, Drummond had already ruined things by showing up in Wind River, but Rose couldn't think about that now. Drummond wasn't here, and Stanton was. He and the other two outlaws were going to bear the brunt of her anger . . . not that she could actually *do* anything.

Or could she? There were only three of them to deal with now. If she could get her hands on Stanton's gun . . . if Lucy and Irene could somehow get the drop on Lannigan and Reyes . . .

Maybe they could get out of this alive after all, Rose thought suddenly. She felt her heart began to pound faster in her chest.

She looked at Lucy and Irene. Both of them seemed pretty downcast, their exhaustion finally forcing them to give in to despair. She wished she could have a chance to talk to them privately and fill them in on her rudimentary plan, but Stanton wasn't going to allow that. She would just have to do what she could and hope that the other two women would understand and play along.

She took a deep breath and moved over closer to the small campfire. Stanton was crouched beside it, waiting for the coffee to brew. Rose said, "I sure would like a cup of that when it's done."

"I reckon you can have one," he said.

"I'm sorry I said those things a while ago. I . . . I didn't really mean anything."

Stanton glanced at her in surprise. After a moment he grinned. "So you decided not to be feisty today after all, eh?"

Rose just smiled and shrugged.

"Well, that's good," Stanton went on. "I reckon you know the old saying about how to catch flies."

"With honey instead of vinegar," Rose said. She kept her voice matter-of-fact, not even bothering to try for some sort of seductive tone. She knew Stanton wouldn't believe such an abrupt change of behavior from her. But he might accept the idea that she had decided to be friendlier toward him out of fear and practicality. That was the impression she was striving for.

"Sounds to me like you're getting smart," Stanton said. "Coffee'll be ready in a minute."

Rose glanced over at Lucy and Irene. Both of the soiled doves were watching her now, and while Irene just looked puzzled, Rose thought she saw a glint of understanding in Lucy's eyes. She was sure of it a moment later when the brunette stood up and sidled over to Lannigan, who was adjusting one of the cinches on his horse's saddle. "I want to thank you," she said.

The man shot a surprised glance at her. "For what?"

"I know you've tried to make the ride a little easier on me today. I really appreciate it."

Lannigan grunted. As far as Rose could tell, Lannigan hadn't done anything of the sort, but if he wanted to believe what Lucy was saying—and it appeared he did—that was just fine. Lucy continued making small talk with the tall, lean outlaw.

Irene frowned darkly. Obviously, she hadn't caught on. But it looked like she wouldn't have to, because Reyes took care of the matter for her. He came up to her, pulled her to her feet, and pressed her against him. His hands slid down her back to her buttocks, cupping and kneading them.

"Your friends, they finally got the idea," he said with a leer. "Things go a lot better for you three if you are friendly with us, eh?"

Irene looked like she wanted to spit. "I wouldn't be friendly with you if—"

"Irene!" Lucy cut in. "There's no need to be like that. We're just trying to make the best of the situation, isn't that right, Rose?"

Rose put her hand on Stanton's arm. "That's right," she said, with just the right touch of resignation in her voice.

"Oh, all right," Irene said disgustedly. She looked at Reyes and went on, "Do whatever you want, Pedro. I can't stop you, anyway."

"That is right, little one. But my name is Alejandro, not Pedro." He brought his hand up and cupped her chin, then suddenly tilted her head back brutally as his other arm pressed tightly around her waist. "You remember that, eh?"

"S-sure," gasped Irene. "I'm sorry, Alejandro."

"Hey, Lew," Lannigan said as he looked at Lucy, "what say we just wait right here until the other boys catch up to us. They ought to be along soon."

"Yeah," Stanton said slowly. "That's a good idea." He looked at Rose. "What do you think?"

She managed to smile a little and shrugged. "You're the boss."

"Yeah, I am, aren't I? Come here." He reached out, snagged her arm, and pulled her against him. His mouth came down hard on hers.

Stupid bastard, Rose thought as her fingers closed around the butt of his gun.

She bit his lip as hard as she could, at the same time jerking the gun from its holster and throwing herself backward. He let go of her instinctively as her teeth tore painfully through his lip. Rose spat blood from her mouth as she stumbled back and tried to bring the gun up. This might not get her anything except a quicker death, but that was worth something.

Stanton howled and lunged after her. Rose saw flickers of motion out of the corner of her eye, heard Lannigan and Reyes shout angrily. She got her finger through the trigger guard of the gun and both thumbs looped around the hammer. As the barrel came up, she pulled the hammer back with a grunt of effort.

The next instant, Stanton crashed into her, his face a twisted mask of fury as blood welled from his torn lip. Rose wasn't aware of pressing the revolver's trigger, but suddenly it roared and kicked heavily against her hands. Stanton's face was only inches from hers, and she saw his eyes widen in shocked agony.

Then Rose's feet went out from under her and she fell. Stanton landed heavily on top of her.

For a moment she panicked, unable to get her breath. She pushed frantically at Stanton and was finally able to roll him off of her. He flopped loosely to the side, his head lolling on his shoulders. There was a large blackened spot on the front of his shirt. Looking at that, Rose knew the gun had gone off right over his heart.

She didn't have time to reflect on the luck that had guided that shot. Lucy screamed, "Look out, Rose!"

Her head snapped up and she saw Lannigan aiming a gun at her. She threw herself to the side just as Lucy leaped on the outlaw's back. Lannigan's gun roared. Rose didn't know where the bullet went, but she was fairly sure it hadn't hit her. She came up on her knees as Lannigan threw Lucy off with a curse and tried to swing back around and aim the revolver in his hand.

By that time, Rose had Stanton's gun cocked and lined up, and she pulled the trigger again.

The bullet ripped into Lannigan's midsection and doubled him over. He went backward a couple of steps, then caught himself. With a shaking hand, he tried to lift his gun again, but it was too heavy for him. The gun boomed, driving the slug into the ground at his feet as he fell.

"Oh, my God!" Irene shrieked. "Somebody help me!"

Rose looked around and saw Irene backing up rapidly from Alejandro Reyes. The half-breed staggered after her. His own knife was buried in his chest, and Rose knew Irene must have snatched the blade from its sheath and plunged it into him when the shooting started. As the three women watched in horror, Reyes grasped the hilt of the knife with both hands and slowly pulled it free. A ghastly grin stretched across his dark face as he slashed at Irene with the blade.

Only the fact that she was practically running backward and tripped over her own feet saved her life. As she fell, the knife ripped through the air where her throat had been an instant earlier. He loomed over the fallen Irene, raising the knife above his head for the next stroke.

"Shoot him! For God's sake, shoot him!" screamed the blonde.

Rose wanted to. She already had Stanton's revolver cocked again. But as she pulled the trigger, the hammer fell with a maddening click. Either the chamber was empty or the cartridge had misfired. Desperately, Rose reached for the hammer to cock the gun again.

She didn't need to. Reyes kept lifting the knife, and when he had both arms high above his head, a great shudder went through him. He went over backwards, dropping the knife as he fell. His legs sprawled out and kicked spasmodically as death claimed him.

Irene started to cry.

Rose slowly lowered the gun and looked around. Lucy was on her hands and knees, panting from exertion and fear, but she seemed to be all right except for a bruise forming on her face where Lannigan had knocked her aside. None of the outlaws were moving.

"Are . . . are they all dead?" Lucy asked.

Rose took a deep breath. "I think so. I . . . I'd better check."

She forced down the sickness that gripped her as she knelt beside each of the bandits in turn and searched for a pulse. Lannigan was the only one still alive, and just as Rose found the pulse in his neck, a horrible rattling sound came from his throat and the beat ceased. He was gone, too.

Rose stood up, trying to make her brain work. They were out of immediate danger—although they were on their own miles from nowhere—but there were still the other outlaws to worry about. She shook her head, clearing it a little, and looked around. The horses were not far off; they had bolted when the shooting started, but they hadn't gone more than a hundred yards or so. "We'd better catch those horses," Rose said, "unless we want to walk all the way back to Wind River."

"We won't have to worry about that," Lucy said hollowly as she helped Irene to her feet. "Look over there."

Rose looked, and she felt her blood freeze in her veins. Riders were coming. Seven riders. She tried to remember. Had there been seven of the outlaws in the group left behind to ambush the posse? That seemed right to her.

But suddenly, as the horsebackers came closer, relief flooded through her, the emotion so strong that it almost made her fall to her knees. She recognized the big golden sorrel being ridden by the man in the lead, and one of the other riders was so big that he could only be one man.

"It's the posse," she said, her voice little more than a hoarse whisper. "It's Cole and Jeremiah and . . ."

Then she could make out the other men a little better, and once again she almost stumbled, but not from relief this time. *He* was with them. After everything she had gone through, *he* was there to torment her with the fact that nothing had really changed.

John Drummond.

*   *   *

Cole already had Ulysses moving at a run. The sound of the gunshots a few minutes earlier had prompted that. But when he saw the three women standing there with the bodies of the outlaws sprawled out on the ground around them, he slowed the sorrel a little. "Looks to me like they're all right," he said to his companions with a smile.

"How in blazes did they manage to turn the tables on those owlhoots?" asked Dan Boyd, his voice mirroring his amazement.

"The Lord was on their side," Jeremiah said. "That's the only explanation."

That might be true, Cole thought, but he figured that grit and good luck had also had something to do with the outcome of this near-tragedy. Of course, some folks would attribute those two factors to the Almighty, too, and Cole wasn't going to argue with them.

Right now, he was just glad to see Rose Foster standing there unharmed, her thick strawberry-blond hair blowing in the wind, a gun clasped in the hand that hung at her side. As he and the other men came closer, he lifted a hand in greeting and began to rein in Ulysses with the other.

"No!" Rose screamed as she lifted the gun.

"What the hell!" exclaimed Cole.

Rose pulled the trigger and the gun in her hand boomed. One of the men with Cole let out a yelp of pain.

A glance over his shoulder showed Cole that John Drummond was clutching his left arm. Blood welled between his fingers as he swayed in the saddle. "She's gone crazy!" Drummond shouted.

"Keep him away from me!" Rose cried. "I'll kill him!"

Cole was close enough to her now that he was able to

leave the saddle in a dive that sent him crashing into her. His arms went around her, cushioning her as they fell to the hard ground. He grabbed the wrist of her gun hand and forced it down. Her fingers opened and the gun slipped from them. To his surprise, Rose began to cry, huddling against him and shaking miserably.

She was murmuring something, and Cole had to put his head closer to hers before he could make out the words. She was repeating, "Don't let him get me . . . don't let him get me . . . "

"Nobody's going to hurt you, Rose," Cole told her. "Nobody."

He pushed himself into a sitting position, bringing her upright with him. Comforting a crying female was something that didn't come easy to him, but he managed to pat her on the back and mutter that everything was going to be all right. He looked up at Lucy and Irene and silently beseeched them for help.

The two women got Rose to her feet and led her several yards away, where both of them tried to get her to stop crying. Cole stood up as well and brushed some of the dust from his clothes.

Boyd had dismounted and was checking the three outlaws. "They're all dead," he reported. "Don't know how these women did it, but it looks like they took care of their own problems." He glanced at Drummond. "Some of them, anyway."

Cole went over to Drummond, who had been helped down from his horse by his men. Saul was cutting away Drummond's sleeve, revealing a nasty-looking gash caused by the bullet cutting across his arm. The wound wasn't serious, though, Cole judged, and looked much worse than it really was.

"You all right?" Cole asked Drummond.

"I suppose I will be," he snapped. "The woman's gone insane. She tried to kill me."

"I'd say after everything she's gone through, she's got a right to let the reins slip a little," Cole said. "I don't want any trouble about this, Drummond. I just want to get these women safely back to Wind River."

Drummond nodded. "Don't worry, Marshal . . ."

Cole grunted in satisfaction and started to turn away. Jeremiah had dismounted and joined the women, where he was talking in low tones to Rose, who appeared to have regained some control over herself. Boyd was gathering up the weapons that the dead outlaws would no longer need.

Then Drummond went on, "No need to worry, because none of you are going back to Wind River."

Cole froze at the sound of guns being cocked.

Inside, he cursed. His surprise and relief at finding the women unharmed had caused him to let his guard down just long enough for Drummond to seize the advantage. Slowly, he turned and saw that Amos, Lige, and Saul all had their pistols drawn and aimed toward him, Boyd, and Jeremiah.

Drummond smiled despite his wound. He, too, had his gun out, and it was aimed directly at Cole. "Go ahead, Marshal," he said. "Try it. That'll just give us an excuse to end this quickly."

"You son of a bitch," breathed Cole. "Boyd was right. You just came along to make sure that Rose died."

"Of course. All of you were watching her so closely in town that we couldn't get to her easily. We missed the only real chance that we had."

Boyd spoke up. "So you were responsible for that ambush behind the café after all."

"Naturally. Lige did his best. He knocked out that old man, knowing that Rose would probably come to check on him when he didn't return. After it didn't work out, he was able to hide the rifle and get back to the hotel in time to change clothes and shoes. You didn't really think someone else was trying to kill Rose, did you? That would have been too great a stroke of luck for me to be believed."

"You got your luck," Cole said harshly, "when those outlaws grabbed her. But that didn't work out for you either, did it?"

"Unfortunately, no. Unfortunately for you and your companions as well, Tyler. Because now the three of you have to die as well. If the outlaws had killed Rose, I might have let the rest of you live." Drummond shrugged casually. "As it is, I can't afford to do that. But Marshal Boyd has been quite a troublemaker in the past. I'll be glad to get rid of him. So I guess I *am* lucky after all."

Rose spoke up, her voice calm now. "You don't have to kill the others, John. I'm the one you want. Just take me."

"Oh, I think not. Then they could testify that I killed you, and I'd be just as bad off as when I started looking for you, my dear."

Rose stepped forward, her expression bleak but determined. "You might as well get it over with," she said. "You killed part of me when you murdered Nick. You can finish the job now."

To their surprise, Drummond laughed. "As always, you're wrong, Rosemary. I didn't kill Nick Murdoch, although I gladly would have if I had gotten my hands on him. No, your paramour had the bad luck to be set upon by thieves there in the French Quarter. The way I heard it, he was robbed and killed for his money. I didn't have a thing to do with it."

Rose stared at him in disbelief. "I . . . I thought—"

"It didn't really make any difference," Drummond said. "I would have killed him if I'd had the chance. I did kill that fellow in the parlor that night, and once you had seen that your own fate was sealed. You just couldn't ever accept the sort of man I am, could you?"

"Accept?" repeated Rose in a shaky voice. "Accept the fact that I was married to a murderer? My God, John, how did you expect me to *accept* that?"

He shrugged again. "You just never did know what was good for you, did you, Rosemary?" He glanced at his men. "Let's get on with it."

"Wait a minute!" Lucy said suddenly. "Let Irene and me get out of the way."

Drummond looked surprised. "Why, Lucy, you don't think that I can allow the two of you to live, do you? It's going to be quite a shame, but those horrible bank robbers killed all three of their hostages, plus the marshals and our big blacksmith friend over there, before my lads and I were able to dispose of them. At least, that's the story we'll tell when we get back to Wind River, and no one will ever be able to prove otherwise."

"My deputy will know different," Cole warned. "He'll come after you, Drummond."

"That old man doesn't frighten me, and neither does anyone else in that backwater town of yours, Tyler. Now, I'm tired, my arm hurts, and I want to be done with this."

"John, don't," Lucy pleaded desperately. "We won't say anything to anybody, will we, Irene?"

The blonde frowned, looking as surprised at her answer as the others did. "Hell, yes, we will," she declared. "If you're going to shoot Rose, John, you might as well shoot me, too."

Lucy came toward Drummond, her hands held out imploringly. "Don't pay any attention to her, John. I'll do anything . . . " A cunning light appeared in her eyes. "I'll even kill Rose myself. That'll give you something to hold over me, to make sure I don't talk."

Rose and Irene stared at her, aghast, while Cole and Boyd looked disgusted and Jeremiah shook his head in dismay. Drummond appeared to be considering her suggestion for a moment, but then he shook his head. "I don't think so, Lucy," he said. "You've always been hard to figure, but I think you're just trying to get your hands on my gun. You wouldn't have been thinking about shooting *me* instead of Rose, now would you?"

The sudden flash of despair on Lucy's face showed that Drummond had guessed correctly about her ruse. But even so, he had made the mistake of letting her get too close to him, because without any warning she threw herself toward him, blocking his gun. "Get them!" she cried.

Drummond's gun went off, throwing Lucy backward. At the same instant, he yelled, "Kill them all!", and Irene flung herself in front of Rose. Cole threw himself forward to the ground, palming out his Colt as he fell, and Boyd pivoted, his hands flashing toward the ivory-handled Colts. Jeremiah sprang at Drummond's men with a full-throated roar.

Gunshots slammed through the hot air. Irene went

spinning off her feet as bullets ripped into her. Cole triggered his gun twice, saw the bullets drive into Saul's chest, then rolled to the side and came up on one knee. Boyd staggered back, hit by one of the flying slugs, but the twin Colts in his hands were roaring. Bullet after bullet smashed into Lige's chest, sending him jittering backward in a grotesque dance of death. Jeremiah batted Amos's gun aside and swung a hammerlike fist at his head. The blow shattered Amos's jaw and slewed his chin around almost under his ear. His head jerked around seemingly farther than the human neck could twist, and he fell limply to the ground.

Drummond was still on his feet, trying to get a shot at Rose. Lucy was at his feet, curled up in a ball. She managed to reach up and grab his leg, throwing him off balance. Drummond smashed at her head with the gun, knocking her grip loose.

That distraction gave both Cole and Boyd time to line their sights on him, however, and the two lawmen fired at the same time. They triggered until all three guns were empty, the slugs hammering into Drummond's body, making him stumble backward. He dropped his revolver and sat down hard as the guns abruptly fell silent, the eerie stillness that marked the end of most gunfights. Drummond's chest heaved as he looked down at himself. His torso was riddled, and his shirt was already sodden with blood. He looked back up, opened his mouth to say something, but crimson gushed from it instead. He toppled over onto his side and lay unmoving.

"Well, I would have rather seen him hanged," Dan Boyd said into the silence, "but I reckon justice has been served."

Cole didn't give a damn about that right now. He

stood up, quickly reloaded his gun, and checked the other three men. They were all dead, including Amos, over whose body Jeremiah stood, slowly shaking his head and holding his right hand in his left. From the way his fingers were swelling already, the blow had broken at least a couple of them.

"I didn't mean to hit him that hard," the blacksmith was saying. "I swear, I truly didn't."

"His neck's broken," Cole said, "and if I was you, I wouldn't waste a minute's time worrying over it, Jeremiah. I imagine that fella's got plenty of blood on his hands."

Jeremiah looked at Cole. "Vengeance is the Lord's, not man's."

Cole took a deep breath and said, "Listen, Jeremiah, I seem to remember you saying something in one of your sermons about how God wants us to smite evil. Well, that bastard was plenty evil, and you smote the hell out of him. I'd call it a good day's work." He clapped Jeremiah on the shoulder, then went to tend to the women.

Rose and Irene were kneeling beside Lucy. Cole was surprised to see the blonde up and around like that, since she had been knocked off her feet by the burst of gunfire. The right sleeve of her dress was bloody, and there was a bullet burn on her cheek that would leave an ugly scar. But other than that, she didn't seem to be hurt too badly. Luck had been with her.

Cole wasn't sure the same could be said of Lucy. There was a large patch of blood on the right side of her dress, just above the waist. Her forehead had an ugly gash on it, too, from being struck with Drummond's gun. She was pale and unmoving.

"Do something!" Rose said as she looked up at Cole. "God, somebody do something!"

Boyd came over, took hold of Rose's shoulders, and gently moved her away. The federal man was limping from a bullet in the leg received in the shoot-out. It would likely heal up all right with the proper attention, Cole thought, but Boyd might have to limp the rest of his life.

He turned his attention to Lucy, ripping away the blood-soaked dress and examining the wound. What he saw gave him reason for optimism. Drummond's bullet had ripped through Lucy's side, all right, but the wound looked clean and not too deep. Cole looked up, met Rose's anguished, anxious stare, and said, "I think she'll be all right."

Rose closed her eyes. "Oh, thank God!" she breathed. "Thank God!"

Jeremiah came over and put a hand on Cole's shoulder. "We might not be out of the woods yet, brother," he said. "More riders coming."

Cole got to his feet and looked to the east, where Jeremiah was pointing. Sure enough, a couple of dozen riders were racing toward them, dust boiling up from the hooves of the galloping horses. Cole didn't know who the newcomers could be, since the gang that had robbed the bank were all dead and the rest of the posse had headed back to Wind River.

But then a grin split his face as he recognized the three men in the forefront of the group. Kermit Sawyer, Lon Rogers, and Frenchy LeDoux . . . and as usual they were riding at the head of the Diamond S punchers.

Boyd came up beside Cole and nodded toward the riders. "Who are they, Marshal?"

"A bunch of proddy Texans," Cole replied, still grinning. "And for once, I'm damned glad to see them!"

20

As it turned out, Lon Rogers had ridden into Wind River a couple of hours after the bank robbery, and when he heard that Rose had been taken hostage by the gang as they escaped, he had immediately raced back out to the Diamond S and raised a posse of his own. Kermit Sawyer had been glad to come along, since some of his money had been in the bank, too, and the rest of the Diamond S cowboys had been more than willing to join in. Chasing down a band of bank robbers was just the sort of break those hell-raisers needed from ranch work.

Unfortunately—at least as far as the Texans were concerned—all the snake-stompin' had already been done by the time they caught up.

The money stolen from the bank had been recovered, everybody's wounds had been patched up, and Rose Foster was out of danger at last. For the first time in two years, she wouldn't have to live life always looking over her shoulder.

By the time they got back to Wind River the next day, Rose wanted a bath desperately, but she waited until Lucy and Irene had been cleaned up and their wounds treated by Judson Kent. The doctor shared Cole's opinion that both women would be fine. When they had been placed in narrow beds in one of the rooms of Kent's house, Rose sat with them while the doctor went to check on Dan Boyd's injury.

Rose's chair was between the beds. She reached out with both hands and took the hands of Lucy and Irene. "Thank you both," she said fervently. "You . . . you turned out to be my friends after all. The best friends I've ever had."

"I don't know about that," Lucy said. "From what I've seen, you've got plenty of friends right here in Wind River, Rose Foster. Mighty good friends, at that."

"I guess you're right," Rose said with a smile.

"You're going to stay here, aren't you?" asked Irene. "I would, if I was you."

Rose thought about the question, but only for a moment. "There's no reason for me to go back to New Orleans, nothing for me there. This is home now. I'll stay."

"Good," Lucy said fervently. "I'm glad to hear it."

"What about the two of you? I mean, with John dead, you don't have to go back, either. You could stay—"

She stopped as both of the women shook their heads. "Not here," Irene said firmly. "Too many folks know what we . . . used to be."

"But that doesn't matter—"

"Yes, it does," Lucy broke in. "I don't want to go back to New Orleans, either, but we can't stay here. We need to make a new start somewhere else."

"San Francisco, maybe," suggested Irene. "I hear it's mighty pretty out there, and there's plenty of places for a girl to work." She put her fingers to the bandage on her cheek. "Although the way both of us are going to have scars, we might ought to look for a new line of work."

"You can do whatever you want with your lives," Rose told them. "You'll have the reward for helping to recover that money from the bank. It'll be enough to help you start over."

Lucy frowned. "What reward?"

"The one that Simone McKay is going to give you," Rose said.

"I hadn't heard anything about a reward."

"Neither has Simone . . . yet. But she will."

All three women began to smile.

Lon was waiting outside the doctor's house when Rose emerged a little later. He came forward eagerly to meet her.

"Rose, I . . . I sure am glad you're all right," he said as he walked alongside her while she headed toward the boardinghouse. "I was worried sick about you while those outlaws had you."

"So was I," she said with a smile. "But that's over now, Lon. It's all finished."

He took a deep breath and gathered his courage. "What about you and me, Rose? That doesn't have to be finished, does it? I mean, now that that fella Drummond isn't looking for you anymore . . . "

Rose stopped and looked solemnly at him. "Lon, you're just about the sweetest boy I've ever known, but—"

He held up his hands. "You don't have to say it. You still think I'm just a boy, that I'm not good enough for you."

She reached out, put her hands on his shoulders. "That's not true. You're a man, Lon Rogers, and you're good enough for any woman." The image of Cole Tyler appeared in her mind. She gave a little shake of her head to banish it . . . for now. "But the feelings you'd like for there to be between us . . . just aren't there. You're my friend, Lon, maybe my best friend. And that's saying something, because I realize now . . . I've got a lot of friends here in Wind River."

He swallowed hard. "You sure do, Rose. And I reckon it's an honor for me to be among 'em." He nodded. "It'll be like you say. It sure will. And this time I mean it."

She leaned forward, brushed a kiss across his cheek. "Thank you, Lon," she whispered. She smiled again and whispered, "Now, I've got to go clean up. I feel like I've been wearing this dried mud all my life. Will you walk on with me to the boardinghouse?"

He grinned and linked his arm with hers. "You bet I will, Miss Rose. Let's go."

A few days later, Cole was sitting on the boardwalk in front of the jail, his chair tipped back and his boots resting on the hitch rack. Billy Casebolt sat beside him, whittling, while Cole read the latest edition of the *Sentinel*. The story of the bank robbery and the resulting string of shoot-outs had succeeded in crowding Michael Hatfield's clamor for elections off the front page.

"Michael did a pretty good job of reporting the facts for a change," Cole commented as he folded the paper and placed it on his lap. "He didn't make that mess sound like the biggest battle since the War between the States."

"It was bad enough," Casebolt said. "This arm o' mine still hurts like the dickens sometimes. And Marshal Boyd was limpin' pretty bad when he got on that eastbound train the other day."

"Judson says he'll likely have that limp for the rest of his life, but I don't reckon it'll slow him down much."

Casebolt chuckled. "Not hardly. That's one fella who's plumb dedicated to upholdin' the law, whatever it takes. He's a mite too hardheaded sometimes, though."

"Aren't we all," Cole mused. "Speaking of hardheaded, here comes Jeremiah. He was still upset about breaking the neck of that gent Amos, last time I talked to him."

Today, though, Jeremiah was beaming as he strode along the boardwalk, coming from the direction of the Union Pacific station. Cole and Casebolt stood up to greet him, and he held out a piece of paper in his uninjured hand. "Look what I've got," he said excitedly.

"'Pears to be a telegram," said Casebolt.

"That's what it is!"

Cole asked, "Who's it from?"

"The company back east that owns the land I want to buy for the church," Jeremiah said. "They've agreed to negotiate with me about buying the property." A frown suddenly creased the blacksmith's broad brow. "The only trouble is, they say they have another offer on the same land. I'm willing to bet it's from Hank Parker."

"Could be," Cole said with a shrug. "What are you going to do about it, Jeremiah?"

"The same thing I've always done," Jeremiah said. "I'm going to trust in the Lord."

Casebolt clapped a hand on the blacksmith's massive shoulder. "I reckon there's a good chance He'll come through for you, Jeremiah."

Jeremiah nodded solemnly, then said, "And if I have to, I'll kick Hank Parker's ass from here to Kansas."

A few minutes later, Cole and Casebolt were still chuckling about that when Simone McKay came strolling along the boardwalk, a folded newspaper under her arm. She smiled and said, "You gentlemen seem to be rather amused."

"We was just talkin' to Jeremiah," Casebolt began, then shook his head. "Aw, you'd have had to be here, ma'am."

"I'll take your word for it, Deputy," Simone said dryly. She gestured at the newspaper Cole had dropped on the chair where he had been sitting. "I see you've read the latest edition."

"Just the front page," Cole said.

"Then you missed the biggest story. Michael had to put it on the inside after that bank robbery and everything else that happened. He's getting what he hoped for."

Cole frowned. "Those elections, you mean?"

"That's right. A committee of the local civic leaders got together, and we've agreed to hold an election for mayor and town council in the fall."

Cole nodded slowly. "You've got to do what you think is best for the town."

"I agree. That's why I've decided to take one more step."

Cole felt a sudden twinge of worry. "What do you mean by that?" he asked.

"Well, as you may know, the legislature in Cheyenne agreed earlier this year to give women not only the right to vote, but to hold public office as well." Simone smiled and went on confidently, "Gentlemen, if I have my way, you're looking at the first mayor of Wind River. And when I'm elected, things are going to be different around here!"

JAMES REASONER lives in Azle, Texas.

▲ HarperPaperbacks *By Mail*

To complete your Zane Grey collection, check off the titles you're missing and order today!

- ❏ Arizona Ames (0-06-100171-6)............................. $3.99
- ❏ The Arizona Clan (0-06-100457-X)........................ $3.99
- ❏ Betty Zane (0-06-100523-1)................................. $3.99
- ❏ Black Mesa (0-06-100291-7)................................ $3.99
- ❏ Blue Feather and Other Stories (0-06-100581-9)....... $3.99
- ❏ The Border Legion (0-06-100083-3)..................... $3.95
- ❏ Boulder Dam (0-06-100111-2)............................. $3.99
- ❏ The Call of the Canyon (0-06-100342-5)............... $3.99
- ❏ Captives of the Desert (0-06-100292-5)............... $3.99
- ❏ Code of the West (0-06-1001173-2)..................... $3.99
- ❏ The Deer Stalker (0-06-100147-3)........................ $3.99
- ❏ Desert Gold (0-06-100454-5)............................... $3.99
- ❏ The Drift Fence (0-06-100455-3).......................... $3.99
- ❏ The Dude Ranger (0-06-100055-8)........................ $3.99
- ❏ Fighting Caravans (0-06-100456-1)................. $3.99
- ❏ Forlorn River (0-06-100391-3)......................... $3.99
- ❏ The Fugitive Trail (0-06-100442-1).................. $3.99
- ❏ The Hash Knife Outfit (0-06-100452-9)............ $3.99
- ❏ The Heritage of the Desert (0-06-100451-0)....... $3.99
- ❏ Knights of the Range (0-06-100436-7).................. $3.99
- ❏ The Last Trail (0-06-100583-5)............................ $3.99
- ❏ The Light of Western Stars (0-06-100339-5)........ $3.99
- ❏ The Lone Star Ranger (0-06-100450-2)................ $3.99
- ❏ The Lost Wagon Train (0-06-100064-7)................ $3.99
- ❏ Majesty's Rancho (0-06-100341-7)...................... $3.99
- ❏ The Maverick Queen (0-06-100392-1)................... $3.99
- ❏ The Mysterious Rider (0-06-100132-5)................. $3.99
- ❏ Raiders of Spanish Peaks (0-06-100393-X)......... $3.99
- ❏ The Ranger and Other Stories (0-06-100587-8)... $3.99
- ❏ The Reef Girl (0-06-100498-7)............................. $3.99
- ❏ Riders of the Purple Sage (0-06-100469-3).......... $3.99

❑ Robbers' Roost (0-06-100280-1)............................. $3.99
❑ Shadow on the Trail (0-06-100443-X).................... $3.99
❑ The Shepherd of Guadaloupe (0-06-100500-2)..... $3.99
❑ The Spirit of the Border (0-06-100293-3)............... $3.99
❑ Stairs of Sand (0-06-100468-5)............................. $3.99
❑ Stranger From the Tonto (0-06-101174-0)............ $3.99
❑ Sunset Pass (0-06-100084-1)............................... $3.99
❑ Tappan's Burro (0-06-100588-6)............................ $3.99
❑ 30,000 on the Hoof (0-06-100085-X)..................... $3.99
❑ Thunder Mountain (0-06-100216-X)....................... $3.99
❑ The Thundering Herd (0-06-100217-8)................... $3.99
❑ The Trail Driver (0-06-100154-6)........................... $3.99
❑ Twin Sombreros (0-06-100101-5)........................... $3.99
❑ Under the Tonto Rim (0-06-100294-1).................... $3.99
❑ The Vanishing American (0-06-100295-X).............. $3.99
❑ Wanderer of the Wasteland (0-06-100092-2)........ $3.99
❑ West of the Pecos (0-06-100467-7)....................... $3.99
❑ Wilderness Trek (0-06-100260-7).......................... $3.99
❑ Wild Horse Mesa (0-06-100338-7)......................... $3.99
❑ Wildfire (0-06-100081-7)....................................... $3.99
❑ Wyoming (0-06-100340-9)..................................... $3.99

MAIL TO:
HarperCollins Publishers
P.O. Box 588 Dunmore, PA 18512-0588
OR CALL: (800) 331-3761 (Visa/MasterCard)

For Fastest Service

Visa & MasterCard Holders Call
1-800-331-3761

Subtotal..$_____
Postage and Handling...$ 2.00*
Sales Tax (Add applicable sales tax)................................$_____
TOTAL:...$_____

*(Order 4 or more titles and postage and handling is free! Orders of less than 4 books, please include $2.00 p/h.
Remit in US funds, do not send cash.)

Name_____

Address_____

_____

City_____ State_____ Zip_____

(Valid only in US & Canada)   Allow up to 6 weeks delivery.
                                   Prices subject to change.   H0805